The Heart's Most Wanted

Books by Mary Connealy

THE KINCAID BRIDES

Out of Control
In Too Deep
Over the Edge

TROUBLE IN TEXAS

Swept Away
Fired Up
Stuck Together

WILD AT HEART

Tried and True
Now and Forever
Fire and Ice

THE CIMARRON LEGACY

No Way Up
Long Time Gone
Too Far Down

HIGH SIERRA SWEETHEARTS

The Accidental Guardian
The Reluctant Warrior
The Unexpected Champion

BRIDES OF HOPE MOUNTAIN

Aiming for Love
Woman of Sunlight
Her Secret Song

BROTHERS IN ARMS

Braced for Love
A Man with a Past
Love on the Range

THE LUMBER BARON'S DAUGHTERS

The Element of Love
Inventions of the Heart
A Model of Devotion

WYOMING SUNRISE

Forged in Love
The Laws of Attraction
Marshaling Her Heart

A WESTERN LIGHT

Chasing the Horizon
Toward the Dawn
Into the Sunset

GOLDEN STATE TREASURE

Whispers of Fortune
Legends of Gold
Riches Beyond Measure

ROCKY MOUNTAIN MARSHALS

Ambush of the Heart
The Heart's Most Wanted

The Boden Birthright: A CIMARRON LEGACY *Novella*
(All for Love *Collection*)

Meeting Her Match: A MATCH MADE IN TEXAS *Novella*

Runaway Bride: A KINCAID BRIDES *and* TROUBLE IN TEXAS *Novella*
(With This Ring? *Collection*)

The Tangled Ties That Bind: A KINCAID BRIDES *Novella*
(Hearts Entwined *Collection*)

2

ROCKY MOUNTAIN MARSHALS

THE HEART'S MOST WANTED

MARY CONNEALY

BETHANYHOUSE
a division of Baker Publishing Group
Minneapolis, Minnesota

Published by Bethany House Publishers
Minneapolis, Minnesota
BethanyHouse.com

Bethany House Publishers is a division of
Baker Publishing Group, Grand Rapids, Michigan

Printed in the United States of America

Library of Congress Cataloging-in-Publication Data
Names: Connealy, Mary, author.
Title: The heart's most wanted / Mary Connealy.
Description: Minneapolis, Minnesota : Bethany House Publishers, a division of Baker Publishing Group, 2026. | Series: Rocky Mountain marshals ; 2
Identifiers: LCCN 2026003930 | ISBN 9780764246005 paperback | ISBN 9781493454143 ebook
Subjects: LCGFT: Romance fiction | Thrillers (Fiction) | Christian fiction | Novels
Classification: LCC PS3603.O544 H43 2026
LC record available at https://lccn.loc.gov/2026003930

Scripture quotations are from the King James Version of the Bible.

Cover design by Dan Thornberg, Design Source Creative Services

Baker Publishing Group publications use paper produced from sustainable forestry practices and postconsumer waste whenever possible.

26 27 28 29 30 31 32 7 6 5 4 3 2 1

To my grandchildren:
Elle, Isaac, Luke, Katherine, Lauren, Adrian,
Quinn, and Harrison

It's an almost freakish coincidence that they ended up being the brightest, most beautiful human beings ever.

1

SEPTEMBER 1872
THE ROCKY MOUNTAINS OF COLORADO

If he could've done it, he'd've left them all behind.

Well, maybe not Owen. But everyone else was slowing him down.

Not as far as speed went. Rosalind Beck, his old childhood friend he'd found living alone in the wilderness with her son, was keeping up all right. Roz, the little pill, could ride her horse like an Indian warrior. Her little son, Jesse, stuck on his horse like a bur. But *little* was the key word there—for both of them. Roz was a pint-sized blonde. The kid was ten. Not really the trained, sharpshooting, ice-in-their-veins lawmen U.S. Marshal Morgan Sawyer wanted at his side.

Morgan wasn't that thrilled to have Owen's wife, Delaney, along either. Yet the Rileys appeared to come as a package. He had accepted a few days into this search that there was no shedding them, so he didn't even try. He did try not to think about the newlyweds, though. He had a trail to find, after all.

Together, they were setting off into the Colorado Rockies,

a wilderness that was the most rugged on the entire face of the earth. They'd be combing through the mountains in search of U.S. Marshal Tex Mitchel, who'd been missing for two weeks now, maybe three. Morgan was losing track of time. And yet, as impossible as that task sounded, he had little doubt that he'd be able, somehow, to find his friend.

First, he needed to figure out a way to skirt the north side of the steep-sided river Tex had fallen into. When they'd tracked Tex to the cliff he and the runaway outlaw Stella Duncan had gone over, he couldn't see a break in the canyon walls on the south side. His hope was that there was one to be found on the north. And finding a way to ride along that north side wouldn't be easy. Of course, if it had been easy, Tex could have just walked right out of the wilderness . . . and he hadn't.

Finally, after hair-raising trial and error, close to a week after they'd set out, Morgan found what he'd been hoping for. Not Tex, but a chance that his friend had indeed survived.

"This has to be where Tex came out of the river." Morgan saw no tracks and for certain no sign of his friend, yet it was the only place that looked likely. That was assuming Tex got out there rather than drowned, in which case he'd've surely floated all the way south to Mexico.

Owen Riley, his boss—even if Morgan wasn't that good at taking orders, while Owen seemed mighty good at giving them—rode up beside him and looked down.

He didn't ask what Morgan's reasoning was, but Morgan told him anyway—more for the crowd that was hanging around them. "This is the first place where there's a bank on this rattlesnake of a river."

They'd been walking along the river for days now, up and down treacherous trails and narrow passages.

Owen eased back and looked around. Neither of them spoke. Owen's wife, Delaney, wasn't a big talker. But both of them were skilled trackers. Not as good as Morgan, but mighty good.

Owen saw it first. "That's Tex."

Morgan saw Owen pointing and followed the direction with his eyes. Tex had left an arrow made of rocks in a way that was his alone, with a T shaped out of smaller rocks, as well as an S. They all had tricks like this to communicate with each other whenever they got separated in the wild for some reason.

"He's alive." A smile broke out on Morgan's face. That didn't happen often.

"Stella made it out, too." Delaney's comment reminded Morgan that he'd focused on finding Tex, not the runaway outlaw who'd led him on a dangerous chase that ended abruptly at a cliff.

"Will Tex keep leaving signs, do you think?" Roz asked.

Morgan had to admire her for how she'd bought into their quest to find their friend without making a pest of herself or slowing them down. Just weeks ago, the woman had no idea she'd be a part of any of this.

"Absolutely. He'll expect us to come after him, and at the same time, he'll be trying to find his own way out of this endless, rugged country."

"And to get out, he'd have to head east. The arrow confirms it." Roz reined her dapple-gray mustang toward the east and started out. They'd come from the east themselves but by way of a different trail than the one Tex's arrow pointed to. And that was mighty generous to call them trails, since there wasn't much indication of any such thing.

Tex hadn't gotten back to Fort D. A. Russell, the destination Tex knew they were headed for, or they'd've met him on their ride back from the fort near Cheyenne, Wyoming, where they'd recently traveled to deliver a prisoner, Clive Duncan, to the authorities. Ultimately, Clive ended up being innocent of all but his being broken out of jail by his family, of which Stella was a part.

After a quick wedding for Owen and Delaney, who'd fallen in love on the way to Cheyenne, here they were out in the wild again. Fortunately, Morgan had no great objections to a long ride in the mountains. He planned to search for as long as it took. They'd brought along two packhorses loaded with supplies, and if needed, Morgan and Owen knew how to live off the land indefinitely. A Marshal needed to be prepared for anything, including bringing a kid along on this latest mission.

Morgan glanced at little Jesse, who seemed to enjoy company. With his dad having passed years ago, the kid had probably never seen another human being besides his mother since his earliest memory. So the boy often rode at Morgan's side.

Morgan thought back to the day they'd found Roz in the spectacular mountain meadow where she'd lived with her parents, then her husband, Herman Beck. A modest but beautiful ranch not far from where Morgan had grown up. Not far, that is, if you didn't count the death-defying mountains and valleys, with trails so perilous that Morgan was astounded his horse could handle them. Somehow those trails had seemed less perilous back when he used to go to

Roz's house as a youngster. They'd known each other since they were children. Then he'd gone off to war when he was absolutely too young. He'd started as a drummer and ended up a sharpshooter. He hadn't been in the war for very long before his rifle skills had shown themselves.

And he'd never gone back home. He hadn't seen the need.

His father had left him a note in Elk Point, Colorado, the closest town to where the Sawyers had lived, though it wasn't close at all. His brother Gavin had died fighting for the South, while Morgan had fought for the North. In his father's mixed-up head, he blamed Morgan for Gavin's death. Morgan hadn't been welcome to visit the place he'd once called home.

Truth was, Morgan wouldn't have returned to his old stomping grounds this last trip if it weren't for the charge to transport Clive Duncan on horseback from Denver to Fort Russell after the only train track had been washed out on account of the rains. Morgan, Owen, Tex, and two other U.S. Marshals had barely begun their journey when a group kin to their prisoner had arrived to bust him free, driving the Marshals and others deep into the Front Range of the Rockies.

With no other good options, Morgan had led his group to his former home, and there'd been no sign of Pa. While being pursued by the Duncan clan, who'd been unsuccessful in rescuing Clive, Morgan had led the way to Roz's house, where they found her and Jesse there all alone. She'd been quick to decide to come along with them to deliver their prisoner to Fort Russell. Before long, they'd rounded up the whole Duncan family and had them all in custody.

Then the Duncans had made a break for it. The rest of

them had all ridden off after their prisoners. It was then that Tex, chasing after Stella, had likely fallen over the cliff into the river. Now the two of them were out here somewhere and no doubt in great trouble. They were probably without guns, horses, food, and other necessary supplies.

Morgan had to fetch Tex home as soon as possible. If only dozens of people hadn't come along, slowing him down. All right. Four people besides himself, but still . . . it was far too many.

Morgan caught up to Jesse, who followed after Roz, then took the lead. She smiled at him as he passed her with a glare. "Why'd you take off?" he demanded. "You don't know where we're going."

"Sure I do. You saw that arrow spelled out in rocks. From here east should lead us back down to the lowlands along the Front Range. Honestly, the whole world is downhill from what feels like must be the top of the world."

That got a tiny smile out of Morgan. "Every step of this journey, when I've thought I was at the top of the world, I find out I can go higher."

She chuckled as she rode up alongside him. "Since we've got all this time in front of us, why don't you tell me what you've been doing for the last ten or so years. The war's long over."

"Sometimes it doesn't feel that long," Morgan said. "When it ended, I came close to home, but Pa left me a letter in Elk Point saying I wasn't welcome there anymore."

"Hate to mention it, but your pa was an aggravating old goat."

He nodded. "Pa was that for a fact. As you can see, I ended up becoming a U.S. Marshal. I started south of Denver around Colorado City. It's not a very interesting job if all you do is deliver papers and transfer prisoners from place to place."

"This last job seemed mighty interesting, though."

"Yeah, you have me there. Mostly I stood guard in court for federal cases in Colorado City. But later I teamed up with Owen, and he got assigned jobs that included traveling, some investigating, searching for runaway prisoners, men who rob stagecoaches and such. Stealing the mail is a federal crime. I get a lot of good out of my tracking skills, and it doesn't hurt none to be a crack shot."

"Morgan is the best we ever had," Owen said from behind them. It figured Owen would be listening in on their conversation.

"Best tracker?" Roz asked.

"Yep, never knew one better. He can move like wind across the tall grass, only quieter. He slips through the forest like fog."

Roz was close enough that she reached over and whacked Morgan in the arm. "Sounds like you've remembered everything I taught you."

Morgan laughed. "I did at that."

The group then picked up their pace as they set off toward the east.

2

Roz looked over her shoulder to see where Jesse had gone.

Her son had dropped back and was riding alongside Owen and Delaney through a wide stretch of forest.

She pushed forward a bit to catch up with Morgan. "It's so strange to be around people other than Jesse."

Morgan looked away from the trail briefly.

"It's been just the two of us for so long," added Roz.

"I can't imagine," he replied.

She gave a sigh. "You know, Herman died when Jesse wasn't yet two. He has no memory of the man, and I've had no interest in fostering a love for him that might bring grief to the boy. Herman was a useless, itchy-footed wastrel of a pa. Talk about an aggravating old goat." Roz didn't talk about her husband much. But what she did say sure wasn't complimentary.

Morgan looked away from tracking again. "Seems you had it hard when with a husband, and then you had it hard without one."

"Lonely at least. But I lived in the mountains well enough; it's not much different from what I've always known. Of course, Herman was no help." She hadn't exactly hated him. That was a feeling with too much heat behind it.

"Ma had long since moved on to heaven when Herman came along. He was a wandering mountain man who took a shine to me and married me. I got to know pretty quick what kind of fool he was, and soon after our getting married, he abandoned me. Pa was still alive then, so I didn't miss Herman much. Honestly, we did better without him.

"Jesse was on the way, and Pa bore a lot of the weight through the first year of Jesse's life. Then Pa died, and Herman came back. He stuck around for a while until his itchy feet got to bothering him, and he wandered off again. The last time he came back, he had a leg wound that had suppurated. I ushered him from this life to the next. He was lucky I didn't give him a boot to hasten him along his way." Roz shook her head as she thought of that dreadful time.

"You've got a mean streak there."

"Mostly I don't, but I made an exception for Herman." Even so, she tried not to speak ill of the deceased man in front of their son.

Nodding, he studied her. Perhaps that was why she saw a chance for some fresh meat before he did.

"I see signs that a herd of elk passed through recently, Morgan. I'll go fetch us supper." She rode off the path they were on, glad for an excuse to quit talking about Herman.

But it wasn't that easy to shake Morgan; she heard him tailing her. She said over her shoulder, "This is the first real trail I've seen. I'll bet Tex took this route." Yet she didn't spot any telltale footprints on the ground.

"Let me up there, Roz." Morgan had to bump into her horse to slip past her on the narrow trail.

Roz couldn't exactly let him pass as he'd requested. The trail they rode on was just too tight. Still, he somehow managed to squeeze to the front, and she let him go. She doubted he was a better tracker than herself. No doubt he was good enough, though, just slower.

They hadn't ridden long when Morgan reined in and dismounted, walking several yards away. "Owen," he called, "looks like they had a meal here."

Owen carefully squeezed past her to see what Morgan had found.

Morgan pointed at the carcass of a bird and the remains of a fire. "They might be feeding themselves, but that's only a single grouse."

Roz knew that a scavenger could have carried away bones and such and left evidence of just the one bird, but chances were they'd've taken all the remains.

"They?" Owen said. "You're certain it's two people?"

Morgan answered, "I'm sure. Why else would he include an S alongside the T. Besides, I see the footprints of two people here."

Roz couldn't see any such footprints, nothing that confirmed this. But if Morgan was sure, then she accepted it as true.

Beside the remains of a campfire lay another arrow made of rocks, much like the one they'd found at the top of the canyon running alongside the river. Next to the arrow were the letters T and S. Tex and Stella had definitely been here.

"You can't hike for hours across this kind of terrain and

live on one little grouse for two people," Morgan said grimly. "Tex knows that, so he'll keep hunting."

"It's a wonder there's any sign of the bird left over." Roz glanced sideways to see Delaney looking around, assessing the situation for herself.

Roz had been impressed by Delaney's family when she met them at Fort Russell. Colonel Bridger and his family were a tough bunch. She wouldn't have minded if a few of them had come along. But Delaney's pa and ma had stayed back at the fort. And her brother, whose head was still recovering from being grazed by a bullet during the Duncans' ambush, had waved them on their way without much interest in hunting up the missing Marshal and his missing prisoner.

Morgan and Owen were still on foot, searching for anything they might glean from the meager campsite. Roz wasn't sure why. Unless maybe they expected to find Tex himself tucked under a scrub pine, but the man had obviously been here and moved on. They needed to move on as well.

To her disappointment, there was no sign of an elk herd either. She wasn't about to take the time needed to find and bring down an elk, but at least the herd had guided them to the right trail. She was a good shot, but once Herman died, there'd been no means with which to buy more bullets, so she'd been sparing with them.

While living out in the wild, Roz hadn't gone to town in years, not since before Jesse was born. But she'd traveled to town a few times with her pa when she was younger, and she remembered the way there. The fact that these tougher folks—the Marshals, the Bridgers, even the Duncan clan they'd hauled to Fort Russell—had all followed *her* out of the mountains gave her a deep satisfaction.

They probably oughta be following her now, but then she remembered how grouchy Herman became if she acted like she knew best, so she'd learned to keep quiet and let him make his own mistakes. After all, he was more of a mountain man than her pa or Morgan's pa. Except her pa was always kind, while Herman had been far from it. There'd been no way of being sure what one word said wrongly might do to that man. It had gotten to be a habit to keep her opinions to herself, even when she thought she knew better.

As she waited for the others to scour the area, she took a few moments to pray for her son, Jesse. He was a fine boy and her shining pride. She asked God to help him grow up to be more like her pa rather than Herman. Since the boy had never known either of them, maybe he'd turn out to be more like her. With his white-blond hair, he certainly resembled her. All she could do was hope and pray that the boy would develop into a truly good man and for her to set a decent example for Jesse to follow.

Finally, Morgan and Owen determined they'd found every possible bit of information available from the camp they'd come upon, slim though it was. It appeared Tex was indeed alive and well enough to hunt, and Stella had survived, too. Tex had done right to mark his trail so that if Owen and Morgan rode by, they'd be able to follow him. In the meantime, he was doing his part to get himself and Stella out of these mountains.

Roz knew how to live off the land, let it care for her. Based on what Morgan and Owen said of their friend Tex, she figured he did as well. Tex and Stella could be wandering out here for a long time, but surely they'd be all right.

A rock that looked as steady as, well, as a rock rolled under Tex's foot, and he pitched forward and careened down one of these blasted mountains. A cry tore loose from his throat so quickly he didn't have time to be embarrassed. He slammed into a scrub pine that snagged the waist of his pants. Jerked to a stop, he dangled like a fat spider. He had only seconds to glimpse just how far he had left to fall, and the sight was sickening. Scrambling to get a solid hold on the pine, his hand clutched its abrasive bark.

Just then he heard Stella scream, "No!"

Before her scream faded, the tree Tex was gripping broke loose of the rock wall where it shouldn't have been able to grow.

The cliff was sheer, not a handhold in sight. With a sickening twist of his stomach, he knew it was likely he wouldn't survive the fall ahead and quick prayed for a miracle from heaven.

And then he smashed into something else that stopped him cold. Was this his miracle? But before he could get too excited, whatever he'd hit crumbled and sent him plunging again to what had to be certain death. Next, he struck a ledge of some kind, which stopped him like a lassoed calf.

Unable to think, at least not clearly, Tex was afraid to move. He fought to breathe as he waited for this new spot to break loose and send him downward yet again.

But he remained there, deathly still, wondering where he was. At first, he'd thought it to be the cliff, yet it was more of a steep slope. The cliff was far higher than this. Did that mean if he moved even a single inch, he'd fall off whatever he'd landed on? He couldn't decide.

He had a few seconds to think of Stella. She needed him. She could probably survive on her own, but her chances were far better with someone with her, helping her. With his thoughts spinning, Tex stayed right where he was, trying to figure out what to do next as he stared at the rock wall in front of him. He should maybe turn his head to look behind him instead of at the rock, to assess his chances of getting off this slope.

That was when he noticed the rock wall facing him had an odd black frame around it, sort of a circle, and that circle narrowed. Startled, he realized he was looking into a tunnel.

The tunnel closed, and so did his mind. His dazed thoughts went dark.

Stella Duncan dropped to her knees and carefully peered over the edge of a slope off to Tex's right. A moment ago, they'd been planning to hike down what had struck them as a perfectly reasonable monster of a slope. Their whole world had become nothing but monster slopes—hiking up them, then down, then up again, and on and on like that. Then, without warning, she watched Tex tumble downward and skid, hit something hard, stop for a bit before suddenly falling again.

When Tex was about halfway down the killer slope, he hit a ledge so narrow she hadn't noticed it at first. Up until then, he'd been doing a fine job of falling to his death, leaving her alone in the wilderness. Dread warred with terror as she thought about being out here in the middle of nowhere without him.

She knew it was as selfish a thought as a human being could ever have, and the fact that she was having it only made it worse.

Then he moved his head, and she felt an ounce of relief before a few stones pelted him, stones he'd knocked loose when he hit them during his descent. The ground in front of her, which had looked solid, then crumbled like dry week-old bread.

She flopped down onto her stomach, so that if the fragile piece of rock crumbled again, she wouldn't go right over. She hoped anyway.

Her eyes locked on Tex. He was definitely alive. He moved gingerly, though, his hand grasping a ledge not much wider than himself. He lifted his head to look around, and what he saw made him pull back for some reason. He then rested his head as if it weighed a thousand pounds, and every bit of movement ceased. It looked to her as though he'd passed out.

Which was unfortunate in that he was halfway down an ugly-looking cliff—thirty feet at least and that much farther to go. Stella wondered if he was unconscious or possibly, though not likely, asleep. Whichever it was, if he made one wrong move, he'd fall again for certain.

Given the situation, she saw no way to reach him from where she was. Then she looked on past him. The cliff appeared a little less steep there. She saw another outcropping of stone and a stand of juniper trees. She had to get herself down the slope they'd planned to walk down, then make her way around to the area below him and see if she could climb up. It would take hours. And if he was unconscious, well, he'd have to wake up and help her. Even if she could climb up to him, he'd need to cooperate in climbing down.

Her plan only worked if Tex woke up.

Stella lay there for a long stretch of seconds. The wind whistled, rustling the branches of nearby trees. She was utterly alone, not counting the man she had to somehow get to and rescue. It was the most frightening moment of her life. The loneliest moment of a lonely life.

She was hungry and thirsty and devastated to think he might be so badly hurt he could die.

She closed her eyes and begged God for strength. And for faith. "To live is Christ, and to die is gain." Her ma had taught her that this life wasn't the end of each man or woman's story. She thought of her brother Leland, lying on the ground, dead, shot by one of the U.S. Marshals who'd been transporting her other brother Clive to Fort Russell to be hanged.

Leland, the headlong fool, had opened fire in an attempt to free Clive, killing a Marshal. Without hesitation, the other Marshals in the group shot back at him.

And now she looked down at the very man who might have killed her own brother. She'd never asked which of the U.S. Marshals had taken that shot because she didn't want to know.

Tex's life now hung in the balance.

She pushed away from the crumbling edge of the mountain that sloped to her right and to the east, then got to her feet and walked down a much more civilized slope.

Stopping, she thought about the markers Tex had left behind. She'd watched him lay out the stones in the form of letters in those places where they'd changed directions.

So strange to be trying to communicate with people who might not be anywhere around here or who might not come by at all. Even so, she took a moment to arrange some stones on the ground in the shape of an arrow, showing the direction she was going to walk. She then decided to lay out the words TEX FELL before adding a second arrow.

There was a whole lot more to tell, but there just weren't enough stones in these mountains for that. And considering the whole world was made of rock around her, that was saying something.

Stella set out down the slope again as quickly as she could safely go, praying with every step that the man who'd possibly killed her brother was still breathing.

She planned to do everything in her power to save Tex.

3

"They're supposed to be heading east." Roz stared at the tracks she'd found while climbing the mountainside. The tracks followed a number of rugged bends, so that now they were moving almost straight north after following Tex's last arrow.

It'd taken them most of a week to locate where Tex had left the river. Since then they'd been following him for three days more. It'd been three weeks at least since the day he was separated from their group.

Roz drew her horse to a stop and looked at Morgan.

He rubbed one brow and closed his eyes, almost as if their mistake was causing him pain. Owen looked disgusted, too.

"The fog can get real thick up this high," said Morgan. "We had a few overcast days. And not even a tree to check for moss. You know good and well that directions don't mean much up above the timberline."

Roz nodded. "If they went all the way to the top and figured out they were facing straight north, would they have turned around and come back down, hoping to go east by another route, or would they have forged ahead?" She knew plenty about tracking, but she didn't know these folks, their habits and such. So far, following Tex and Stella had taught her the pair were doing well at surviving, so she wasn't overly worried about their starving to death. But she was real sure they were lost out here.

Tex and Stella weren't the only ones.

"Hey! Over here." Delaney waved the others to her side. She pointed at another arrow on the ground, this one pointing down and toward the east.

"He figured it out and is saving us a lot of steps." Morgan gave his head a firm nod, then started following this latest arrow. Apparently, he was leading now.

Roz shrugged it off. She figured she was better than him at tracking but decided not to say so. Instead, she just fell in line.

Jesse rode beside her at times, going ahead and riding with Morgan once in a while, then dropping back to ride with Owen and Delaney some, too. No doubt he was liking all the company. She'd seen Jesse talking with Morgan, with Morgan pointing in one direction or another. He was teaching her son to track just like she'd been doing, which was a good use of their time.

It reminded her of the day she first met Morgan. They were both about eight years old. He'd come trotting onto their land, and when she caught sight of him, it was like being struck by lightning. Until that day, she hadn't hardly met anyone her age.

"You must be Rosalind?" he'd said. "My pa is a Sawyer. He talks of your pa sometimes and mentioned he had a daughter. I came to meet you."

Roz knew Mr. Sawyer. He came around and talked and

drank coffee with Pa some. "I didn't know Mr. Sawyer had a son."

What else to say? She had no experience talking to a boy her age. In fact, with her pa being a quiet man, and since she lived alone with him, she had precious little experience talking to anyone.

"You want to go riding? Show me your meadow? It's uncommonly pretty up here. We live in a ragtag kind of place."

Almost like he wanted to talk to another child . . . just like her. "Let's walk instead of ride," she'd suggested. "Our mare just had a foal, a little filly, and she's the one I usually ride."

Morgan's eyes lit up. "Can I see it?"

They'd hiked together, studied tracks, and gone hunting. Later, Morgan had helped break the little filly for riding and had a rare talent for it.

They used to challenge each other to move around silently in the woods.

Roz still remembered that lightning strike when she first met him. It'd felt the same when he'd come galloping into her meadow, running from outlaws while transporting prisoners. That lightning strike had shocked her back to life.

They were hours following the tracks slanting to the east. This was a rugged, rocky, rattlesnake of a mountain range. Roz had never been in this particular stretch of mountains, but she'd lived all her life in the wilderness, so she knew how difficult and dangerous it could be.

Morgan turned at an unexpected angle, and now Roz, despite feeling twisted around by all the trees and rocks and slopes up and down, was sure they were going straight east.

Riding in the wilderness might be hard, but it was also beautiful. She tried to imagine what life would look like away from her pa's ranch. Her ranch and home. Because it was so terribly lonely at her mountain home, she felt she couldn't go on staying there. Jesse needed more than that. Yet it was all the home she ever knew, and this big wide world beyond her ranch was full of fearful things. Of course, that world had Morgan in it as well, and she wasn't about to let her childhood friend ride away from her again. If he hadn't figured it out already—and she'd told him quite bluntly—she was never going to leave his side, not ever, for the rest of their lives.

How he felt about that didn't matter. It was how it was going to be, and that was that.

She had to wonder if Tex and Stella were as lonely now as she'd been. She suspected it was a shock at first to be so stranded, so lost, and stranded with an enemy to boot. After all, Stella had been taken prisoner, and it was during her escape attempt that they'd gotten lost.

But it looked as though they had stayed together and were surviving. By now they were used to it and had realized these might well be the most precious days of their lives, surrounded by beauty. The soaring mountains, the majestic trees, the sunrises and sunsets. The teeming wildlife and the gushing springs. In such a rich and fertile land, survival should be easy, even comfortable.

They were living off the land, discovering that they could survive through their own wisdom and hard work—that was a fine gift.

Surely, Stella and Tex would one day reflect back on this time with wonder and awe.

Estella Duncan peered back up the slope at Tex's unconscious body and wondered grimly if he was already dead, and if not, if she'd end up killing him in her attempt to get him down from there.

And kill herself while she was at it.

Far as she could tell, it looked as though he'd stopped bleeding. The vivid red that was dripping from the ledge earlier had now ceased. One of his arms dangled, scraped raw and bleeding. The heavier bleeding had come from near his head, which she could no longer see. But the sight of so much blood was enough to spook anyone.

Fighting tears, she studied her route up to Tex. She was terrified she was going to climb up there only to find him dead. Studying the slope, she noted the handholds and footholds she'd use. One wrong move and she'd drag him off that ledge, and he'd flat-out plunge to his death for certain.

After taking a deep breath, then blowing it out slowly, she started up the slope. Thirty feet, she judged it to be. She could walk most of it, or at least sort of walk it. She leaned forward and steadied herself with her hands against the rough cliffside.

Stella saw no way to get him down if he remained unconscious. Not only did she not have the strength to tie a rope around him and lower him down, but she didn't have the rope to begin with. Which meant Tex was going to have to help. She'd just have to sit up there with him until he woke up. If, that is, he woke up.

After what felt like an hour but must have been far less than that, she reached the ledge. He lay there flat on his belly, facing the rock wall.

"Tex, can you hear me? It's me, Stella."

He didn't move. She moved to rest a hand on his back and felt his chest rise and fall. Seconds later, she felt the steady beating of his heart.

He was alive!

Tears spilled over just a bit. She was embarrassed to cry, but since no one in the whole wide world could see her, she decided she wouldn't let it bother her.

She bent over to look at his face; it was scraped and had a nasty gash. That was where most of the blood must've come from. And his arm that dangled, swollen and bruised, it didn't look right. She'd taken the better part of an hour climbing down from above and then climbing back up to him, yet no blow to his arm should have bruised this deeply, this fast. She was afraid his arm might be broken. For sure it'd need a splint put on it. And she'd have to be even more careful now about moving him with that arm so injured.

Stella became aware all over again that there wasn't much room on the ledge. Mindful of Tex's hurt arm, she pushed him closer to the rock face so she wouldn't have to cling to the cliff like a scared cat as she decided what to do next.

"Tex, if you'd wake up, you could sure help me figure out how to get out of this tangle we're in."

She didn't see him so much as flicker his eyelids, but it made her feel better to talk to him, so she kept at it. They might well be up on this ledge all night long. Tears helped nothing, while the talking braced her spirits. Swiping her arm across her eyes, she said, "I need to bind up your arm, but how? I suppose I could climb back down and gather some sticks to make a splint. I could maybe find some bark or vines to strap it in place." She examined his bruised arm again and prayed for a sprain. That would be easier to deal with. "And I'll cut fabric off my petticoat or your shirt to make a sling with."

She wished there was water available. A cloth soaked in cool water to bathe his face might help Tex to wake up. She might as well wish for plaster to make a decent cast for his hurt arm, the skill to apply it, a staircase to walk down to level ground to rest beside a blazing fire, and an elk haunch to roast for dinner. And while she was at it, why not wish for a horse with wings to fly up here and fetch them both to the nearest town with a doctor.

"Tex, come on and wake up now." She gently rocked his right shoulder, leery of even touching his left. When he showed no response, she sighed and leaned back, unsure what else to do.

"How about I tell you stories of when I was a youngster, living with my ma and my little sister, Geraldine, who we called Sissy. Aunt Ethel and Uncle Gordy lived next door, and Pa and Gordy always rode off into the mountains most of the spring, summer, and fall. But they'd live at home for the winter—not quite the tough mountain men they liked to believe they were. At the time, Sissy and I were the only females born of the Duncans, and we came along after a passel of brothers and boy cousins."

It occurred to her that she was wasting her breath, but then breath was about the only thing she had in abundance. Yet if she quit talking about her past, there wasn't much more to talk about.

"Once Pa and Uncle Gordy decided the boys were old enough, off they'd go out into the wilderness, not to be seen again for months. Honestly, life at home was better with them gone. As each brother rode off, the house would be a little easier to keep up, the meals easier to prepare. Sissy and I, along with Ma and Aunt Ethel, would hunt our own food. We came upon some beautiful land while out exploring and wondered if any other people had ever set foot on it before.

"So every fall, Pa and Uncle Gordy would come back home, but after a few years, again one by one, the boys started not coming back with them. Pa would announce that another of them had struck out on his own. We'd never see them again."

Stella stopped talking and seriously considered climbing back down to search for water. "But what if you shift around in your sleep?" She shook her head. Tex looked more like he'd been knocked out cold. Cold as a snowcapped mountain in January. "I can't have you falling off this ledge. Now that I'm up here, it just doesn't seem wise to leave you."

She needed to figure out what to do and quick. "So far the only ideas I have are to sit here with you or climb down to fetch some water. That amounts to doing nothing or doing something stupid. How's that for a pair of miserable choices?" She leaned back against the rock face again, thinking the Scriptures might give her inspiration.

"'The Lord is my shepherd; I shall not want. . . .'" Slowly, Stella recited Psalm 23. Today it held more meaning than she'd ever realized. She had learned to read with the Bible. It had been the only book in their house; it had been Aunt Ethel's until she died, so really it was the only book in two houses. It was a wonder she didn't speak in Thees and Thous.

Stella had saved that Bible when the fire broke out in Pa's cabin. Pa had returned from a trip to find his wife and younger daughter badly harmed from the fire and his older daughter trying to care for them. He'd built a new cabin, and they'd moved Ma and Sissy into Uncle Gordy's. Then after a terrible month in which Ma and Sissy both died, and after a winter alone with all the menfolk, Pa had taken Stella into the wilderness with the dwindling group of brothers and cousins. She didn't want to go but she didn't want to stay alone in the cabin either. It would have been a terrible choice, so Pa settled it for her, and she'd carried the Bible along with her.

That Bible had been left with her pa when Tex had captured her and taken her prisoner. She wondered what had become of it.

As she spoke the words of Psalm 23, she wondered what other verses she knew by heart. She was sorely afraid she'd have plenty of time to recite them all. The holy words seemed to drift upward as if in prayer, lifting her spirits while also giving her something to do besides fret over doing nothing or doing something stupid.

4

Tex woke up inside an Indian war drum.

After long minutes unable to do more than listen to the pounding, he finally realized it was happening inside his head. A head that ached something fierce.

Had he suffered any more damage? He'd learned long ago to think before he moved. It was an even better idea when he hurt this bad.

Where was he anyway? What had happened?

It came back a little at a time. First, he remembered Stella, and that made him want to jump up and find her and make sure she was all right.

After tensing his muscles to move, he discovered that was all he was capable of. Just this threatened to rip him apart. He breathed deeply, listening, thinking. He managed to hear exactly nothing and think exactly no thoughts. He was breathing steadily, though, and that was good.

He cracked his eyes open and stared at sheer rock right in front of his face. He realized he was lying on rock, too. His face hurt something terrible, matching the feeling inside his head. He hurt all over, in fact, though his head was the worst, and his arm felt like a hungry wolf was hanging from it.

He noticed it was daylight. How long had he been lying here? And lying where exactly?

"Stella?" His voice was little more than a whisper. He tried again, louder this time. "Stella?"

Something moved, or someone. Then something besides rock appeared before him. A pair of familiar eyes, blond hair flying every which way and knotted up, reminded him that he'd been stranded in the Rocky Mountains for what seemed like forever. Sure enough, it was Stella—leaning down to stare into his face.

"Tex, you're awake! Thank the Lord above. I was so worried. I've recited every prayer and every Bible verse that came to mind. It turns out I've memorized a lot of Scripture in my life. God used those verses to keep my spirits up while I waited for you to come to."

Their eyes met. Hers were blue like his, but his weren't such a pretty bright color as hers. Truth be told, he'd never thought much about eye color before meeting Stella.

"What happened?" he asked. The words slurred. Moving his lips was a challenge.

"It was so sudden, Tex. The ground caved away under your feet, and you fell off a cliff." Stella shook her head as if she still couldn't believe what she'd witnessed. "You've been unconscious for most of the Psalms I had memorized, although I couldn't promise you I didn't miss a few verses."

She was talking too fast for him to make much sense of.

"You ended up on this ledge after smashing into who knows what all. By the time I looked over the edge of the cliff, you'd already landed here, about thirty feet down. I'm real glad you didn't fall the whole way to the bottom. I then ran down part of this wretched mountain that isn't a cliff and climbed up here, another thirty or so feet up. I'm here to help bring you the rest of the way down. And here I sat, waiting for you to wake up and help."

She straightened until he couldn't see her anymore. But he could feel her hand on his back, which kept him from being frantic that she'd vanished or wondering if maybe he'd dreamed her up.

Then she poked her head forward so he could see her again. "I'm afraid your left arm might be broken. Can you move it?"

He concentrated on that just long enough to suspect she had it right.

"If it's not, it's terribly sprained. And the sun is setting. We've got to get you down off this slope, and I can't do it without your help." Her brow furrowed. "Which means you'll need to get on your feet, then do some mountain climbing."

Tex winced in pain. "Broken arm, huh?"

"The bone isn't at an unnatural angle, but we can't go jostling that arm. If it is broken, you could make it worse and end up with a bone sticking out of your skin, and I'd just feel sick about having to amputate. Does that get your gumption up to climb down a mountain?"

"It does." Tex pondered for a minute just how he'd manage to do so.

As if she'd heard his thoughts, Stella said, "You can start by rolling onto your right side, being very careful of your left arm, then sit up and see if your head is clear enough to allow you to stand. Fortunately, the slope below us isn't a cliff, but it's still steep. Maybe you can slide off this ledge, sit down, and scoot the rest of the way."

Tex nodded. That was the only move he made for a while, not counting his mouth. He gathered himself, gritting his teeth from the pain, and rolled slowly onto his right side. He got a better look at his left arm and shuddered at the sight. It was so swollen, she had cut his shirtsleeve up to his elbow. Tex still had his knife, thank heavens. He'd hate to have lost the only proper tool they had with them.

Using his right arm, Tex pushed himself up an inch at a time. Stella boosted him up as best she could.

Finally, he was in a full sitting position. He'd never known such misery. He closed his eyes tightly as he breathed hard, then leaned his head back against the rock face as the world went black again.

"Tex!" Stella wrapped her arms around his chest as he began to slide.

He howled in agony. His arm! She was quick to shift her grip, and the pain of that had his eyes flying open.

"Careful, Tex. You're going to fall."

Tex moved his left arm, or rather he tried to move it. He braced his right arm against the narrow ledge they were sitting on.

"If you can't make it, you're going to have to stay up here until you can." And if that was the case, Stella would have to stay up here with him. She was exhausted, but that had been the story of this whole disaster.

Exhausted. Hungry. Hurt. Scared.

She was so tired of it all. What if she went to sleep in

the night and he rolled off the ledge? She decided then they couldn't stay. It was too much of a risk, so a little straight talk to rouse and encourage him was called for.

"Tex Mitchel, you get ahold of yourself. You're going to climb down this mountain even with one working arm, a dizzy head, and every muscle and bone in your body demanding that you stop. And you're gonna do it *now*." She liked to think she'd stopped short of outright abuse but had perhaps gone beyond simple encouragement. Call it a scolding like only a mother could give.

Tex, his eyes open only a slit, slid his gaze to lock with hers.

She saw a cranky man, but more than that, a man who knew what she was up to. He seemed to gather his strength. Then he sat up again and slowly, moving as little as possible, leaned forward and looked down.

That was when she realized he hadn't opened his eyes to mere slits by choice; he was so battered, that was the best he could do.

He swallowed hard, his voice sounding rough and muffled. That might be the best he could do, too. "If I scoot to the right without using my left arm . . ."

Stella was on his right side. That meant she'd need to slide off the ledge and go back to clinging to the side of the cliff. She didn't mention that if he didn't scoot right, she'd need to catch him, and she was sorely afraid she wasn't strong enough. If it came to that, they'd both plunge thirty feet down and land on jagged rocks.

Talk about *"the valley of the shadow of death."*

Peering down the slope, he said, "If I can get to that first foothold and sit down, then I'll lie on my back, hold my left arm across my body, and scoot down slowly all the way to the bottom. I think I can do it."

She most fervently hoped and prayed he was right, but she wondered if maybe he was talking through his plan to put off the moment he had to carry it out. They really needed to get moving. He needed water and some food, and he needed a safe place to rest.

"Let's do it," she said, nodding. Trying not to look too spry lest she make him feel his limitations more fully, she eased herself off the ledge, found a firm foothold, then stepped a bit farther to the side. "Now it's your turn." She dreaded this first step on their journey down. Honestly, she dreaded every step, but she'd worry about each of them in turn.

Tex hesitated at first, as if he had to work up the nerve to use every bit of his body. At last, he moved off the ledge and lay flat on his back.

"Tex, this is going to work," she assured him.

He groaned and said nothing more.

She feared getting below him, but she didn't think he could do much better than a controlled fall. She knelt beside his feet, lifted one leg, and guided it down to the next foothold. When that foot was steady, she lifted and guided his other leg.

Inch by inch, step by step, they moved down the mountain until, at the ten-foot mark, she realized he'd passed out again.

She paused to let him regain consciousness, but then she changed her mind. It might be more merciful if he stayed knocked out. Stella took a deep breath, working up her resolve. The remaining distance should be doable.

Her strength, along with assistance from gravity, helped to get Tex the rest of the way down.

They reached the rocky base of the wretched mountain, where finally she stood on somewhat level ground. Looking around, she saw they were tucked between a jumble of rocks and the slope they'd come down. A few paces beyond the rocks were trees. Rocks and trees—this land didn't hold much else, it appeared.

A warm breeze made a nearby stand of aspens quake, their leaves spinning as if they loved to dance. Among the aspens were oaks and a few ponderosa pines, with smaller trees and a century's worth of fallen branches and leaves taking up any spare room.

The hushed breeze seemed to whisper of their isolation. Or was it desolation?

Her stomach growled, reminding her they could sure use some food. And right now, everything they needed had to be provided by her, using Tex's trusty knife and the slingshot.

Stella turned to check on Tex. He was still unconscious, reclining against the side of the cliff. She tugged on his right arm to shift him a bit lower. That way, if she was going to leave him, he wouldn't fall any farther and cause more injury to himself. She hoped he didn't slump over onto his hurt arm.

If the bone was indeed fractured, they couldn't take the chance of it shifting and breaking the skin. In the wilderness, with no doctor around, an injury like that could leave him in terrible danger of serious infection, even costing Tex his life.

When she'd sat beside Tex on the ledge earlier, she'd spotted a trickle of water nearby. She'd use the knife to cut free the remainder of his shirtsleeve since she'd already cut some of it due to the swelling of his arm. She'd then go and soak the sleeve in water and wipe the blood off his face. Next she'd need to find sticks for a splint . . . well, one step at a time.

Eventually they were going to get out of these mountains. She'd begun to believe it was best to aim to do so before winter set in. And though she was pretty sure it was August, winter came early up here.

They'd been hoping to get out and catch up with Tex's Marshal friends, but she let that idea go. Better now to just hope they avoided any blizzards.

Demoralized, she found the spring and wet the sleeve thoroughly. Returning to Tex, she began cleaning his face gently with the cloth. She saw his throat work as he swallowed a dribble of the water.

No sign that it was waking him up.

She urged all the water she could squeeze out of the cloth as she washed his wounds. When she pressed the cloth against his forehead, his eyes flickered open.

Smiling, she said, "We got down."

"Thank you," Tex said, looking at her through eyes still swollen.

The moment didn't call for encouraging talks or scoldings or dire warnings. She simply replied, "You're welcome."

His eyes closed again, and Stella decided to let him sleep while she went and contrived splints for his arm. And food and a fire. She'd moved him enough for now. She might have to set up camp around Tex's battered body. As badly as he was hurt, she might as well plan on building a cabin right over his head.

With a knife, a slingshot, and a shirtsleeve as her only tools.

5

Morgan laid a hand silently on Owen's shoulder.

Owen's eyes popped open, but the two of them had worked together long enough for the touch not to startle him. He didn't move. He didn't speak.

Morgan pointed. "Someone's out there."

Then he got up to investigate. Whatever Owen did was for him to decide, and Morgan was sure he'd decide right.

As he left, Morgan got down low and slipped through the woods that surrounded their camp. Morgan, fighting a surprising protective instinct to go see if everyone was all right, turned to the woods. The night birds had gone silent. There'd been a rasp of cloth against stone. A rustle of leaves that sounded like the step of a man and not a critter. Little things, but Morgan had been in the woods near all his life, and he just knew someone was out there. And whoever it was had no good purpose. Especially no good purpose being silent like this.

There was a right way and a wrong way to approach a camp. The right way was to make yourself known at a distance. Come in slow but only after you've been invited. Keep your hands empty and in clear sight at all times.

Or there was this way. And no one this quiet could fail to know both ways. Which meant trouble.

Another brush of something against a tree. Fabric maybe. As silent as the wind, only not quite. In fact, this intruder was so skilled, so careful, Morgan had to wonder if he was deliberately making noise, maybe to lure Morgan away.

He dropped to the ground and felt more than heard something fly overhead. His heart sped up. Who was it? Indians maybe? There were mostly Cheyenne and Arapaho in the area. While Morgan thought he was as good as anyone in the woods, he didn't count the Native folks. They seemed to be born with woodland skills.

But no. This felt threatening, and the Indians around these parts were peaceable for the most part. His heart pounded so hard, he wondered if it would give him away. Whatever had been thrown at him, another object might come flying, so he flattened himself to a low crawl to make the smallest target possible. His hearing was as keen as a colony of bats, so he lay still and listened, watched. Every one of his senses was on edge. He had no idea where to crawl next because their intruder had given him no clues.

Slowly, one small bit at a time, the tension left the woods. First an owl flew by, then he heard a cricket chirp, followed by another.

A chill raced down Morgan's spine. Something about this intruder made him doubt the man was that careless. It seemed every noise the man had made, he intended to make. Did that mean he was just trying to torment them, let the camp know they were being watched?

It was spooky, like a ghost hovering near them. Morgan didn't believe in such things, but didn't it figure that if there was a Holy Ghost, there might very well be such a thing as an *unholy* ghost?

He shrugged off the shudder he felt and settled in. He was no longer hunting; now he was hiding. And he didn't like it.

Time stretched on. They hadn't posted a night watch. Near as they could tell, there were no people out in these woods except maybe Tex. But Tex knew the right way to approach a camp. And anyway, Morgan wouldn't mind one bit if Tex snuck up on them.

Now they'd have to post a guard. Morgan was bothered by his carelessness. It'd been sloppy on his part, thinking it to be safe bringing along two women and a child. Well, safe if one didn't count the risk of falling over cliffs and being swept down rivers or being hopelessly lost in a trackless wilderness.

Another strange sound, but not one that belonged to the night. It was far enough away that the man—or the unholy ghost—was either leaving them, or it was one from their camp moving around.

That was when Morgan noticed the sky turning from starlit-black to dark gray. The night was fading. And come sunup, Morgan would be out searching for tracks. While he'd usually been able to track anyone or anything, for the first time in a long time, he had his doubts.

Minutes later, the sky lightened and suddenly a burst of twittering echoed as the morning birds welcomed the new day. The owls found the nests they burrowed into, either in the notches of trees or in the abandoned nests of other birds. The grass rustled as the grouse hunted for their breakfast, and there was the scurrying of little critters after having survived the night, keeping their distance from the night predators roaming the mountains.

Morgan saw Owen come out from his hiding place and walk back into camp to build up the dying fire. It wasn't just the small birds and animals that were stirring with the daylight. Their group began stirring, too.

The day ahead would be filled once again with the group's searching for their friend. And now Morgan was afraid they'd somehow gained an enemy—an especially dangerous enemy.

Delaney joined Owen at the campfire, where she started a pot of coffee. As Owen got a skillet out, Roz and Jesse joined the others around the fire.

"What did you find?" In the past, Owen would have known better than to ask. Anything he needed to know, Morgan would tell him without hesitation.

Morgan was finding out that being married had made his friend into a regular chatterbox. Morgan hadn't known too many married men. He wondered if this was a particular new quirk of Owen's or if all married men acted this way.

"I found nothing," answered Morgan, "but someone out there threw something at me. I've got a feeling he did it on purpose too, maybe to make sure I understood he was out there and that he had his eye on me. I need to spend some time today tracking whoever it was. Learn all I can from whatever trail he left behind. But I need full light first before I can scour the woods for our mysterious visitor."

Delaney pressed a tin plate into Morgan's hands. Piled onto the plate were steaming fried potatoes and crisp side pork. How she managed to cook so well out here in the wild was a wonder.

"Well, it should be full daylight by the time we're done eating," she observed.

Morgan met Owen's eyes. Both of them chafed at the delay. They needed to find Tex and soon. But if their ghostly intruder was planning trouble, they'd first have to round him up before the group could move on.

Stella continued to bathe Tex's face, wincing at all the cuts and scrapes.

He was asleep again—or unconscious. She was sorely afraid it was the latter. No matter how tired, not a lot of men slept through having their battered face washed. Whichever it was, it was just as well he was out because she needed to splint his arm.

She'd never set a broken arm or leg, but she'd heard tell of it, and the concept seemed simple enough.

Tex's injured left arm had swollen to about double its normal size. She'd gathered a few branches thick enough they wouldn't bend but thin enough they wouldn't weigh too heavily on him. Or so she hoped because they still needed to walk out of these blasted mountains.

To fashion the splint, she began by stripping the bark from the branches. Then, taking a deep breath, Stella whispered a prayer as she gingerly lifted his wounded arm. Using the bark, along with some vines she found, she wrapped the branches so as to hold them securely against the arm. Once finished, she very gently lowered the now splinted arm to the ground beside him.

She'd kept a close eye on Tex's face as she worked. He flinched a few times and made a feeble effort to pull his arm away, but she was able to overpower him, which was a terrible shame. They needed two strong people to get through this whole ordeal.

"All right, Tex, I'm going hunting now. I'll try and be back soon." She grimaced as she pictured a hungry wolf or mountain lion wandering by and eyeing Tex as its supper.

With a heavy sigh, she grabbed the slingshot and left her traveling companion behind. She figured they would have to stay put for a couple of days to give Tex time to rest and heal a bit. She sure hoped he wouldn't need longer than that.

After hunting awhile, she came upon a bush with berries. She gathered a few cups of them and tied them in her skirt. She recognized the berries and knew she'd eaten them before, yet her pa had never told her what they were. But he'd sent her into the woods to pick them, then taught her how to use them to make pemmican.

It wasn't long before she brought down two rabbits. She also found a piece of curved bark to hold water while she heated it.

The sun had dipped low in the sky by the time she got back to Tex. Mercifully, no wolves had stopped by. He was still unconscious. Kneeling beside him, she said, "Tex. Time to wake up now."

No reaction at all.

She started reciting Scripture verses again, loudly this time, thinking it might help him not to feel so alone. She liked the sound of it, even if it was just her own voice, and the words were always reassuring.

Then after a while, she stopped reciting and said, "You know, Tex, there's a rock wall not far away that will block the wind and hold in heat from the fire. It gets a bit too cold up here for comfort, even in the summer. A fire will feel nice once I get it going. But you're going to have to wake up and move there to be the most comfortable."

Looking at him, her heart clutched. Though she knew he was alive, she couldn't stop herself from going over and watching his chest rise and fall.

Then she went back to work. She got a fire going by striking Tex's flint against the knife blade, creating enough sparks to ignite the kindling she'd placed in a little pile.

"Now I'll soak this piece of bark thoroughly, then pour a bit of water in it to stew the berries and rabbit meat. If I pound on it until it's all mixed together, you'll be able to chew it more easily." She left the slab of bark under the spring that poured out of a crevice in the rock and turned her attention to building up the fire. Once it started to crackle, she went and turned the bark over to soak both sides of it.

"My aim is to get some food in you, Tex. It'll help to get your strength back. I can probably get you to swallow some water even if you're unconscious, but you'll need to be at least a little bit awake to eat."

She arranged a tripod with sticks to hold the pan made of bark, then started the pemmican. It was all she could think to make in a nearly flat pan of bark; she hoped to get the meat cooked through before the pan caught fire. If she had to, she'd somehow keep the pemmican from burning up, knock off the ashes, and eat.

Later, she could try weaving birchbark to make a pan. If kept soaking wet, it too would hold water for heating. But Tex needed to wake up and eat something now. A more elaborate pan would have to wait.

Looking over at Tex, she feared she'd have plenty of time.

With the meal cooking, she longed for a few things that would make their camp more comfortable. A real pot. Blankets. A few supplies for doctoring. And while she was at it, she might as well wish for a doctor and a coffeepot full of the hot brew, a couple of horses, and those horses might as well be tied outside a hotel near Fort Russell. She admitted to herself that wishing for such things was a waste of time, but then all she had was time.

When the meat was nearly ready, she went to see if she could get Tex to wake up enough to get on his feet and walk over to the fire.

That was a lot to ask in his condition.

Dropping to her knees beside him, she rested a hand on his right shoulder. "Tex, wake up. Please—"

He groaned.

She felt that fullness in her throat that she knew not to show because the first thing he'd felt was pain. She hadn't even cried when her brother Leland was killed. She for certain wasn't going to break down now.

"You've been asleep for a couple hours or more." Most of the day, in fact. "I know you're tuckered out, but I need to be sure you're gonna be all right."

He blinked, his eyelids fluttering open for just a few seconds before drifting shut again. Still, he was waking up, even if slowly. She was determined to get him some shelter near the fire.

"I've got a meal on for you. C'mon, wake up." She kept up her encouragement until his eyes opened and stayed open. "Tex." This time, his glassy eyes met hers. "I've got a splint on your left arm. That's the best I know how to do. Now I'm going to help you sit up. We need to get you closer to the fire. We'll eat, I'll fetch some water for you to drink, and then you can sleep the whole night away."

His eyes closed again, but she saw him gather his strength, roll onto his right side, then shove himself up to a sitting position.

"There's a boulder right there beside you. Maybe you can raise yourself enough to sit on it. Then when you're sure you're not going to keel over, you can try walking. It's not very far."

Saying the words, Stella had some vague memory of believing it wasn't going to be very far to walk out of these mountains either. That'd been a few weeks ago. She hoped it didn't take that long to get Tex to walk the ten steps to the fire.

6

Tex's jaw went taut. This was going to hurt real bad, but staying put hurt as well.

Slowly, he shoved himself up, fighting back the dizziness, the sharp pain in his knees, his head, his back, and most especially, his arm. He was sure he hurt in other places too, but he couldn't keep track of all the aches and pains.

Tex had made it to sitting on the boulder, but then he wobbled, his vision narrowing. Stella slid an arm across his back, and the agony of that jerked him back to full consciousness. She looped his arm around her neck.

He straightened his legs, trying to take a deep breath that stung enough he wondered if he had broken ribs. He took a small step, then another. One at a time. Lifting each foot brought a new wave of pain.

He remembered skidding down the mountainside until he felt as though he'd had his skin grated off, every inch of it. Stella had set up camp nearby, bless her heart . . .

The two of them inched along toward the warmth of the fire. Tex bit down hard to keep from crying out. On wobbly legs, his teeth clenched the whole way, at last he made it to the crackling fire.

Leave it to Stella to have contrived some kind of cooking pan. The wet bark wouldn't burn, or at least not burn easily. Food could be cooked in it over the fire for quite a while.

She helped move Tex so he could lean back against a boulder. Yet he hesitated to sit, knowing that doing so was only going to increase the pain.

"Here's a nice spot for you next to the rock," said Stella. "It'll shelter you from the wind. And I made the fire close by so this will be a good place for you to rest, too. If we can get a bit of food in you and some water, maybe you can get yourself a decent night's sleep and—"

"If you're going to say I'll feel better in the morning, just go ahead and cling to your sweet hope."

Stella gave him a wry smile, and then with her assistance, he sat all the way down on the ground. The boulder did make a nice backrest, if only his back wasn't killing him. Once he was somewhat settled, Stella hurried back to the bark pan. Using her skirt to protect her hands from the flames, she lifted the pan away from the fire and set it on the ground right next to him.

He couldn't help but marvel at what she'd concocted. His head was a bit addled, so he couldn't exactly identify what she'd made, but it sure smelled good. It was meaty with something sweet added in. His belly was beset with collywobbles, but that might be more from hunger than anything else. The food was worth a try to help settle his gut.

She'd set a second small slab of bark beside the fire, and he saw it held water. It was a nearly flat bowl, and she came with the bowl and tilted it slowly so he could drink from it.

After a few swallows of the cool water to relieve his parched throat, Stella pulled the bowl away. If it hadn't hurt so much to move, he'd've wrestled her to get the water back.

But being a wise woman, once she gave him a pause, she brought the water back to him so he could drink again. When he finally had enough, she put down the bowl. The smell of hot food had lured him away from having just water.

Using a thin strip of bark for a scoop, Stella dug into the pan and brought a bite of food to his mouth. "It's a rabbit stew of sorts. I gathered some berries to add in, along with a splash or two of water."

Tex nodded as he chewed, then swallowed. "Tastes real good. Thank you."

He ate for a while. His stomach went from so empty it echoed to overfull of the stew.

"I'd better stop," he said, and she set the makeshift pan aside.

"If you're done, let me help you lie down now."

Tex suspected she spoke mostly to warn him of what she was going to do, not so much to ask if he needed the help. And as she eased him to the ground, he appreciated not needing to ask for her help. He'd never been very good at that.

Today had proved again that Stella was a strong, smart, kindhearted woman. How had she ever ended up riding in the wilderness with her featherbrained family?

He wondered where the Duncans were. Last he and Stella knew, her brother had been on his way to a hanging . . . his own. He knew she wanted nothing to do with her family again, but that didn't mean she liked the idea of Clive being hanged for a crime Stella swore was no crime at all but self-defense, even if he had been convicted of cold-blooded murder.

"Stella, we'll get out of here and make it to Fort Russell, I promise you."

"But probably not in time to save Clive," she said and then sighed. "I know Clive can be foolish, but I sure hope my pa and Uncle Gordy and brother Johnny don't end up getting tossed into the stockade with him. Or worse, end up getting executed."

Lawmen wouldn't take well to her family helping to break Clive out of the fort's jail, but Tex wanted to reassure her that they wouldn't all end up getting their necks stretched. But his mind was starting to do an odd swooping thing that made it hard to gather his thoughts. He kept his eyes open as he lay there, then wondered if maybe he should shut them in the hopes of getting some sleep. Just now, though, every breath hurt enough to keep a man wide awake.

He shifted, and his arm dropped to the ground beside him, causing him to grit his teeth in agony. Finally, he managed the one thing he had the strength left to do. "Thank you, Stella. Thank you very much."

"You're welcome."

He said a prayer and then drifted off to sleep wishing she'd lie close to him through the night. She wouldn't, and he shouldn't want her to. But they were the only two people he knew in the biggest world he'd ever imagined, and he was sore and worried and ached with loneliness.

As Morgan studied the ground for some hint of last night's intruder, he thought of Tex and Stella and was surprised by a wave of fear.

And Morgan wasn't afraid of anything.

"That's a human footprint," Roz said, "but it's not exactly normal."

She dragged his thoughts away from Tex, and for the first time, he was happy for the interruption. Then he saw where she'd pointed and approached the spot.

"Have a care, Morgan. There could be other tracks around here."

She was right, and he appreciated the reminder, though it embarrassed him a little to need to be told. Where was his head right now?

He dropped to his knees to study the single print, then looked up sharply. "How did you recognize this? Now that I'm right on top of it, I know you're right, but . . ." He shook his head. "Well, I'd've never picked it out."

The footprint was little more than an indistinct dent in ground covered with fallen leaves from years before.

Looking up at Roz, he noticed how pretty she looked in her black riding skirt with a dark green broadcloth shirt-waist. The clothing was plain but new and sturdy and clean, all things she'd purchased while at the fort. When he'd first seen her, stranded with her boy, Jesse, in their home by that beautiful mountain meadow, she'd been wearing a mishmash of worn-out, ill-fitting men's clothes, almost certainly left to her from her pa and her husband.

Upon recognizing him, she'd dropped her rifle and hollered his name, then ran to him and jumped into his arms, smiling to beat all.

Morgan had to admit he'd been glad to see her, too. It was a memory he wouldn't soon forget. Roz, his childhood friend, all grown up.

He turned his attention back to the footprint. "Have you seen a track like this before?"

"I have," Roz said simply, then rose, no doubt to search for more tracks.

Before he could think it through, he caught her wrist and pulled her back beside him. "Tell me about it. Where did you see it?"

She looked at him and smiled. Her fine blond hair was neatly tied in a bun, and her blue eyes shone like the Colorado sky at midday. She held his gaze. And he held hers.

"When I first saw you in your meadow, you might've been happy to see me, Roz, but seeing you was like finding I still have a place in this world. I'd forgotten how well we got along."

A faint pink tinged her cheeks, and her wide smile shifted to something more intimate. A smile just for him.

"I'd settled in for life, I reckon. I was going to start making clothes with buckskins before this winter. My clothes were coming apart, and Jesse was growing with precious little of Pa's or Herman's clothes left to rework for him."

"And you didn't think you'd ever go to town? Not ever in your life?"

Roz gave one shoulder the tiniest shrug Morgan had ever seen. "I'd've had to go someday, I suppose. But I had no money."

Morgan stopped and looked around. They'd come quite a way into the woods. Back at the campsite, he saw Jesse hanging on every word Owen said. The boy had never met a grown man before Morgan had ridden into the canyon where he lived with his ma.

"I considered trapping," she continued. "That's how Herman earned money. As for Pa, well, he did a bit of trapping too, so he must've had furs. But if he went to town, he took me along only a couple of times in my whole life. He did go once a year or so. He'd come home with a few canned goods and a bit of coffee and flour. I didn't pay much mind to where he got cash money."

"He never drove a cow to town to sell?"

"No, and I never asked him about paying for things. Mostly we lived off the land. I guess the thought of town was overwhelming to me. I just managed with what I had."

Morgan had no idea where she'd found the money for her riding skirt or the clothes Jesse was now wearing. It struck him that he should have bought them for her. Delaney had handled it most likely. Morgan felt ashamed by that. He needed to stop being such a lunkhead.

"Now that I'm out in the world again, I suppose I'm going to need some money. Can we go fetch my livestock after we find your friend and Stella? I aim to drive the cattle to town and sell them."

Morgan had been hunting for his nighttime intruder all morning and half the afternoon. A short break wouldn't be out of order. "Let's sit down for a bit, Roz."

He caught her wrist again and pulled her around so that they were sitting side by side.

"I don't know if we can get your cattle out of that meadow. Some of those trails we went down, skirting the sides of canyons, trails I still can't believe my horse was able to follow . . . well, I'm sure a longhorn could tackle any trail a mustang could, but how would we make them go?"

"The horses did all right."

Nodding, Morgan thought the trail over carefully. "We'd

never get them out if they doubled back toward my old house. That trail was a pure hair-raiser. I remember two bad stretches in particular. One not so deep, and if we got them moving down, they'd be loose at the bottom of a canyon. We'd have our hands full getting them to walk back up the other side of that gully. And the other one is worse still."

"Can we do some pathfinding? Find another trail out?"

"Your pa had to get those cows in there somehow."

Morgan tried to imagine doing it. It might take them months, a lot of trial and error. Like hunting for Tex. Nothing was easy out here in the wild.

He paused and looked around at the staggeringly beautiful world God had created. Still, all of it came with challenges. Nothing was easy anywhere, it seemed.

"We'll do that." He turned to face Roz. "I might just quit the Marshals Service and find a new way to make a living. With Owen settling in Wyoming, with no plans to take these jobs transporting prisoners and being an investigator and heading off to explore new places, it's not going to be much fun anymore."

Roz gave him a rueful smile but didn't respond.

"What is it?"

"Fun? Morgan, are you talking about that last assignment?" Then Roz managed a quiet laugh. "Was it fun to get shot at? Was it fun to climb up and down those steep gorges? Was it fun to sneak around in the night until you had captured five prisoners, then move the ones that didn't get away to the fort? What part of any of that was fun, would you say?"

Morgan laughed. "Showing up at your place and seeing

you again after so many years was fun. Getting to bring you out of the mountains with us has been fun. Meeting Jesse—he's a fine boy, Roz—that was fun."

Looking so deep into her eyes he could see her goodness and loneliness and the kindness in her heart, he leaned forward, then caught himself and pulled away from her. "I've missed you, Rosalind Sutcliff. And I've had a hard time believing you're a widow lady."

"Does my boy Jesse help boost your belief?"

"A little." He rose and then helped her to her feet. "You're blue blazes on a trail, Roz."

Then he hesitated and felt stupid to say what he wanted to. And yet he trusted his instincts even when it sounded ridiculous. "Last night, when I heard someone in the woods, I—" he paused and gave his head a hard shake—"I was spooked."

Roz's eyes sharpened. "Spooked? You?"

"There was something wrong about it. I can't even say what. I've been on the trail or been followed by skilled woodsmen. But that man last night . . ."

"Are you sure it was a man?"

Morgan considered that. "I'm not certain, no, but that's how it struck me at the time. Anyway, except for being surprised when I catch up to some *woman*, I'm going to act the same while I search for whoever it is."

"Could that person be Cheyenne or Arapaho, do you think?"

"It's possible, but it didn't strike me as such. Even so, it's someone with that much skill for a fact. There sure haven't been any signs of any Native folks out here up until now, though. Did you see any in your meadow? You said you'd seen that footprint before."

"I've not seen any man, woman, or child since Herman died. Only Jesse."

That hurt Morgan's heart. She'd been a happy youngster when they played together long ago. Nothing about her seemed to make her the kind of person who'd want such a solitary life. He wondered what her husband had been like. He sure as certain hadn't ever taken her anywhere in the few years they were together.

"I don't reckon anyone came to our cabin either. How did our pas ever find their way up to that high country? I'd've never found it on my own. It wouldn't have occurred to me to even try riding up that first steep slope."

"Maybe they saw a herd of mustangs run up it. If they'd seen a mountain goat, neither would've thought to follow." Roz reached out and took his hand, drawing Morgan out of his dark thoughts of how remote they'd been during those years. "You were telling me about being spooked?"

Morgan wished he'd never started this. But he had to tell her and Owen as well. They needed to be warned. "There's something about whoever was out there last night. Something, I believe, very dangerous." He looked down at the oddly misshapen dent in the ground. Not like any track he'd seen before. It was all too easy to imagine something not quite human. "I felt cold chills. I felt malice." He swallowed hard. "I felt that, just outside my sight, whoever was out there was evil. Like a ghost . . . though I don't believe in such things. But last night, for just a few moments, I believed."

Roz very quietly wrapped her arms around her waist, then slid her hands up and down her arms as if she were cold. She didn't otherwise respond.

Morgan found himself wishing he could have done the

wrapping. If he was going to scare the sweet woman, he oughta be there to hold her in case she passed out with fear. Then again, this was Roz; she wasn't exactly a fainting wallflower.

"You recognized something about the track," he said. "What was it?"

She nodded. "That footprint was a trick I learned from Herman. He'd bind his feet in a gunnysack, and it'd disguise his prints."

"Now you said it, yes, that's exactly what it is. I've heard of that, but I've never seen it before." He longed to rub her arms. He'd chilled her with his fear, and she needed him to soothe that chill. But he knew touching her was the wrong thing. She'd spent her life more alone than with someone, and she didn't need the attentions of a man whose whole life was about wandering.

"Now," he said, going back to studying the track, "let's see if we can follow these prints."

7

Roz guided Morgan.

She felt solid, possibly even undue satisfaction that she was better than him at tracking. After all, she'd found the footprint before he could.

And as Morgan was busy studying the one print, she'd found four more. Then Morgan had struck out on his own and had found the next one. He peered deeper into the woods away from the camp. "I'm going to search for where he left his horse."

Roz fell in beside him. "I'm coming with you. Of course, the intruder might have walked to our camp from a long distance."

They were following their mysterious visitor more easily now, though Roz had to admit it wasn't *that* easy.

"Morgan, Roz, come on back now," Owen called out. "We need to get moving." He'd been more patient than Roz had expected.

Morgan pointed at a tight grove of aspens. "His horse was right there."

Roz saw the torn spot on the bark of one aspen. Another tree had a tuft of gray horsehair caught in a low branch.

"No tracks, though. He must've brushed them away. Looks like our ghost is no ghost at all but flesh and blood. A ghost wouldn't ride a horse, and it was a real horse that stood here."

"Let's go talk this over with Owen. He was studying the other side of the camp all morning." Morgan started back.

"Why do you think Jesse tagged along after Owen and Delaney this morning?" Morgan sounded a little disgruntled, hurt even. She was probably imagining that, but she hoped that Morgan would take a liking to her son.

"What we really need to talk over," Roz said, "isn't who or where to find him. It's *why*. Why was this stranger roaming around our camp last night?"

"And why did he throw something at me?"

Roz had heard all about something sailing over Morgan's head. Yet they hadn't found anything that looked like it'd been thrown and left behind. Had it been a rock or something else natural? Something that would land on the ground and fit right in like it'd always been there? And had he missed or just meant to scare the man who was coming after him?

"So it all comes down to why."

Roz and Morgan exchanged looks.

"Yep, we've got a lot to talk over," Morgan agreed.

They walked out into the clearing around their campfire. Roz knew it was very likely they'd sit here and play a guessing game while they ate before heading on down the trail after Tex.

Because answers seemed as hard to find as ghost tracks.

Tex jerked awake, looked around for about five seconds before Stella was there with water, then some of the food from last night. It wasn't like any concoction he'd had before, but it seemed to fill his aching belly in a way that didn't upset his stomach. The perfect food for a badly battered man.

He still winced with every breath, and after a long night lying on the hard ground, his back was paining him something terrible. He'd broken a rib before, and that didn't seem to be the source of his back pain. His knees were hurting too, especially the left one.

Yet it was his arm that felt the worst of all. And his vision was still blurred, his eyes seeing double. He'd moved just enough to know it was going to be a misery to get to his feet.

It struck him then that the pain was starting to separate itself. Up until now, he'd been in agony all over. Now he had a localized sense of different aches and pains. It wasn't good, but it seemed like an improvement.

"That food gives me just enough strength to fall asleep again," he said.

Stella frowned as she pressed a cool cloth against his forehead. He hadn't a fever, but it sure felt good.

"Wait . . . is that the sleeve of my shirt?"

"'Fraid so. I was forced to cut it off because of your arm being so swollen. We don't have anything else to spare, and so I'm reusing it." Stella gave him a closer look as she shifted the rag. "Your eyes are open a bit more this morning, more so than the slits you managed last night. That's a good sign. But if this is progress, we're going to be here long enough I should probably consider building us a cabin. Maybe I could round up a mustang or two and build a barn while I'm at it. Catch and tame a few longhorns, get a herd started."

Tex chuckled at the idea. "I'd like to see that. But as soon as my arm stops feeling like a wolverine is hanging from it by its teeth, I'll be up and moving."

She nodded like a woman who didn't believe a word he'd said. "The swelling in your arm looks as bad as ever. I caught two more rabbits this morning. I scraped the skins and washed them. Sure wish I had some salt to tan them properly, but I think they'll work in a pinch."

"It's gonna take a lot of rabbits to make a tepee. Maybe blankets."

Stella laughed. "Don't be getting any ideas. I'd need about a hundred rabbits to do all of that. I'm working hard to find two or three each hunting trip. It's summer—we can get by without blankets. But there's no sense wasting a nice warm rabbit fur. I've got four now, and I've worked the hides a bit and stretched them using branches. They could make a sling for when you're walking again. Sturdier than the one I worked up yesterday."

"That's smart thinking." He looked up at Stella. "I appreciate all you're doing. I'd tell you at length and in detail, but . . ." Tex lost his train of thought and felt himself fading.

"As soon as your jaw isn't swollen, I'll cook the rabbit on a spit. You'd have trouble chewing meat right now."

It was as if he were listening from inside a dark cave. "I'm sorry, but I have to rest again, Stella. I'm worse than nothing when it comes to helping out around here."

"Nope." She brushed his hair back off his forehead.

She smiled—a sad smile, yet it was for him.

8

"Is there any more to learn, or are you ready to pack up and head out, Morg?"

Morgan had learned pretty quickly in their working relationship that Owen had a knack for getting people to do what he wanted. He could snap out orders whenever he felt the urge, but he was also good at convincing others somehow—smart, tough, independent people—to do things his way.

Just like Morgan was going to do right now. "Nope," he said, "let's get after Tex."

"And Stella," Roz reminded him with a sniff.

Morgan had to admit he and Owen were focused mainly on their missing friend, but they'd go ahead and haul the woman with him back to civilization. Honestly, Morgan was looking forward to telling Stella her brother hadn't been hanged, her family wasn't in jail, and she wouldn't be arrested. She oughta be thrilled to see them.

Owen started packing up the bedrolls. They'd brought a lot with them, knowing they were going to be roughing it in the wilderness for a while. And that could be a long time because they were not giving up until they either found Tex alive or found his body.

Morgan saw Roz narrow her eyes at him, then at Owen. "All right," he said. "If you'd've pushed for it, we'd've come, Roz. Probably would have anyway." He reached over and patted her on the shoulder.

Jesse hopped up and started rolling up his blanket. For a youngster, the kid was mighty handy. He couldn't tighten the cinch on his saddle yet, but he could get it over the horse's back and get the cinch threaded through the iron ring. Tightening it was someone else's job, though it wouldn't be for long.

Morgan wondered if Roz had spent time teaching him. He recalled her as being a real hands-on girl, ready to go on whatever adventure he proposed. He didn't remember her ever reading much of anything. As youngsters, they'd spent all their time outside, so there wasn't a lot of book learning when they were together.

With everyone helping to break camp, they were on the trail in a matter of minutes. Morgan trotted forward to take the lead, Owen riding alongside him. That wasn't usual. These days, Owen and Delaney stuck together like burs. He'd never known the man to be so ridiculously happy. He even flat-out smiled once in a while.

While Morgan thought Owen's cheery mood to be a bit irritating, he didn't say anything but tried to ignore it. Seeing as his friend hadn't been married long, he was probably still getting used to it.

He glanced over at Roz and wondered if he was ever going to get used to having her around again. He'd forgotten just how much he enjoyed her company.

"What do you think was going on around our camp last night?" It wasn't like Owen to waste words when he had something on his mind that was niggling him.

"Well, you heard what I said about feeling spooked by whoever it was out there. And Roz's notion that he'd likely wrapped his boots to cover his tracks."

Owen nodded and shifted the reins to his other hand. "Maybe it was someone who lives out here in the wild. A hermit kind of person who was just curious but didn't want anything to do with us."

Morgan turned that idea over in his head. "Seems like a lot of trouble to go to. It'd be an odd kind of hermit."

"I think *odd* is probably guaranteed. It probably doesn't need to be said, but . . ." Owen fell silent.

Morgan wondered what was going on in that head of his. "Just say it, Owen."

"You don't suppose he could be . . . um, your pa?"

Morgan whipped his head around so hard he jerked on his reins. His horse tossed its head and pranced toward the trees they were riding through. Morgan had his hands full getting the horse under control. And himself too.

His heart threatened to pound out of his chest. His breath sped up until he was nearly panting. He felt flushed with heat. He might have even felt his eyes burn with tears, which he would never let fall.

Under the almost mad overreaction, Morgan recognized that what he was feeling wasn't rational. Was he afraid of his pa? He knew Pa didn't want him to come home. In some twisted way, Pa blamed Morgan for his brother Gavin's death.

Twisted . . . He thought of last night and the evil he'd sensed around the camp. Would that qualify as twisted? Was his pa running mad in the woods? Maybe it was just a hermit like Owen had first suggested. That was another kind of odd, although that might describe Pa as well.

Morgan realized at that moment that he'd figured Pa for dead, or maybe he was forever gone off somewhere in the wilderness. Either way, he'd expected never to see his pa again. Morgan hadn't considered that Pa might still be alive, close by even. He hadn't considered that his pa might be following him. But for what reason? It made no sense.

Morgan thought of the letter Pa had left for him at the general store in Elk Point. Also in the envelope, Pa had included the letter from the U.S. Army informing him his son Gavin had died. And then Pa wrote that he blamed Morgan for Gavin's death, making it clear that if he came home, Pa would shoot him on sight.

Morgan had taken it hard. His heart had been broken by his pa's words, and it'd never worked quite right again. There wasn't even a flicker of happiness in the letter at the prospect that his other son might make it home from the war alive. In Morgan's young mind, Pa had too much stubborn pride to let himself think differently. He'd wanted to ride on for home and force Pa to—

A firm grasp on his forearm brought him out of the strange spinning of his mind and heart. Morgan realized he was staring into the distance, and his eyes focused on Owen with a snap.

Owen watched him, concern leaving furrows in his forehead. But he didn't ask. He knew. Somehow he was reading everything that had surged and stormed its way through Morgan.

The grip on his arm gave him a chance to get ahold of

himself and return to the here and now. That and a profoundly heartfelt prayer that soared straight up to God. He knew then he'd risk anything, even death at his father's own hand, to see his pa again.

Which was pure stupid. Why would a man want to see a father who hated him?

Yet the fact that he *did* wasn't the point. The truth was that he *shouldn't* hate his son. He forced himself to regain control. Go back to the life he'd led for years of simple acceptance that his pa was either dead or gone somewhere. And Morgan should never want to see him again.

"What makes you think of my pa being the intruder?" he asked Owen.

"I'm not sure. But, Morg, if you want to try and track down your pa, I'd be glad to help. Word gets around among folks, even in this vast wilderness. We may be able to find him."

Morgan seriously considered that, then shook his head. "I've figured him for dead. But whether alive or dead, it doesn't matter. He wanted me to stay away, and so I have."

"Maybe, but your pa's had a lot of years to calm down."

"He was of an age with Roz's pa, and that man's been dead for almost ten years. Since Jesse was a baby. I know I acted a bit addled when you suggested it, but no. I'm not going to hunt for my pa after all this time. I've figured him for dead, and I'm going to go on that way." Once Morgan had shoved aside the notion that his father might be the one haunting their camp at night, he could think clearly again.

"All right," said Owen. "I just—"

"Look at that," Morgan said, cutting him off. "On the ground there."

Owen turned his head to follow Morgan's gaze.

"I have gotten so used to Tex's markers, I've come to expect them at certain spots."

A gust of wind had cleared the fallen leaves from another arrow, this one shaped with smaller rocks, once again pointing the direction Tex had gone. They were at the low point between two more mountains. The rugged land seemed to be endless, but they all knew to keep an eye out for the arrows, which had turned up regularly.

"Looks like that arrow's been there awhile. I wonder if we're closing in on him at all." Owen removed his Stetson and wiped his brow with the back of his hand. It was a warm day, and the sun was especially bright.

Morgan heaved a sigh. "It ain't easy sticking to an easterly direction when cliffs and gulleys block your way." They started riding again, everyone following behind.

"Nope," Owen said, "nothin' is easy up here in the mountains." He then lowered his voice and said, "I'll be leaving your side now, Morg. I think Jesse wants a turn riding next to you for a while." Owen pulled on the reins and dropped back so he could ride alongside Delaney.

Morgan heard him chuckling just as Jesse and Roz caught up to him, Roz riding on his right and Jesse on his left.

He tried not to think about the wild reaction he'd had to the suggestion of his pa maybe following them and instead started talking to the boy about tracking.

Stella wandered farther from Tex today. He'd slept through the night for the first time and with no nightmares to speak of.

The first two nights after his fall, he'd been awakened by a nightmare, and she had as well. His murmured words and cries sounded as though he were falling over a cliff all over again, which seemed highly probable. Hardly surprising when he'd had that same awful experience twice in three weeks' time.

Though Tex was still seeing double, he could now get to his feet—that is, with her lending him a hand. He'd eaten more pemmican this morning. She had collected six rabbit furs but had no way to sew them together. She hoped to weave them together by using the knife, cutting slits and strips of hide.

Today she aimed to bring down a deer or an elk, and she was on the hunt for a flat stone that curved a bit at the top, so she could use it to cook on. She kept burning through the pieces of bark.

Her pa and his brother Gordy had prided themselves on being able to live off the land like the Arapaho people did near them. They'd always admired the tribe for their skills and self-sufficiency and their respect for the land and the wildlife.

But Stella hadn't had the same respect for her pa and Uncle Gordy, nor her brothers and cousins. The men in her family rode off and stayed away most of the time, and it had annoyed her that they left her and her ma and aunt and Sissy. They did come home for the winter. To Stella, though, that made it seem more like children playing a game, who came into the house when the going got rough.

She wondered where they were now. Had they ended up getting hanged? Were they sitting in jail? She hoped they were all okay. Sometimes family could bring an awful lot of heartache.

She pushed that thought away and turned her attention to her slingshot, then made plans to fashion a bow and arrows. Building those wouldn't be easy, as she didn't have all that she needed. Yet she was working on it. For now, she had the slingshot and Tex's knife. She'd've preferred a rifle, of course, but she'd save her hopeless wishes for when she didn't have to keep a sharp eye on the woods around her.

A shudder of fear raced up and down her spine to think of getting far enough from Tex that she wouldn't be able to find her way back. Because of that, she very carefully marked her trail. She was surprised by the depth of her fear of being alone.

She was at it for hours and starting to feel like she shouldn't leave Tex by himself for so long a time. By now she'd hunted down several rabbits and the place a herd of deer had bedded down for the night.

She'd burned up the afternoon hunting their supper and getting it home, but when she got there, the campsite was deserted.

Fear swept through her all over again.

"Tex, where are you?" Her heart raced as she imagined someone coming into camp, finding him helpless, attacking him. What if they'd—

"I'm coming, Stella."

The rabbits dropped to the forest floor, and she sank into a heap. The sound of his voice brought such relief that tears burned her eyes, which she didn't let spill over.

Tex came from around a nearby tree, limping and moving

slowly, one knee still badly swollen. His arm was clutched against his chest.

"You washed up." She didn't bother to add that now she could see his cuts and scrapes better. The swelling in his eyes had gone down, but his face was so scraped and battered, he didn't look like himself.

His hair was sopping wet. She could only hope he hadn't studied his reflection in the puddle of water that formed out of the spring near their campsite.

"Yep, I . . ." He'd reached the edge of the fire, where his knees buckled. He hit his swollen knee so hard he cried out. He reached out to break his fall with his bound-up arm and shouted again before falling on his backside, where he gasped in pain yet again before passing out.

Stella rushed to his side. Gritting her teeth, she checked his arm. Thankfully, the fracture hadn't come unset, and the bone hadn't broken through the skin. As she touched his face, she felt the heat rolling off him and gasped.

He had a fever. Wickedly hot. His skin was flushed, and any damp she felt was from the water, not a drop of sweat to cool his body.

She choked back a sob. She should never have left him. She should have hurried to his side when she saw him standing up. She should have . . . Shaking her head, she quit dwelling on the past and hurried to dampen their faithful sleeve rag.

Quickly, she rinsed the sleeve and filled one of the shallow bark basins with an inch of cool water. Carrying the water to his side, she knelt. And as long as she was on her knees, she prayed as she began the job of fighting to keep the only other man in her world—the only other *person*—on this side of the Pearly Gates.

9

"We need to stand watch tonight, Morgan, both of us," Owen announced as he peered into the woods around them. The party had finally stopped riding, and Roz was already setting to work with Delaney to make supper while Jesse collected firewood.

"It'd be better if we took shifts. After a long day today and a disturbed sleep last night, neither of us will make it with no sleep. I'd prefer two sentries." Morgan shouldn't have said that out loud.

Roz for sure didn't like hearing it and glared at Morgan to make sure he knew as much. His eyes landed on her long enough, she knew he understood her meaning.

Delaney, standing beside Owen, turned and frowned at him, her brow creased with worry.

Because they'd ridden as late as possible, they were setting up camp in full dark. The only reason Owen had called for them to halt was because he was afraid they might overlook Tex's markers. They'd gotten a slow start that morning, searching for tracks and other signs of intrusion around the campsite, and so they'd tried to make up for it. Now they stood with the first flickering of light from the campfire.

Fretting about Tex and Stella was making them all restless.

Roz came up beside the men. "Delaney and I will take a shift."

"No," Morgan said. "I don't want—"

Roz put a hand up in front of his face, an inch from his nose. "You just said you need to get some sleep. You know Delaney and I are more than capable of standing watch."

Roz met Delaney's eyes and gave a firm nod.

"If you don't like that, how about I stand guard with Owen, and you stand with Roz?" Delaney rested a hand on Owen's arm. "My hearing is keen, and my sense of the woods is dependable." She looked at her husband. "You know there's no choice unless you and Morgan stand watch alone, and you can't do that. We need two people standing guard. You'd best let us help. You've no choice, Owen."

Roz watched them together. Owen's strong desire to protect Delaney was obvious. The mutual respect and love for each other. She wanted that for herself until it was a deep ache inside her. Mainly because she knew she was going to marry Morgan whether he loved her or not. Well, she didn't know for sure, but she wasn't about to let him leave her behind, never again. Eventually he'd have to marry her, that or he'd have a saddle partner for life. But she longed for him to want her . . . to love her.

She hadn't gotten anything close to love with Herman, and she'd accepted that. At the time they married, she hadn't been thinking of romance. She'd simply thought him to be a decent man, the kind who would work alongside her to raise a family up there in her family's remote mountain valley. Having lived such a self-sufficient, lonely kind of life, she came to see how very lacking it was. And now here she was, planning to snap Morgan up whether he liked it or not. Even so, she sincerely hoped he *liked* it.

Morgan stepped forward and said, "Roz is right. Besides, she and Delaney are as good as we are, Owen. It goes against the grain when we've been working as lawmen for so long, but yes, we'll let them stand guard."

Owen, his jaw tense, nodded. "Sounds like it's decided. Let's eat first and then scout around to find the best places to post a watch. We're set up well here."

Roz had been pleased to be the one to spot this good-sized clearing next to a rocky outcropping with a bit of space behind it, which ended in a rock wall on one side and a cliff on the other. No one could get up from one side or close in on them from the other side. And the outcropping made a shelter they could sleep behind. Nobody could get close to them without stepping out into the open.

Whoever had been slinking around last night had slipped up close but without attacking. She hated to bet her life that the stranger was only curious, especially with Morgan's instincts about bad intent riding him so hard. But her saddle partners had agreed this was a decent spot to bed down for the night.

They ate quickly in the cool air. Owen and Delaney would take the first shift while she and Jesse slept on one side of the fire, Morgan on the other.

When they walked off in two different directions, Roz felt a pang of fear for their safety and knew her turn was coming to go out into the darkness.

The night insects fell silent. Once Owen and Delaney

stopped moving, they would likely go right back to their chirping. The owls would start their hooting at the moon.

Roz heard a wolf howling in the distance and wondered where in the world Tex and Stella had gotten to. What must it be like, surviving night after night without so much as a blanket? With only the food they could hunt or pick off a berry bush? It was a land full of food, but it took hard work to find it.

Lying with Jesse between her and the fire, her eyes met Morgan's as the flickering light died down. "Any idea how close we're getting to Tex? I'm surprised we haven't caught up to them yet, with them being on foot."

She spoke quietly. Jesse was breathing slow and steady, already deep asleep like children tended to sleep. Or at least like Jesse tended to. She'd never been around any children besides him, at least not since she was a child. It struck her many times a day how little she knew about the world.

Morgan shook his head. She could barely see the motion amid the glowing embers. "They've had near three weeks' head start. At least we know we're still on his trail."

"Where do you work most of the time, Morgan? Where is your home?"

He gave a soft chuckle. "I've been roaming mostly back here in Colorado. My work takes me hither and yon. But Colorado is where I'm based out of. I've not had a home, not since I left Pa's cabin for the war."

She let that sink in. "Do you really think it's impossible to get my cows down out of my meadow?"

"I've ridden in high valleys where no buffalo has ever gone. There are elk up there, but no buffalo. An old-timer told me they couldn't make the climb. They just never found a trail in. If there are places no buffalo can go, it stands to reason no cows could go there either."

"Then how'd Pa get the cows up there to begin with?"

"I have an image in my head of him carrying a calf draped over his saddle, and probably your ma carried one, too. One a bull, one a cow. The foundation of a herd."

"We have an old bull I call Big Red, and a black-and-white longhorn I call Patch. They've been around from my earliest memory. But up and down those gullies? Could my parents have made that journey each carrying a calf . . . and carrying me, too? Carrying as well whatever supplies they'd need to start a ranch?"

"Well, longhorns are known to be agile and good on rough terrain, so maybe they found a way. We'll do our best with your cattle. I suppose if we can't get them out, we could carry a couple of the calves down the slopes draped over a saddle."

Roz yawned.

"Get some rest, Warrior Woman. You've got to stand guard in a couple of hours."

Warrior Woman. She liked the sound of that. She was tuckered out, yet she wanted to keep talking with him. She wanted to know Morgan better.

But a warrior woman was no doubt more practical. Yes, she'd spend her life with him. In a very practical way, not so much a love match like Delaney and Owen shared.

"Good night, Morgan." And like any exhausted, practical warrior woman, Roz fell straight to sleep.

Stella had no idea where the fever was coming from. It had been the most frightening day of her life. Yes, Tex was scraped and cut and battered, so maybe his overall terrible condition was enough to bring on a fever, but none of his many wounds, including the broken arm, looked infected.

She'd bathed his forehead with steady determination and gotten a few sips of water down his throat every hour. And she'd mashed the food mixture into something soft enough for him to swallow—that is, if he ever woke up enough to eat.

"You may have noticed, Tex, I'm no doctor." Stella had taken to speaking every word that came into her head out loud.

"I noticed." She was relieved to hear his voice and quickly brought him more water. Not easy without a cup.

She had found a short branch and was attempting to whittle a cup without harming Tex's knife, their only tool except for the flint. But she'd never whittled anything before now and was proving that with every passing hour.

She'd heard that willow bark could be made into a tea, which helped to bring down a fever. Unfortunately, she hadn't come across a willow tree. And with Tex feverish, she was hesitant to leave his side to go looking for one.

"I'm going to roll up your pant leg. I'll try to be careful, not cause you any further pain. But I haven't checked your knee since I decided it wasn't broken."

"All right," he said, nodding.

Kneeling beside him, Stella slowly rolled his pant leg up the calf area. She soon realized his leg was more swollen than it had been at first. As she reached his injured knee, her stomach swooped. The knee was double its normal size, though she could see no sign of a cut.

She paused to count. "Have we been out here two days or three days?"

He gave her a look that was purely sarcastic. Quite a talent for a man so close to unconscious. Of course, being mostly unconscious made it hard for him to keep count.

"I stayed up with you all night the first night," she said. "I think you slept badly enough, the next two days blurred together. Then there's the day I hunted and came back to find you feverish. Now that I think on it, that wasn't last night—it was the night before." She shook her head. "I'm losing track just talking about it."

"If we stay put in these woods long enough, I figure Owen and Morg will come fetch us out of here."

"Do you really think they'll come, Tex?" She grabbed the curved piece of bark, took it over to the stream, and came back with a bit of water in it. She got most of the water into his mouth, and any water she spilled on him, well, she hoped it'd help to cool him down.

"They'll come, I'm sure of it. They'll be out looking till they find me or find my body."

He fell silent for a stretch, as if speaking had worn him all the way out. Or maybe speaking about finding his body had cast a pall over the mood.

"No doubt they know by now where it was we fell into the river," he continued, breaking the silence. "They'd follow the river, find where we climbed out. Because I marked our trail, they'll find us. I just don't know when exactly."

She went back to tending his wounded leg but didn't see anything that would explain a fever. "Roll on your side if you can. I want to see the back of your knee."

Tex struggled but managed to roll over.

"Maybe . . ." Then she noticed his dark shirt was stuck to his back. "Yep, looks like you've got a wound in your back."

Tex groaned. "Well, how bad is it?"

"I can't yet see the wound clearly enough." She tugged on the shirt a bit, which was stained with dried blood. "Your shirt is stuck to your skin. I have no idea what's under there, but if you scraped your back and we haven't tended it, that could be the source of an infection and the cause of your fever. I've got to get a better look at it." She leaned so she could look down into his eyes. "I need you to roll over farther."

"I apologize for all this trouble," he said. "I shouldn't've been standing so close to the edge of that cliff."

"I shouldn't have made a break for it back when you were escorting me and my half-wit family to jail."

"I should've packed more supplies in the event I got injured or lost out in the wild."

"I should've looked over your wounds more thoroughly that first day you fell."

Tex sighed. "We could keep rewriting the past until we're blue in the face. How about instead you fetch more water? I'll try and roll all the way over."

"Wait. I have something that'll help." She hurried over to the rabbit hides she'd been working on. They were as soft as mink. She folded the hides together and brought them to him. "Rest your head on these. Your poor bruised face could probably use a soft pillow."

Tex looked up at her. His eyes were glassy, though otherwise much improved. But his face looked hot and feverish. Wincing, he rolled toward his right to protect his broken arm. Once he managed it, he asked, "Is this enough? My left arm isn't going to like me resting on it even a little."

"It's enough. I'll be right back." She went to the little

spring and soaked the handy sleeve and came back to press it against his back. The black shirt with the dried blood on it turned red as the fabric got wet. “I’m going to let things soak for a while before trying to get at the wound. Your shirt is stuck to your back pretty tight.”

“I can lie like this for now. It’s not too bad. The rabbit furs help.”

She nodded. “Maybe you can sleep for a bit in the meantime.”

He didn’t respond, yet she could hear his breathing deepen until it was a gentle snore. She took the sleeve and soaked it again at the spring, then filled her growing collection of bark basins to heat over the fire. Because the basins were overly flat and had little brim on them, they didn’t hold much water. Which meant she would need to use warm water and change it frequently.

She went over and rested the soaked sleeve on his back for a few minutes, then tugged on the fabric. It had loosened around the edges but was still stuck to the skin in the center. She rinsed out the cloth and pressed it over the wound again.

Stella repeated the routine on his back for a long time, trying desperately to cause as little pain as possible. So far she hadn’t hurt him badly enough to wake him. But the time came when she knew she either had to tug harder or just leave it alone. And feverish as he was, she didn’t dare leave it.

She needed to pull the shirt free of the wound, no matter the pain.

Her jaw clenched, she tugged the drenched fabric harder. Finally, it gave, then stopped, then gave again, then stopped. Tex groaned in his sleep. Then, forcing herself to go on, she gave it one last firm tug, and it came free.

The groan changed to a growl, followed by a shout.

"I'm sorry." She leaned forward and saw his teeth gritted, his eyes open and bloodshot.

"Hot, feverish. Water . . ."

She rushed back to the spring and rinsed out the shirtsleeve. On her way back, she stopped at the fire for the bark basin of water. It was warm now. She brought everything to him and knelt. Using the clean sleeve, she bathed his lips and encouraged him to suck water from the wet cloth.

"I don't think you'll be able to get any water down unless you sit up."

Tex tensed, and with agonizing slowness he pushed himself to sit up. Stella held the shallow basin to his mouth and let him drink. Slowly at first, then faster. He drank nearly a full cup of water before turning his head away.

"I can get you more," she offered.

"Not now, but the warm water was good. It soothed my throat and warmed me inside. Thank you."

"I need to get another supply of water." She moved to the spring, refilled the bark, and took it to the fire. Coming back with clean water, she said, "I haven't looked at your back yet. I got the shirt loose and stopped. Lie back down on your side."

He didn't so much lie down as topple over. But she helped him go down easily. "I'm hoping the worst of the pain is over."

She nodded, knowing full well his pains were far from over. "I had to tug to get the shirt unstuck from your back. I've been soaking it for a long time, and it just wouldn't come loose without a fight."

"B-but you got it?"

"I did, yes." She finally got a good look at his back wound and shuddered. "It's scraped up worse than I'd ever imagined." She sighed so deep it felt like she pulled air all the way up from her feet. "It's really angry and red, but we have to get this wound cleaned up."

"That sounds bad," said Tex.

Her hands trembled. "Your whole back is scraped raw, but there are also deeper scrapes and cuts with a few bits of gravel that have to be dug out." Much more than a few, but she didn't bother with that ugly detail.

She stared at the knife she'd been using for everything under the sun, and after some thinking, she went and held it to the fire. When it was nearly red hot, she pulled it away to let it cool. Then she got to work.

Tex was tense as a bowstring right before the arrow flew, but he made no sound, nor did he move or jump and try and run for it. Probably because he just wasn't up to it.

Minutes later, she'd gotten out every bit of gravel and sand from the scrapes and cuts that she could. She then spread the soaked sleeve gently on his wounds.

Her rough doctoring had made his back start to bleed, so she bathed the wounds again with warm water until the bleeding stopped. She hoped it was all enough to ease his fever.

If she woke up in the morning to find red streaks stretching away from any of the cuts, their situation would go from serious to life-and-death. Grimly, she saw nothing more she could do.

There was no way to bandage his back without cutting up the rest of his shirt. She didn't want to do that, and leaving the wound open seemed better anyway. If she wrapped it, the dressing might just stick to his back again. While she considered, she realized his muscles had relaxed some. Exhausted from her torturing him, he was falling asleep again.

Stella folded the back of his shirt out of the way of the wounds so it wouldn't stick again. She didn't like the idea of his resting on the tattered and bloody shirt, nor did she want him rolling onto his back in his sleep and lying in the dirt. Looking around, she saw one of the rabbit skins had slid out a bit from under his head. She slipped it the rest of the way free and laid it on the ground so that if he rolled onto his back, he'd have a meager cushion.

"Are you done?"

His voice startled her. She realized only then how bitterly alone she felt. "I was hoping, for your sake, you'd sleep awhile."

"What about for your sake, Stella. I wish there were something I could do to help you." He looked over his shoulder. His eyes met hers, both of them bloodshot. He gave her a weak smile.

She brushed his dark hair off his forehead again. "I think it would be best for your back if you didn't sleep on it. And best for your arm if you didn't sleep on your left side."

"It'd be best for me if I just lay on a cloud and didn't move a muscle."

She chuckled. "Well, then you'd be all set. You know, Tex, you're about the unluckiest man I've ever known. Matched only by me and my unluckiness."

"We survived falling over a cliff. That's awful lucky."

"True, but don't forget—we fell over it to begin with."

"True, but we landed in a river instead of on jagged rocks."

"True, and then you had to go plummet over a second cliff and bruise yourself and break your arm."

"True, but I lived through it."

"True." She sighed. "I'm not going to point out any more bad luck."

He swallowed hard. "How bad is my back, Stella?"

"It's mostly just scraped raw, but there are four gashes that are especially inflamed."

"All this pain from four little cuts?"

There was a long pause before she said, "I didn't say they were *little*." Stella patted the shoulder of his good arm. "Try and sleep a little more. I'll get a meal ready for you and fresh water."

"I'll sleep, then eat, then rest some more, and then maybe we can start moving again."

She left him to his optimistic plan, then sank to the ground across the fire and watched him and prayed for him, scared to death he wouldn't survive the night. She asked God to give her some idea of what to do next.

Stella wouldn't have recognized it as an answer to prayer, but she was so exhausted she didn't notice it when her chin, bowed in prayer, sagged deeper until her whole body slumped sideways, and she stretched out for desperately needed sleep.

10

Morgan came up to Owen's side and spoke just above a whisper. "We need to talk."

They'd been standing watch, defending against a ghost for three nights now. He was out there, Morgan knew it, and yet he never spotted the man.

Owen, sitting on the ground by the fire, eating some of Delaney's always-tasty stew for supper, nodded once and said to his wife, "Excuse me," then got to his feet.

Delaney took his plate from him. "Be careful out there, both of you."

Owen took her hand for a long moment before following Morgan into the darkness beyond the firelight.

"What are we going to do to get this guy?" As a rule, Morgan had very little trouble finding the path forward that suited him. Right now, though, he was stumped.

Owen arched both brows in genuine surprise. "Don't you know?"

"Do you think I'd be asking you if I did?"

"We've been standing guard every night. He leaves enough

signs we know he's there, but not enough that we have a hope of catching him. What is he doing out there? And why has he latched on to us?"

"The Ghost is playing with us." They'd taken to calling the stranger the Ghost, which suited him well. "If he's here to do us harm, why hasn't he done anything other than snap the occasional twig or leave one of his mysterious footprints? How long is he going to keep this up before we know what he's planning?"

They stood in full darkness, ready for Owen to take his first watch with Delaney, with Morgan and Roz spelling them for second watch.

Suddenly, Morgan stood straighter and looked around. The Ghost was out there right now. There was such a tiny indication that the man was near, Morgan could have kidded himself that he wasn't. "We know you're there," he called out. "Come on in and talk to us. We'll give you a bite to eat."

No response.

Morgan stood there silently. Though he couldn't see the Ghost, he felt he knew exactly where he was. Morgan wanted to launch himself straight at their intruder, but he held himself back. The man could be moving away deeper into the woods even now, but Morgan didn't think so.

Time passed.

As suddenly as it'd come, the chill that nearly made him shudder faded.

"He's gone," Morgan declared.

"For now," said Owen. "Only for now."

Morgan nodded, turning to his friend. "Well? What are we going to do, Owen?"

"I figure it's best to keep doing what we've been doing.

Keep finding camping spots that are hard to approach undetected—"

"If we're able to, you mean. Sometimes it's hard to find what we need."

Owen continued, "We do our best. But we need to keep pushing as hard as possible to find Tex. I think we're getting closer."

"I believe we are. We're finding the signs he left behind, and I can tell they're not as old. I think we're within days of catching up to him."

"And then we'll all start working our way back to civilization. Instead of two groups lost in the wilds of Colorado, we'll be one."

"One lost group being followed by a ghost." Morgan sighed. "I was hoping you'd have a few more ideas than that."

"And I was hoping you'd come up with something yourself."

Shaking his head, Morgan clapped Owen on the shoulder. "It's your shift to keep an eye out for the Ghost."

The Ghost.

He smirked. The moniker suited him. He'd use it from now on. At least when he was away from people he knew. And he knew mostly no one. Weren't ghosts dead, though? That sent a shudder down his spine. He didn't like that idea.

He'd let Morgan know he was here. Yep, he'd listened and learned names. Then he'd let Morgan know he was leaving. The fool should have figured out that the Ghost would let Morgan think what the Ghost wanted him to think.

Morgan had looked him right in the eye. The Marshal might be good, but the Ghost was better.

Now he watched Owen and Delaney as they stood watch. Such a beautiful woman. But it wasn't the brown-haired woman that drew his interest; it was the little blonde. He knew her. It sped up his heart to see her here, away from that high meadow.

For years he'd gone there to see her. He'd met her pa, too. But he'd never bothered her. She had nothing worth stealing, and he'd stayed well back to keep from scaring her.

But that was when he had his boys at home. Since they'd left him, there was an empty place inside that itched for someone of his own. He itched, in fact, for that pretty yellow-haired woman and her young son.

He could have a family again.

For now, he would do nothing, waiting as deep into the night as he could. He didn't want to do anything with Morgan on guard either. He could consider a man a fool and still respect his talent. And Morgan had plenty of talent, though obviously not as much as he needed.

When Owen and Delaney had settled in and had let down their guard after their shift was nearly at an end, the Ghost slipped up to where they'd tied their horses and approached the one he'd been considering. A calm, easygoing critter, he liked the look of it. He took a few minutes to cover and bind the horse's hooves with leather to hide the animal's tracks. And by handling it, he learned the horse's nature and introduced himself to it. Then he led it away with no complaint from the horse.

No saddle. No bridle. He didn't need them, and he didn't want to take the time or make the slightest noise. All he wanted was just one packhorse. A critter he'd recognized as unusually calm and tractable. There was another just as calm that he planned to come back for later. Let them get nervous, watch closer. He'd still best them.

Tonight he was satisfied with one.

He led the animal to where his own horse awaited.

He couldn't stay up day and night, but he could get by with very little sleep. It made him chuckle to imagine those Marshals waking up in the morning to find one of their horses missing.

He'd've liked to take the pretty blonde, too, and especially liked the idea of having a son again. But taking the woman without also taking the boy bothered him. He'd been separated from his own ma young and still felt the ache of that.

Besides, there was no way he could take the child in utter silence. In fact, knowing they'd make noise had held him back from taking either woman. He could have snatched Delaney up while she was standing watch, but he didn't want her. And both women would be much harder to keep quiet than the horse.

Add to that, a woman would be noticed missing almost immediately and then the chase would be on.

But the day for the blonde and her boy was coming, and soon. For now, he was enjoying tormenting their camp.

The Ghost, huh?

Yep, he liked it.

Tex's survival was between him and God. Stella had done everything she knew to do, yet it seemed it wasn't enough. His fever wouldn't go down. The wounds on his back remained inflamed, and every time she touched them, she caused agonizing pain. He was more unconscious than awake, and she'd gotten very little food and water into him.

She'd stopped thinking of herself, how terribly alone she'd be without him. Instead, she only worried about him.

Stella had tended him all through last night, along with spells when she'd dozed. All through the day, she'd circled between bathing his head with cool water and his back with warm water; she'd crooned over him, prayed for him.

He surfaced from his stupor now and then, took a drink, murmured a few garbled words before sinking back into unconsciousness. Each time he seemed to sink deeper. Each time she'd feared he'd never surface again.

He'd been hot with a fever for two long days.

Now, kneeling at his side, praying and tending, her mind foggy from exhaustion, she only distantly noticed a man slip into the camp. So silently and moving in such a way that she felt no threat. Was he a dream maybe? Too tired to ponder it, she fell into a deep sleep for the first time in days.

He wasted no time in getting to work.

Bright blue eyes so sharp, he saw nearly as well in the evening as in full daylight.

A bearded face that hadn't seen a razor yet in his life.

Clothes made from the world around him. Furs and leather. Moccasins on his feet. Hair so long he'd quit paying attention and kept it tied back with a leather thong.

He had all the supplies he needed. He'd been watching these two for two days and could tell they'd been here longer.

He'd been taught doctoring by the Arapaho and had

herbs to drink and others to use as ointments and powders that drew sickness out of the body. He had willow bark and feverfew. But he didn't have any leeches and regretted that. He'd seen leeches clear up infections like the one this man Tex had; he'd overheard the woman call him by name.

He built up their fire just enough to brew the herbs in his own kettle. He had a pot of stew from his own fire that he put on theirs. Then he left the makings for another meal so the woman could have more when she awoke.

This man Tex was terribly wounded. Seeing the U.S. Marshal's badge pinned on his chest, well, he never considered riding on. But he was the solitary type, so he was hoping he could help without having to talk to either of them, leastways not much.

As exhausted as she was, and as sick as the Marshal was, he thought he could do what needed to be done with little interference from them. They'd sure wonder what happened tomorrow morning, though. He started by lifting the Marshal enough to put the cup of warm brew to his lips. The pain roused him enough that he swallowed the fever-reducing concoction. Tex's eyes flickered open but didn't focus.

He kept on working and was at it for hours. Packing moss on the ugly scrapes on the Marshal's back to draw out the infection. Next, he started on his arm. He had gypsum and strips of cloth to make a proper plaster cast for the broken arm. That took some time, and the cast would be a while drying.

By the time he had the cast wrapped in a sling to protect it while it dried over the next few days, the Marshal's fever had dropped. His patient opened his eyes and focused on him, fully awake now.

He touched one finger to his lips and gave a quiet "Shh. Drink this. Willow tea and feverfew. I'll leave some for you."

He'd been there for hours working since the first dose, so he gave a second drink of the tea.

Tex soon dropped off into a sleep that seemed more like true sleep and less like unconsciousness.

He'd heard the name Tex, but her name was still a mystery. Tex had done almost no talking, and though she talked some, enough to mention his name, she'd certainly never spoken her own name.

Whoever she was, he knew she'd see they had a visitor. Being exhausted didn't make her stupid.

To give her a bit of help, he'd leave some of his supplies behind. She'd make good use of the pot for the next meal, and he had an extra. He also left the empty cup with a leather bag holding tea tucked in it. He hoped she had the sense to dose Tex now and then.

When he'd done all he could, he drifted off into the darkened woods. Far enough away she wouldn't come upon him when she went hunting. Although he'd left her enough food, she could take at least a day off from that. If only he had a gun or bow to spare. Hard to survive in the wilderness without one, but somehow these two had managed to so far.

He'd stay close and keep an eye out in case Tex needed his help again tonight. And while he'd come out in the daylight if the need was urgent, he preferred the solitude of night.

11

At least now, Morgan didn't need to ask Owen what he should do. He had a plan that Owen agreed was a solid one. He was just annoyed with himself for not thinking of it sooner.

It'd only been a few days, of course, and the Ghost hadn't stolen a horse before last night. It occurred to Morgan that he thought better when he was mad.

Probably not true, but right now it suited him to believe it because he was as mad as a rabid badger.

He'd had a long talk with Roz earlier that day and gotten her cooperation. As he settled in to sleep through Owen's first watch, he studied their camp. He'd carefully picked this spot, knowing exactly what he was looking for.

The camp turned quiet for the night, and as usual, Owen and Delaney went out to stand guard.

Roz, Jesse, and Morgan went to sleep. Well, they were all supposed to. Jesse slept like a tired-out kid who'd been in the saddle for long hours. He was asleep within a minute of lying down.

Roz lay awake still. Morgan could hear her breathing and

was surprised he recognized the difference between sleep and her lying still, eyes closed, breathing evenly.

It didn't matter. She wasn't a kid; she wouldn't ask questions.

Quietly, Morgan got up and moved without making a sound the way he'd learned to.

Using darkness, shadows, shallow dips in the ground too small for a man to fully hide in, Morgan kept low to the ground, trying to remain unseen. He wore clothes that matched the colors around him. Not a speck of metal to reflect off the moonlight, nor clink if it hit a stone as he crawled past. He didn't know where the man had set up camp, but he knew not to take this search lightly.

He was a long time finding one of those misshapen tracks in the dark. But it was generally where he thought it would be, even though the Ghost might've gone on past them to his camp. But he'd been after them for days, hanging back. Morgan had hoped the man was letting down his guard just a bit, and Morgan had hit it right.

He still didn't know exactly where the Ghost was, but he wasn't looking for their intruder. He'd left the fool to close in on Owen, who had staked himself out close to the horses in case the Ghost tried to steal another horse. Even a crafty man such as this one would find it hard to get past a fully ready-for-trouble U.S. Marshal.

Morgan well knew he wouldn't be back for his turn as sentry. Owen would head back to camp with Delaney as usual, then step behind the boulders that hid their camp, and Morgan would emerge and take over, Roz with him just like every night. Only tonight it would be Owen wearing Morgan's coat and hat, keeping his hair covered and his head down. In the darkness, the Ghost wouldn't notice. They hoped anyway.

Morgan and Owen had supposed the man would wait out the night, looking for a chance to steal another horse. Then when he'd figured his chance had come, he would take the horse and return to his camp. Which Morgan had to find first. When the Ghost came back to camp, Morgan would grab him and end this maddening sneaking around.

Morgan kept at his search, and it was far into the night, the dawn threatening to lighten the sky, when he finally found the site. He moved fast, packing up everything the Ghost owned and leading the horses just beyond sight of the camp. All the while, he swore he could feel the hot breath of the Ghost right behind him. Imagined or not, Morgan took it as the good Lord telling him to hurry, and so he did.

He hitched the horses to a shrub to allow them to graze for as long as it took. Then he set up to guard them, aiming his gun toward the brush, ready for the man to come from any direction.

And he waited and waited and waited.

The Ghost was barely visible, watching Marshal Morgan from behind a boulder. Fuming, he'd wasted the night playing with them. Now he was stumped.

That first night, when he'd used his slingshot to take down Morgan and missed, it'd shaken him. He never missed, not when there was a little light from the moon to go by. Yet Morgan had moved the second before the stone hit, as though he'd heard it in its soundless flight.

That'd done something to the Ghost. It'd both shaken

him and intrigued him. He wanted to see what kind of man this was.

He'd followed and stalked them and observed. Then he'd decided to make something of this game and stole a horse. Mainly to prove he could and to slap Morgan down. He didn't need two horses after all.

He'd gone tonight to steal another one just to goad them with his skill and their helplessness.

He hadn't gotten a second horse tonight.

And he couldn't get his own horse back now, nor the one he'd stolen last night.

Resting his hand on his Colt pistol, he took stock of his situation. He at least had a gun, but he'd left his rifle on his saddle. And now his saddle was gone, his supplies, everything.

He considered solving his problems with bullets. Morgan was behind a boulder, but the Ghost could slip around, get the drop on him.

Probably.

He'd gone into this wanting to prove he was a better man than this Marshal in the wilderness. It had challenged him, and he loved a challenge . . . if in the end he won.

Sure, the Marshal had taken his horse, his food and supplies, but he hadn't lost. He just hadn't won yet. And that meant it was an even greater challenge, which only stirred him all the more. This wasn't over, but for tonight he decided to fade away, ghostlike.

I'll be back.

He stared hard at his foe and thought the man crouching behind the boulder shifted to look right into his eyes. Morgan felt his threat and understood that nothing was finished.

When he was out of earshot, he headed to where there'd be horses and equipment and time to reconsider how best to show Morgan who was stronger, smarter, faster.

I'll be back.

Stella's eyes popped open in shock.

Something had changed. She knew it before she saw anything. The smell of something delicious wafted her way. Slowly she sat up, looked around.

Tex! She spun to look at him. He was fast asleep. Lying on his back when he'd been on his side for days. She tilted her head, trying to make sense of it all. He had a plaster cast on his arm, bound up in a sling . . .

Why had she fallen asleep so near him? Usually, she was across the fire from him at a respectable distance. She liked to keep some space between them, though propriety had been blasted away during this long stretch they'd spent alone together. But they had to behave in a proper way, at least to uphold their own honor, even if no one in the rest of the world believed that.

That couldn't happen again.

She looked at him and saw his eyes flicker open. They focused on her, as bright and clear as they'd been before his fall. Her relief was so powerful, so all-consuming, she wanted to laugh and cry and maybe dance a few steps. But the mystery of how all this had happened held her still.

"Good morning." His eyes shifted from her down to his arm. "You put a cast on my arm?"

Stella shook her head. "No. What on earth's happened? Someone must have come in and done this and . . ." She looked around. "They left a pot of something. I smelled that as soon as I woke up. And look, there's a spoon and a tin cup."

After falling over the cliff with nothing more than the clothes on their backs and Tex's knife, a cup to drink out of and a pot to cook a stew in seemed like grand luxury. Her eyes then slid to a small pile of Indian potatoes, a few wild onions. "We're all set to survive comfortably now. Who did this?"

Tex's eyes narrowed. "I kinda remember someone giving me a drink. I almost slept through it, but about the time he was done, I woke up enough to see it was a man. He said he'd leave me more of . . . whatever drink he gave me."

Stella looked at the tin cup next to the fire.

"It was willow bark tea," Tex said. "I've had it before. It fights a fever. I remember the taste. He said something about drinking more of it later." He glanced down at his arm again. "This plaster's not fully dried. He's got it wrapped in a sling, too. We don't have the fabric for a sling."

Stella scanned the camp, wishing the man were around to thank. "Could it have been an Indian?" she asked. "The Arapaho and Cheyenne are known to be in the area. And I see footprints that look like moccasin tracks."

"I can't remember much about him, except that he had a full beard."

Stella turned back to Tex. She touched the cast and knew he'd have to be careful with it for a while. "I'll leave your back alone for now. You were lying on it, so the pain must have improved. I wonder what all he did."

Tex shifted around a little. "My back still hurts some, but it's much better."

Stella stepped closer to Tex and pressed the back of her hand to his forehead. The skin was no longer hot, and his eyes were bright again. "Tex, you're going to make it. I was so worried. I should have given you more of an examination. I never even thought to check . . ." Her voice broke. Then she lifted her chin, swiped at her eyes, and said, "I-I'll get you more of that tea, and then you should eat something."

Tex gently pushed himself to a sitting position. With some struggle, he got to his feet. "I'd be glad for whatever medicine we have to keep my fever down, Stella. And I'm hungry for the first time in days." With that, he turned, walked a few steps away, then stopped and raised his voice. "If you're out there still, thank you!"

"God bless you, whoever you are," Stella added. "You're the answer to my prayers."

He felt warmth wash over him. He was the answer to someone's prayers. It was hard to forget about God out here, where he was surrounded by heavenly majesty all the time. God was ever-present, his companion and partner, his Redeemer. And right now, those words made him feel overly blessed.

Yes, he'd stay close, though Tex looked to be on the mend now. They could still use a few things, though, and he knew just where to get them. Which meant he'd have to leave, but not for long.

He slipped away into the wilderness.

12

"Look at this. It's a sign left by someone other than Tex. It says Tex fell."

Roz came up with Jesse by her side, all on horseback except for Morgan, who'd seen the rocks and dismounted to study them closer. Two sets, two arrows. Carefully, Morgan looked over the crumbling cliff's edge indicated by the T and the words. He stepped back quickly. That wasn't a drop any man wanted to take.

He pointed down the slope with the S. "That way."

Leading the way down, he smelled woodsmoke and meat cooking before he was halfway down the hill. His heart felt lighter. He was pretty confident they were going to find Tex, although the arrow pointing toward the area that had recently dropped away gave him cause for worry.

The slope they were descending was steep but still passable on horseback. Before he got too close to the campfire, he hollered, "Hello!"

And Stella Duncan came running out of the woods that surrounded the base of the hill. She then stopped and shouted, "Tex! Your Marshal friends are here!"

Tex hooted but didn't show himself. That worried Morgan, but he was still relieved to have found them.

They reached the bottom of the hill just as Tex, looking very wobbly, limped into sight.

It was a reunion for the ages.

Everyone rushed toward Tex.

Stella didn't like such a lukewarm reception, but she understood.

Delaney turned to her and said, "I'm so glad you're both alive and well." She glanced over at Tex. "Alive, anyway."

"Did they hang Clive? Did they hang my whole family?" Stella dreaded the answer, but she'd already waited too long to learn their fate.

Delaney hugged her. "No, you'll be glad to hear they all got out of jail, even Clive. The prosecutor dropped the charge of murder and called it self-defense."

After all her family had risked and lost to secure Clive's freedom—including her brother Leland—Stella could scarcely believe things had turned out so well. "They're really all free, Delaney?" Smiling, she shook her head in wonder.

"Yes, they're free," Delaney reassured her. "I've got so much to tell you. But first, what do you need? What can I do? I suspect you went over that cliff and into the river with hardly anything."

"Well, Tex had his knife strapped down tight, so we had that. He had a flint for building a fire. Otherwise, you're right—hardly anything."

Delaney looked around the camp, her expression puzzled.

"So where did you get that pot and cup or the plaster for Tex's cast?"

But before Stella could respond, Delaney's eyes went wide—so wide that Stella whirled around. A man was coming out of the woods. A very strange, wild-looking man.

"Was it you who brought us the pot of stew?" Stella asked the man. "And the medicine for Tex?"

The man nodded, but he wasn't looking at her. His eyes were riveted on Delaney. "Are you Delaney Bridger?"

Tex and his friends quieted down as they turned toward the stranger.

Owen strode over to Delaney's side.

Delaney answered, "That's my name, though now I'm married, it's Delaney Riley."

Owen moved a bit closer and slid his arm around her waist.

With his long hair and beard, he looked more like a bear than a man. Add to that the deerskin pants and jerkin and wide-brimmed hat. At his waist was a leather holster and a six-gun.

And he spoke as if he hadn't done much talking in a very long time. "I-I am your big brother, Bowie," he said. "Bowie Bridger."

"I don't remember ever meeting you," said Delaney.

"When you were just a tiny thing, I was around for a time. Then I headed west and never came back."

"It's been years, then. How do you know it's me?"

But under all that fur on Bowie's face, Stella saw a resemblance to Delaney's brother Boone, who'd traveled with them from Denver to the fort near Cheyenne. Delaney no doubt saw it, too.

"I've seen Pa twice since I left home," said Bowie. "He carries a picture of you and Boone and him and Ma. He said you were all together in Texas for a spell after the war. I always hoped I'd get a chance to see you again. And now I have."

He moved a step back, as if the mere sight of her had satisfied him and he'd leave now, but Delaney launched herself at him even as Owen made a grab for her but missed.

Delaney flung her arms around Bowie. "I've always wanted to meet you. Stay with us for a time, please? We're heading back to Cheyenne. Pa and Ma are both there now."

"Pa told me when I saw him. But at the time, Ma hadn't come out yet. Ma's there now?"

Stella thought of a better reason than a family reunion to get him to stay. "Do you know how to get out of these mountains?"

Through his thick beard, Bowie gave a big smile. "Sure do."

"Will you help us find our way out?" Delaney asked.

He looked down at Delaney, over at Owen, then put his hands firmly on Delaney's shoulders and held her away from him. "Can I ride along with you, Baby Sister?"

"Oh, yes, I'd love to get to know you. When I left Fort Russell, Boone was there recovering from an injury. I can tell you more about that later. Please come with us and see him. Do you know where Crockett and Jedediah are these days? Maybe we can get them to come, too. It's where Ma and Pa live, so it's home now. After you lead us out of these mountains, I'd like it if you came home with me to the fort."

Bowie's smile faded. "I avoid towns as a rule." There was a stretch of silence, as if he was considering whether it was a hard and fast rule. At last, he settled it. "But I'd sure like to see my family. I'll come for a time."

Delaney hugged Bowie again, and then she took her brother's hand and led him around to meet everyone. "This here's my husband, Owen Riley. And this is Tex and Stella—we've been searching for them for a long time after we got separated. And these are our friends: Morgan, Roz, and Roz's son, Jesse."

It struck Stella that Delaney was being very gentle with the tough-looking man. But given his situation, maybe gentle treatment was called for.

13

Morgan was both fascinated and annoyed. He'd've found a way out of these mountains just fine and never would've asked for directions. It was embarrassing. But then, after spending some time with Bowie Bridger, well, a man could stand a little annoyance and embarrassment in exchange for getting to know a legend.

"I've got a question for you," Morgan said. "Were you by any chance near our camp the last few days? We were being followed by a man who never showed himself. It was eerie. He was mighty skilled with his haunting of our group. We even took to calling him 'the Ghost.'"

Bowie looked thoughtful. "Reckon that was Wildcat Duncan. He's a strange one. You could say he haunts these parts."

Stella gasped. "Uncle Lenny was following you? Did he steal any horses?"

Everyone turned to face her.

Tex spoke first. "Your uncle is Wildcat Duncan? I thought you said your family was honest."

Stella shrugged. "He's from a different branch. Uncle

Lenny is a scoundrel. Most of the crimes pinned to my family name are his doing."

"His name came up when we were talking with your uncle Gordon," said Morgan. "He blamed everything on Lenny, too."

"Wildcat Duncan, huh? Haunting your camp? Yep, that sounds like him. How many men did he have with him?" Bowie tugged the fur on his face.

"Far as we could tell, he was alone," Morgan replied.

Pondering, Bowie tugged his beard some more. "I wonder if maybe it was someone else. Wildcat Duncan usually travels with a pack of men, mostly kin. If it was Wildcat, he likely wouldn't've been alone."

"Pretty sure the Ghost was alone," Morgan said. "I found his horse and took it after he stole one of ours." He pointed to the horse. "That's it right there."

Bowie arched his brows. "You stole his horse?"

Morgan gave a little shrug. "It was probably stolen to begin with. Look at the brand. It's been worked over, so it can't be real. Can a lawman steal a stolen horse? If this guy had a bag of money from a bank robbery, no one would accuse me of stealing that."

"Good point. But as I said, Wildcat's rarely alone. I wonder if it was him."

Stella added, "He always travels with his three sons. They rob banks together and get up to who-knows-what."

"You said he's strange," Morgan reminded Bowie. He was struck by how strange the man seemed who'd been stalking them.

"That I did, and coming from me, that's a strong statement. Is he still following you?"

Shaking his head, Morgan said, "After I set him afoot, it appears he's stopped haunting us."

Bowie nodded. "I think Tex needs another day to get his strength back. The plaster on his cast is almost dried solid, and his back looks better. I got a few rabbits this morning. I've made a stew. I'll go fetch it." As he turned to leave, Delaney grabbed his arm.

He jumped like someone who wasn't used to being around people.

"I'm afraid you'll walk out of my sight and vanish forever," she explained. "Can Owen and I come with you? Help you carry whatever you have back here so you can stay around our campfire?"

"Sure, Baby Sister. Tell me about the family. I heard tell Jed and Crockett had come west. Are all of them married? Any little nieces and nephews?"

"I'm the first one married and the youngest. That doesn't seem right at all. What's the matter with you boys?"

One bushy brow arched. "Been a long time since anyone called me a boy. Pa always talked about his youth in the wilds of Colorado. It was our favorite thing to talk about. It put a hankering in me to come and see it for myself, and the mountains suited me. So I stayed. I reckon Crockett and Jed felt the same."

"Boone and I were stragglers. Pa's talk was more about soldiering when we were youngsters. Boone's been talking of signing up and serving under Pa at Fort Russell. He wanted to learn more about it before he settled on it. He got shot on our way from Denver to Cheyenne, but he survived."

Stella watched them walk away, talking, and then turned to Tex. "Will you be ready to go by tomorrow? Just yesterday you were so sick I feared you wouldn't survive the night. Now Bowie Bridger says you're ready to hit the trail as soon as your cast dries."

"If Bowie thinks I'll be ready to go, well, he could be right about that. I guess I'll have to see how things look come tomorrow morning."

"I want to look myself at those cuts on your back, Tex. I haven't seen 'em since Bowie put those bandages on."

Tex said to Morgan, "That Bowie is a regular miracle worker. He snuck into our camp last evening while we were sleeping and fitted the cast and doctored my wounds, leaving me some willow bark tea. I was mighty sick before he came. I survived that first fall over the cliff into the water and came out battered, but the second time . . . well, it all boils down to, I fell over another cliff. One minute I was standing on solid ground, the next a rock shifted under my feet and I went over. Almost died."

Morgan shook his head in wonder. "You still look mighty rough. Let's go sit down. You can tell us how you've been surviving out here since, and all that went on before you came to be all busted up." The two of them headed for a log close to the fire and sat. Roz and Jesse tagged along.

Stella felt left behind. She paused to give thanks that her family hadn't all been locked away or hanged. It was a pure miracle. That didn't mean she wanted to go back to riding with them. She wondered if Tex remembered his promise to keep her hidden from her family. Surely they'd left Fort Russell by now. Stella asked for more details about what had become of her family, while Roz asked if they should go straight to her meadow and fetch her cows. No reason to go all the way to Cheyenne again.

"Let's ride along," Stella suggested. "Bowie will be a big help moving the cows, and he wants to go see his family." She wasn't sure if *want* was the right word. He was *willing* to, although he'd shown a spark of interest in seeing his ma.

Roz nodded and started stripping the leather off the horses. The others fell in to help out—except for Tex, of course.

They'd brought the two packhorses and the Ghost's horse, saddle included. Morgan well knew that horse thieves were hanged in the West, but he figured he was safe in this case. To accuse him of theft, the Ghost would have to admit he'd stolen Morgan's horse first, so he doubted the man would say anything. He thought again of Bowie's mention of Wildcat Duncan, wondering if he might be their man. Morgan wanted to find out everything Stella and Bowie knew of Wildcat Duncan. But whether it was him or someone else, Morgan had a feeling he hadn't seen the last of the Ghost.

And always in the back of his mind was the question of whether it might in fact be his pa.

They made an early night of it, all of them having had their fill of Delaney badgering Bowie with questions. The man answered them warily, obviously unaccustomed to talking much.

As they bedded down, Morgan felt a measure of relief. A weight had been lifted off his shoulders, one that was dragging down his spirits during this whole journey. Tex was alive and well. He thought that over and decided Tex was only somewhat well.

He rolled onto his side, and across the campfire he saw Roz, also on her side, watching him.

He was going to have to do something about that woman.

Yep, he had some decisions to make.

14

Roz rode closer to Bowie than was probably wise. He didn't seem to care to talk without prompting, which was all right with her because she found herself feeling the need to fire questions at the man.

Once there was a break in Delaney's questions, and Owen's and Morgan's, she finally had a chance to question Bowie about his knowing she'd been living in the remote meadow. Why hadn't he ever gone and spoken to her? Had others done the same? Of course, those who roamed the mountains like Bowie often became the solitary type, not at all inclined to go visiting folk.

This trail out of the mountains wasn't one she'd've chosen. Bowie took unexpected turns and had them riding down tight little gullies, and yet they came out of the endless hills by midafternoon.

"I can't believe we were this close to finding our way out," Tex said to Stella.

"Except we'd've never gone the way Bowie did." Stella shook her head. "We might've been wandering for another week."

Tex nodded his agreement. "Daniel Boone once said, 'I've never been lost, but I was bewildered once for three days.'"

"We're north of Fort Collins," announced Bowie. "We've got a long ride ahead of us, but we should be arriving at Fort Russell sometime later tonight."

Roz wondered if she would ever ride that same trail again. It was tricky and confusing, and it awakened in her a desire to explore the land around her high valley more. Maybe explore the whole mountain range.

Delaney came up to ride closer to Bowie again. Her brother was going to be all caught up with his family by the time he met up with them.

Roz dropped back and rode beside Morgan. It was a wide road they were on, well traveled, and they often passed by other riders, wagons and whatnot. She leaned close to Morgan and whispered, "I've been to Cheyenne once already, but at the time we were fretting about outlaws and captives. It was enough of a distraction that I didn't quite get the chance to consider the crowds."

Morgan peered down the road ahead. They'd just ridden past a farmer driving a wagon. His wife sat beside him on the high seat, a baby on her lap, two small boys in the back.

"I'll grant you there were a lot of people at the fort and in Cheyenne, especially to a woman who'd been living with only her son for company." He twisted in the saddle to look at her. "When you were real young, you said your ma and pa took you to town some, is that right?"

"I have only a few memories of Ma. One is that she liked going to town. Pa used to complain that she couldn't let the summer go by without a trip to town. We'd ride horseback, with me in front of Ma or Pa, sharing the saddle. But then

Ma died the year I was . . ." She swallowed hard. "Do you remember her, Morgan?"

He shook his head. "I don't. My first memory of you was when I was around eight. Back then, Pa spent a lot of time in the wilderness with me and Gavin."

"I hardly remember Gavin. He didn't turn up at our ranch as often as you did."

"Gavin loved hunting from an early age, and there was some land to the south of our place he favored. Even when I told him I'd met you and it was fun playing with you, he wasn't much interested in visiting your place." He smiled at Roz, and the sweet smile touched something deep in her heart. "Guess he figured he was too old for such things, and I didn't push him either. I liked having you as a friend that was mine alone."

"He was never as friendly as you, nor as handsome." Roz gave him a sly look.

Morgan chuckled, and she wanted to say it again, but louder. Demand he understand how much she'd already cared about him back when they were youngsters. Point out how much she was starting to care for him again now.

Instead, she asked, "How old would you say I was when we first met?"

"We were of an age, I'd say. If I was eight, then you were eight, too."

"Well, Ma hadn't been gone long when I met you. From the age of eight, then, it was just me and Pa. And after Ma passed, Pa rode into town no more than once a year. Later, when I turned fifteen or sixteen—you were gone by then—there was trouble in town." Roz fell silent for a moment, suddenly not caring to talk about those days.

"What kind of trouble, Roz? You can't quit your story now."

She'd really prefer it if she could. "Well, there was this man who paid me improper attention. Men, honestly. Three of them."

She saw Morgan's jaw tighten, and anger flashed in his eyes.

"I didn't do anything to try and draw their attention—I didn't talk to them or flaunt myself."

Morgan reached across his horse and gripped her wrist gently. "I know you didn't. I'd never cast the blame on you. I'm angry at any man low-down enough to mistreat an innocent young woman."

That took her fear of his upset away, but it didn't quash the fear she'd felt at that time. "It was frightening. They were in the general store when Pa and I went inside. They said some crude things. One of them had the gall to grab at me."

Morgan's grip tightened, and the anger flashed again.

"As you can imagine, Pa was furious. There was a fistfight, and a gun was drawn. I ducked behind a barrel of pickles. Thankfully, the store owner threw in on Pa's side, and someone ran out and called for the sheriff. I didn't see most of it; I peeked out from behind the barrel only once or twice."

"Did your pa get shot?"

"No, but one of the men shot a hole in the pickle barrel, which made a big mess."

"He shot at you?" Morgan sounded incredulous.

Shaking her head, Roz said, "I think the bullet went wild. I never thought he or anyone else intended to kill me. With the sheriff on his way and the store owner's help, the fight ended and we headed for home. Thankfully, no one came after us. After that, Pa said it was too dangerous for me in town, and I was old enough to stay home alone. He went to town only once or twice more in his life. Once to buy flannel for diapers when we learned the baby was coming. Herman had gone away. Mostly, Pa was determined to live without store-bought things, and he seemed almost desperate to teach me how to live off the land.

"We were all settled into our life in the wilderness when Herman wandered through. He got on well with Pa and seemed like a dependable man, so we ended up married. I look back on that now, and I'm pretty sure Pa was worried he wouldn't live for much longer and so wanted me to have someone around to help. We didn't even go to town for the wedding. Herman went and fetched a preacher, and Pa and I rode halfway to town and met them. We became man and wife out on the trail. But after a couple of months of being married, Herman's feet got to itching. He rode off to go trapping about the time I realized there was to be a child."

"Did you tell him you were expecting?"

Roz nodded. "I'd told him I thought there was a baby coming. I think that news was a big part of what made his feet itch so bad."

Morgan shook his head. "Any man lucky enough to be with you on that beautiful land and turn and ride away would have to be a consarned fool."

"You did, Morgan." The words were out before she knew what she was saying.

His mouth clamped shut, and his eyes narrowed. "We were way too young back then, Roz. And I thought I couldn't call myself a man if I didn't go fight in the war. Then after the fighting stopped . . . well, I've told you how Pa left that note and made his threats. I can admit to you now that it broke my heart. Even so, I shouldn't have let it stop me from seeing you again."

Roz waited, wished, prayed he'd add words like those she was dying to hear from him.

"But we're not too young now, Roz."

A smile broke out on her face as she looked across from her horse into his brown eyes. His hair had been newly shorn in Cheyenne, and his clothes were his usual garb made from buckskin and broadcloth, all brown or tan to match his skin. He said it helped him disappear when he was tracking someone. Well, he wasn't going to disappear from her.

Tears burned in her eyes, yet they didn't stop the smile.

"You're not gonna *cry*, are you? I was hoping you were above that kind of—"

"Shut up, Morgan." She swiped her wrist across her eyes in case any tears escaped and saw he was smiling back at her. Teasing. She remembered that about him from long ago. Pa was a good man, but there wasn't much fun in him. And Herman had quickly turned into a useless, sullen, abandoning loafer. Morgan, on the other hand, made her laugh.

She laughed now. "No, we are *not* too young. Is that a marriage proposal?"

"It for certain is. You need someone to take care of you and Jesse, and I'm just the man to do it."

That put a little hitch in her happiness. She'd wanted words of love. She'd married before because Pa had pushed her into choosing someone to take care of her. At least she liked Morgan. It didn't matter that he didn't love her. He'd offered, and she would accept that offer. But oh, how she'd wanted more.

"And together we can drive some of those cattle of yours to Fort Collins or Cheyenne or Denver or wherever we can find a buyer. Then how about we keep the rest and grow a herd and some children? We'll help Jesse grow up to be a big improvement on his pa, and we'll build a life, Roz. We'll ride to town anytime you want, and any man who pesters you had better be ready to part company with his teeth."

He just kept on talking. Planning their lives. There were plenty of words spoken if he'd wanted to tell her he loved her. But none of that nature were uttered.

She then noticed the people around them, all clearly eavesdroppers. Who could blame them? This was a long ride, and what was going on between her and Morgan had to be the most interesting thing around.

Morgan drew his horse to a stop, swung off it with that animal grace he'd always had, and dragged her off her horse. At the top of his lungs, he yelled, "Roz just agreed to marry me!"

He wrapped his arms around her waist and lifted her off the ground. Roz heard shouts and applause coming from the others.

Morgan whirled her around a time or two before he plunked her back on her feet. Then, while she was still a little dizzy, he turned to Jesse and asked, "Does that suit you?"

Her son was smiling to beat all. "It suits me fine, Marshal."

Morgan tugged on the Stetson someone found for Jesse in Cheyenne. "Call me Pa. It'll be official soon enough."

Jesse lit up like a comet blazing across the sky, and so Morgan grabbed Jesse, lifted the boy, and spun him around, too.

"How about we have a wedding when we get to Fort Russell?" Delaney asked. "I'll see if my family can come."

Morgan looked at Roz. "Okay if we do that?"

Nodding, happy regardless of the quiet ache in her heart, Roz said, "Sounds wonderful to me."

"Then let's ride for Cheyenne. And fast!" Morgan got his family back on horseback, and they set a brisk pace through the rest of the afternoon.

Fort Russell came into sight before the sun went down.

15

The wedding took some time despite Morgan's eagerness.

The Bridgers had to spend time whooping and hollering over Bowie. While they'd been in the mountains, Delaney's two other brothers had come to the fort to see their folks. The whole family chattered until Roz was afraid her wedding had been forgotten. It seemed Hester Bridger could take charge of just about anything.

Roz bought a new dress for the second time in a single month, and she had a second bath as well. The whole idea of new clothes and bathing was strange to her, yet she couldn't help but like it. Being in Cheyenne could be downright pleasant when she thought about it.

Hester Bridger, Delaney's ma, had outfitted her another time when she'd come to Cheyenne wearing a riding skirt and shirtwaist. Hester had tossed her other clothes out, and Roz had to bite her tongue to keep from protesting.

She'd grown out of her childhood dresses and taken to wearing her ma's. Then when they'd completely worn out, she started wearing her pa's clothes, who was dead by then. Then she put on Herman's, though he'd had only one change of clothes. She'd used his second set of clothes to bury him in. She'd had to remake them as best she could for Jesse, too. She knew how to tan hides and would've had to change over to all leather outfits soon, for herself and for Jesse.

Now she had a new riding skirt, a shirtwaist, and a pretty blue dress because Delaney's ma said that blue was a beautiful color on her. Roz had no idea colors could be better or worse on a person. Colors were just colors. Clothes were just clothes. The whole idea was new to her.

She had her freshly washed hair hanging loose. Hester Bridger had lamented that there wasn't time for curls. She'd always just tied it back in a bun anyway.

Stella and Delaney wanted to stand up with her at the altar, yet no one had for Delaney. Roz didn't care where people stood. She half suspected that Stella wanted to stand where she could keep an eye on the back door; she was worried about running into her family.

Fort Russell had a couple of guesthouses that were currently empty, so Roz and Morgan would get their own house after the wedding. Jesse had been invited to join them, but Hester had used pie and coaxing to get the boy to stay with her. Roz didn't think that was necessary, but Hester had a will stronger than her own, and so it had been arranged.

There was room enough for Stella in the Bridger house, even with all the company. Tex got invited to stay with Owen and Delaney.

By the time the ruckus had settled down over Bowie, and Roz had her new dress on, and Morgan had bathed and changed into clean clothes, it was full dark.

Chaplain Brokaw knew Colonel Bridger well and had conducted Owen's wedding to Delaney, and he was delighted to be part of a second ceremony. It was finally all settled, with Owen and Tex—who hadn't yet seen a doctor but probably oughta—standing at Morgan's side.

Roz's whole life was changing. She was about to begin something she'd wanted all her life—well, almost all. She wondered what it would take to get Morgan to love her. As for herself, she'd loved Morgan Sawyer since the day she'd first laid eyes on him as a youngster.

The Bridger family and a few others, most notably the fort's sawbones, were sitting quietly in church pews. Jesse was with Hester and Grizzly Bridger, a nickname the colonel had picked up long ago. Though they were of no relation, Roz heard Hester tell Jesse to call her Granny.

She stood side by side with Morgan and listened to the chaplain, and when called upon, she spoke aloud the vows she'd dreamed of speaking all her life.

Morgan said them right along with her. As the ceremony ended, the chaplain said, "I now declare you husband and wife." And just like that, she was wed to the love of her life.

Morgan smiled down at her, pulling her arm through his elbow and tucking her close to his side. "Hello there, Roz Sawyer. I hope that name suits you, ma'am."

Roz smiled so wide her face hurt. The joy she felt could not be contained. "It suits me right down to the ground!"

Morgan nodded and faced their guests. "Jesse, I'd like your name to be Jesse Sawyer now. I'll put in the paperwork to make it official, if that's all right with you."

"That suits me too, Pa." Jesse was squeezed in between Hester and Grizzly and seemed content there.

Roz felt Morgan's chest expand with what felt like pride.

He was proud to have a son. It was the perfect blessing from God over their marriage.

Hester hugged Jesse as if he were her very own grandson. Had she claimed Morgan as another son? She wouldn't put it past Hester. The woman had a mind of her own.

She just hoped Hester wasn't going to tell Jesse his surname was now Bridger.

16

"I should have brought Jesse with us." Roz looked behind her at the commander's house, still all lit up. They'd been the first to leave, not counting Tex, who'd been led away by the doctor. And Delaney looked to be getting ready to ride off with Owen soon. They were still newlyweds and no doubt craved some time alone after many nights on the trail.

Morgan saw Jesse through the front window, standing between Bowie and Boone Bridger. He was pretty sure he heard the kid laughing, even from where he stood.

He guided Roz inside with a gentle but determined nudge. "I like the idea of having a night alone with you. It's a good way to start a marriage."

"I know what you've been doing since you left—I mean the jobs you've had—but there's plenty I don't know."

"We've got a lifetime to get to know each other." Morgan closed the door, then turned Roz to face him. He kissed her before she could launch into a nice long chat.

But Roz had been married before. It didn't take Morgan long to realize she knew exactly what that meant.

Morgan had lived shy of women for the most part. He

was a busy man with a job that took him to wild places, and no women were anywhere near him. And since he never had much interest in stopping his wandering ways, and women seemed to like putting down roots, he'd never gotten to know one overly, leastwise not as an adult.

Well, he was going to stop his wandering now.

Roz's arms came around his neck, and she stood up on her tiptoes.

Morgan lifted her off her feet, just as he had when she agreed to marry him. She fit in his arms perfectly.

Hester Bridger had sent a bit of food over, the makings for coffee, and supplies for breakfast. They ignored them all. Slowly, they made their way to the bedroom, where Morgan closed the door on the whole world.

And found one of the sweetest facts of life for a wedded couple.

Later, as they lay beside each other, he said, "I'm sorry I didn't come back and find you a long time ago, Roz. Being a married man is the best thing in the world."

Roz propped herself up on an elbow and kissed him thoroughly. "I'm sorry I didn't abandon my pa and my ranch and chase after you to the war."

He smiled. "We were still mighty young. Can't see your pa taking kindly to letting two sixteen-year-olds run off with each other."

"True, he wouldn't have stood for it. But I regret every moment of my life I didn't spend with you. I'm glad to have Jesse, though—he's a fine boy. I reckon God guides our path, and He put Herman in my way so I could have my son. Then He put you in my path so I could have you again. You, Morgan Sawyer."

Morgan ran his fingers deep into her fine blond hair. "Let's head back to your ranch soon. We can live there, unless you're tired of being so far out."

She shrugged, and he felt her move under his hands. Having a beautiful woman close enough you could feel her shrug was a true wonder.

"If we stay, I'll be content. If you want to go, I'll follow. For now, let's go to the ranch. I'm used to the place, but I could give it up. What I can't give up is you."

He pulled her closer, holding her tight, and they fell asleep together.

After many days of hard living, sleeping on the ground, scant food flavored with trail dust, and rugged conditions of every imaginable kind, Morgan was both exhausted and more relaxed and comfortable than he'd ever been in his life. He slept the night through with no turn standing watch, staring endlessly into the woods, half awake and listening for the footsteps of a ghost.

It was the finest night of his life.

"Hester left behind eggs and bacon, and there's fixings for coffee and a loaf of bread." Roz glanced at Morgan, almost amazed that he was still there. It'd take some time to get over being thrilled whenever she remembered she was married to him. "Do you want breakfast here, or do you have plans for the day? I know you talked about wanting to get to know Bowie better while he's around."

Morgan grinned, then laughed. "I expect his family has a lock on him right now, and if he decides to ride home with us, we'll get to know him plenty on the trail. I can't deny the man is a legend, and I'd love to spend time talking to him. Let me help with breakfast. You want to slice the bacon or get coffee on?"

They worked companionably together. Roz had all sorts of hope that they'd have a happy marriage. She'd soon lost hope for such a thing with Herman, and that was the last time she allowed thoughts of her dreadful first husband into this house with her and Morgan.

After they'd eaten their fill, Morgan said, "I can't remember the last time I loafed around over a meal." He poured another cup of coffee. "Or had coffee that didn't taste like trail dust."

"You can go on over to find the Bridgers while I clean up after the meal."

He shook his head. "I'll stay and help, and we'll go over together. We need to talk about supplies for your place."

Roz wondered at that. "Supplies? I have everything there we need." What more could there be?

"We should at least buy coffee, flour and sugar, and a few more changes of clothes for you and Jesse. I've got money set aside, Roz. I can afford to make the cabin a bit more comfortable if you'd like. Have you got enough blankets? I'll bet Jesse has outgrown his winter coat. And we can buy some canned peaches and any other whatnots you'd like."

"Canned peaches?" She laughed. "And Jesse wears Herman's old winter coat, which is plenty big, while I wear Pa's."

Morgan leaned back in his chair, his legs stretched out, the coffee cup held in both hands. "You're not going to be an overly expensive wife to take care of, are you, Rosalind?"

Roz gave a little shrug. "Never needed money, not up at my ranch."

"Won't need much now either. Still, it'd be wise to pick up a few things. I also need to turn the Ghost's horse over to the law; I reckon it's a stolen animal. 'Course, we have a few horses the Duncans stole from your place when they were chasing after us."

"After you stole *their* horses."

Morgan flinched. "Figured them for stolen, too. But we gave them back and got your horses back. Point is, we have plenty of pack animals."

"Now that we've got a plan for the future, how about we go see the Bridgers and find out how Tex is doing?"

The doctor seemed determined to give Tex a thorough examination, and it sounded like he might keep his patient in the infirmary for a while longer. Tex didn't seem to object. He wasn't interested in spending the night anywhere he was offered, and so he'd let the doctor decide.

Morgan took her hand in his, and they walked toward the infirmary. Roz wondered what all the doctor had found out about the poor battered man.

Morgan's Marshal appointment was up in six months. He wrote the man who'd appointed him and resigned. Since Morgan was leaving early, Owen included his own letter saying he would step in if there was work needing to be done by Morgan. And Tex had offered to help as soon as he healed up. While at Fort Russell, a telegram arrived that allowed Morgan to resign. A new Marshal would be hired to take his place.

Morgan found he enjoyed the Bridger family's company a great deal. He was especially enthralled by Colonel Bridger's stories about Morgan's pa. The colonel called him Amzi. Morgan recognized the name when he heard it, and yet hardly anyone referred to his pa as Amzi.

He and his big brother Gavin had called him Pa, and Roz's pa called him Sawyer. But he knew the name, of course. Amzi. It rhymed with *lamb's eye*. That was the joke Pa used to tell. The colonel had spent time wandering in the wild before he'd married, and he'd come to know Amzi Sawyer. It was one of the reasons he'd noted when Morgan joined the Union Army, and it had helped guide them as they were tracking Delaney. When Grizzly had seen where they'd gone running into the mountains, and knowing Morgan was with them, he'd had a good idea where exactly they'd gone off to.

He also wondered if Bowie had known or met his pa, and if he had any idea what had happened to him. A part of Morgan didn't want to know the answer. He wouldn't soon forget the ugly note his pa had left him, telling him not to come home, that Gavin was dead, and Morgan had killed his brother by picking the wrong side in the war. All the while he couldn't deny a longing deep inside to know if his pa was alive or not, and to see him again if he was.

It sent a chill up Morgan's spine every time he remembered Owen asking him if the Ghost could possibly be Morgan's pa. Morgan had to admit he was afraid of his pa. Not physically. He'd be an old man by now, so Morgan could handle him that way. But he also knew his pa had a rare talent for saying just the right thing to break Morgan's heart. He'd figured the man was gone for good and, alive or dead, it didn't matter much.

But the Ghost . . . could it possibly be Pa?

Bowie had suspected their culprit was Wildcat Duncan,

until Morgan said the man was alone. Duncan traveled in a pack of outlaws, apparently.

Tex wanted a few more days of rest and said he'd probably come up to Roz's place before he headed back to work. Owen was staying at Fort Russell with Delaney, newly assigned as a Marshal working at the fort. Bowie promised to come up later as well and bring some of his brothers along. They could show Morgan the trail to town that the longhorns could handle.

That meant Morgan, Roz, and Jesse were heading back to the ranch without the others.

Morgan remembered riding out to search for Tex and wishing he could go alone. Now he'd set up his life so he'd never be alone again. And he couldn't help but smile whenever he thought of it.

After plenty of time resting and eating well, Morgan and Roz and Jesse planned to ride south back into the wilderness. But this time they wouldn't be searching for a lost Marshal. This time they were headed for home. Together.

Roz seemed flustered by all the supplies she'd bought with the money Morgan gladly provided. Hester had come along with them to Cheyenne to shop, seeing as Roz had no idea which store-bought items a household might need.

Hester was a wise woman who understood living off the land, so she didn't overwhelm Roz or Morgan with foolish unneeded fripperies. But she insisted on flour and yeast and salt pork. She'd questioned her about pots and pans, plates and utensils, and added a few items for the packhorses to carry.

When Roz had confessed to Hester that she remembered little of cooking from her mother and they'd never used flour since Pa didn't go to town, Hester spent time with Roz, teaching her to make bread, pancakes, and other things. She also insisted they add to their slim collection of children's and women's clothes, all under protest from Roz. Even so, Hester made certain they bought and packed everything they needed. For once, Morgan appreciated the interference. And now the three Sawyers were hitting the trail, leading five packhorses, all of them going back to the high meadow.

They spent the night in Fort Collins, and then Morgan let Roz take over and lead the way home. When at last they reached their meadow, Morgan pulled his horse to a stop, and Roz reined her horse over to stand beside him. "I can see why your pa fell in love with this meadow," he said, "but I've never been sure why my pa settled where he did. We never had cattle, never raised horses. Just lived off the land. It was a hardscrabble life, but a fine place to grow up."

The meadow before them was a shallow bowl with canyon walls surrounding it. It stretched for a mile or more, its grasses lush and belly high. A light breeze blew, and the grass waved as if God's hand were sweeping across the top of it. There was a stream near one corner of the meadow, its water flowing out of a cave.

"Your longhorns look to have stood your time away well enough."

From massive old mossy horns with an eight-foot spread to razor-sharp horns to frolicking babies born just this spring, and every size in between. A handful of horses grazed among the cattle as well. The Duncans had taken a few for pack animals, but some of them remained. Wild mustangs, too, could be seen with the cows, munching on grass as if they were part of the same herd.

"I'm not sure I want to sell any of these cows. I like them right where they are." Morgan turned and smiled at her.

The scream of a bald eagle drew their eyes upward. The great bird swooped down into the meadow and snatched a fish out of the stream with its golden talons. It screamed again as it rose up into the air.

"This has to be one of the most beautiful places on earth." His eyes shifted to her cabin. "I didn't go inside the cabin when we were here before, and I don't remember going in when I was a kid. I'm looking forward to seeing it. We may need to add on more bedrooms once the youngsters start coming."

He glanced at Roz, and she smiled back. The idea of having more babies pleased her.

"Well, let's get unpacked and settle in." Morgan urged his horse forward. "Jesse, you and I can unload the horses and carry in the supplies while your ma puts things away. Does that suit the both of you?"

"Yes, Pa."

"And I'll get a stew cooking," said Roz. "We're in need of a hearty meal."

Jesse was eager and hardworking. Before long, the day was worn all the way out, and they sat down to the meal Roz had created as she unpacked and put away the supplies. The stew wasn't much, but it was delicious.

Afterward, they lay together listening to the eerie howling of a wolf in the distance. Simple though it was, the cabin was sturdy and kept them safe from the curious or hungry wildlife.

"It's a fine home, Roz. I think we can make a good life for ourselves here."

"If my cattle are in fact worth one thousand dollars, we're set for life."

"Especially since we don't need hardly nuthin' here." Morgan hugged her tight against him. "With how long and hard a trip it's likely to be to drive the cattle to town, there's no sense bringing the whole herd to market and collecting all that money. If something comes up we need to buy, we'll take a cow or two to town, sell 'em, and get what we need. In the meantime, just like your pa did, we'll let the herd grow."

With everything securely planned, Morgan soon fell asleep, and she followed him shortly after. It was the most restful sleep of her life.

Tex was about half dead, and he didn't like admitting it.

He kicked up a fuss when the doctor kept him in the fort's infirmary, but he did that mainly out of pride. Underneath he was glad of it. The quiet. Not having to move. Not fretting about what a burden he was for Stella. The weight of it all had made his poor, battered head ache even more than it did from his fall. He wasn't on the verge of dying anymore. Because of Stella's and Bowie's and the doctor's care, Tex was finally starting to heal from the beating he'd taken.

He was glad to follow the orders of the scolding doctor, who told him to lie in bed and stay there for a day or two at the least. In truth, it'd been longer than that, and Tex might just settle in and live this way.

Every muscle and bone in his body hurt. His arm was still in the cast Bowie had made. His knee was killing him. His back, though not infected anymore, was so tender that Tex could hardly lie on it. And he tended to fall asleep, suddenly and deeply, for too long.

His head was the worst of all. Waves of dizziness swept over him. His vision blurred at unexpected moments. Getting to his feet to use the privy was just flat-out dangerous, and so the doctor insisted on following along to keep Tex from falling and injuring himself further.

Just a few more days, though, and he'd be up and around. He thought even the doctor was ready to let him loose.

Owen came most days to visit him, and usually a Bridger or two stopped in with Owen. Sometimes one of the Bridgers came on their own.

Delaney had two more brothers turn up. Jedediah and Crockett. Grizzly and Hester had a liking for naming their sons after trailblazers, it seemed. It was a wonder Delaney wasn't named Meriwether.

And Stella came by a couple of times a day. She wasn't sure about her future and was afraid her family would turn up and make her go back into the mountains. She was a woman alone in the world, and her pa thought it was right and proper to keep her close. But her pa lived a roaming, rootless life, and Stella had hated that life and didn't want to return to it.

It was starting to feel embarrassing, getting caught sleeping all day, which probably meant Tex's condition was improving.

From his place on the bed, he looked up at Stella. "Why don't you stick with Owen and me when we go out to visit Morgan and Roz?"

She stared at him, concern etching lines on her face. "I don't want to go back into that wilderness, Tex."

Her words gave him an ache inside. "Stay here then. You know Hester would take you in, and if you want work to do, there's plenty of that here at the fort. Maybe you could live with the Bridger family."

"I don't want to stay here with so many people around. Too easy for my family to blend in."

Tex studied her worried face for too long. He probably shouldn't even mention it. But he was in bed and he had a visitor and not much to talk about, so why not? "You don't want to be in the wilderness, but you don't want to be around people. What's left?"

Stella gave him a look so sad he wanted to comfort her, though that'd be pure stupid. But he might mention to Hester that Stella could use some reassurance just now.

"I don't seem to fit anywhere. But I know I don't want to stay in the fort or even in Cheyenne. If Uncle Gordy ever comes looking for me, he'll come here. I don't want to be here when he arrives."

"Owen says he acted real worried about you." Her uncle worried about her more than her own pa did. "He cares about you, Stella. He wanted to come along on the search, but Owen didn't trust him, nor any of your family. He didn't want them to come along, so I guess he understands your concerns. He even threatened to have Colonel Bridger lock your uncle up just for being irritating and to give him a head start on the search. Owen told him if he wanted to look for you, he could do it on his own." Tex sat up and slowly swung his legs off the bed.

"Should you be doing that?" Stella stepped closer, preparing to catch him should he falter.

"Probably not, but today's the first day I've minded spending so much time sleeping. I take that as a sign I'm healing up. The doc seems to want me to stay in bed until every scratch and bruise is gone, but I'm hoping to leave this place today."

His mentioning being restless made him wonder if that wasn't exactly how Stella was feeling. It made him wonder if she was able to make a decision for herself. He decided to take over unless she ordered him to stop. She'd either do as she was told, or it'd clear her head enough to know what it was she should do next.

"Stella, I'd like it if you came with us to visit Morgan and Roz. We said we'd ride up there before heading out for good. Morgan wanted Bowie to come because he knows of a trail out of there they can use to drive their cattle to town."

"But the trail Bowie used to lead us out of the mountains was . . ." Stella shook her head. "Well, I'm not sure we'd've ever gotten out on our own."

"Those mountains are a hair-raiser. I've never been so lost in my life. You've heard of the Donner Party, haven't you?"

Stella flinched. "I promise I'd've never eaten you, Tex. I swear it. You'd be all gristle anyway."

Tex grinned. "I didn't mean we might come to that. I meant the promise of cutting fifty or so miles on that trail was so tempting they risked it. People have been fighting their way across those mountains for years. The men who built the train route did the same. A whole lot of mountain men and other trailblazers spent their lives looking for a way into and out of the mountains. It's never been brought home to me quite how huge the wilderness is until now. What a challenge it must've been for Bowie to find that trail. I for one would like to see how he plans to get those cows out of there. Let's go see Morgan and Roz, both of us. It'll give you more time to decide where you want to spend your life."

"All right, I'll go," Stella said with a deep sigh. Then she gave him an assessing look. "How's it feel to sit up for so long? Is your head still clear?"

"Yep. Now I'm going to stand and move over to a chair, and we can sit at the table there and visit like I'm an adult instead of a kid being tucked in for a nap."

Stella stepped back just a bit, ready to leap forward to catch him if need be.

It should have irritated Tex, but instead it made him feel grateful to have someone there to lend him a hand should he need one. Outside of his fellow Marshals, he couldn't remember anyone doing that for him, not in a long while.

17

Having a husband again was so irritating, Roz wanted to run off to a distant part of the woods and scream. She wouldn't run off permanently; she'd just do so once a day maybe and scream until she didn't want to anymore—hopefully, that wouldn't take long—then come back home.

She was having a hard time getting used to her brand-new life. One that didn't run as it had always run. She had to admit, for a young woman, she was mighty set in her ways. She loved Morgan and was glad he was there, and yet she wasn't settling in as easily as she'd expected.

It had always been *her* job to go hunting for food, and Jesse usually went along with her. Now Morgan brought home a grouse or a pair of rabbits, once a turkey, all cleaned and ready to cook. Now Jesse went with *him*. She liked hunting. She liked the time with her son. They'd hauled a small flock of chickens home, and Morgan had built a strange pen of woven saplings, closed at the top but not the bottom, so he and Jesse could move it to fresh grass every few days.

She should have helped. She hadn't been invited to help,

but why hadn't she gone to them and offered? Instead, she'd stayed in the cabin and felt sorry for herself.

Up until now, Roz was used to preparing meals for two people. She would make a pot of stew, and it'd feed them for a couple of days. Now it seemed she was always having to start something new to eat while feeling pressured to come up with a more well-rounded meal.

The flour and yeast she'd brought home, along with Hester's advice on how to make bread, didn't work like it had with Hester watching. Roz had only vague memories of her ma cooking; she'd been so young when Ma died. Yet even when Ma was alive, they lived mostly on what they grew in the garden and what Pa hunted.

She didn't know what to do with flour. Hester had talked of cookies and cakes and pie. Roz didn't know where to begin with all of that. She wondered if Morgan knew how to bake a pie. But she was reluctant to ask him, feeling like a married woman should know how to handle such things herself.

While there was a stack of fabric at hand, she'd never sewn herself a dress in all her life. After her ma died, Roz had worn out her own dresses. Then she'd worn Ma's. They were too big at first, but she'd learned about hemming and so let Ma's dresses out at the hem as she grew.

Even when she'd switched over to Pa's clothes, all she needed to do was hem them to fit. And while, thanks to Pa, she knew how to tan a deer hide and stitch it with an awl, it was nothing like making a dress. Thankfully, the ready-made clothing she'd bought should last a long while. Still, she should at least make Jesse a shirt. Unfortunately, that didn't seem any easier to sew than a dress.

She could probably figure it out, but she might do it so

badly she'd embarrass Morgan. What sort of frontierswoman couldn't sew?

Worst of all was finding out she never talked. Hadn't she talked to Jesse? Some, no doubt, but they were neither of them chatterboxes. They'd worked well together and had mostly known what was expected of each other to the point where no talking was necessary.

Had she talked since Morgan came back? She remembered being proud that she was leading them all out of the mountains. But did that include much talk? If it had, such talk had all but ceased. She just didn't know what to say about how she was feeling. At its root, she knew that if she'd been sure he loved her, it wouldn't have mattered so much. Maybe she would drive Morgan away with her quiet. Had she driven Herman away? Was everything she'd disliked about her marriage her own fault?

Morgan showed no talent for knowing what she was thinking, and she hoped he didn't develop that skill because she was always thinking cranky thoughts. And now that she knew it was all her fault, she was irritated by him. All the more reason she didn't want to admit it, hoping he hadn't noticed.

Another thing that vexed her was when she saw Jesse talking with Morgan. She had to ask herself if the boy had so often been silent with her for reasons other than by choice. Maybe he'd wanted to talk, but she'd somehow made it hard for him. Maybe she'd scowled or something when he talked so he'd know she preferred silence over talking. And if that was so, it made her an even worse mother than not being able to make her son a proper shirt.

Stepping outside after the breakfast dishes were done and the kitchen cleaned, she looked across her beautiful meadow, which Morgan had taken to calling the Sawyer Ranch. That upset her a little, too. She didn't really mind so much about the name of their place, but still, she'd've liked to discuss it. Even have him ask her permission to name the ranch. Another thing they hadn't talked about. She'd've told him yes, but being that this ranch had long been hers, it just seemed like the kind of thing that should be discussed. All the same, she let it go and kept her inner grouchiness to herself. Anyway, she didn't have another name handy.

She stood outside the door of their cabin, admiring the trees in their fall glory and the grass bending low in the wind. No sign of Morgan or Jesse anywhere. A longhorn had wandered close to the cabin, grazing, and Roz walked out to pet her. Patch, her oldest cow. She had a spring baby that Roz had gentled. The cow had red-and-white patches in equal measure all over—except for her face, which was all red, and her huge spread of horns were white. Patch had been in this meadow from Roz's earliest memory. She remembered Pa saying she was one of his first cows.

"Hello, Patch, how are you today?" She stroked her broad, friendly face. Her calf, called Little Red, was much redder than her mama, resembling her mostly red daddy. The heifer came up to her and sniffed her riding skirt. "I can't get used to having these new clothes, Little Red," Roz said.

Why on earth did she feel so at ease talking to her cattle, but not to her husband? Had she always talked to her cattle? Roz supposed she might not have noticed it while out here on her own for so long.

The calf licked the black skirt. Roz had on her green shirtwaist. Patch seemed more interested in that. Maybe the cow thought she was wearing grass.

She tugged on Patch's horn to get her moving, and the three of them headed toward the rest of the herd. Little Red walked up to her, then away, then came close again. Then, with her small but fast-growing horns, she began play fighting with the other calves.

Her oldest bull was an all-red monster named Big Red. He had black-tipped horns that spanned over eight feet. Big Red ambled over for a scratch between the ears. He was a sweetheart. Roz gave him a hug and then kept moving through the herd, past a couple of her horses and on toward the stream.

Big Red came up behind her, tagging along, and bunted her in the back. She must not have scratched him enough. Smiling, she turned and scratched between his ears again until he lowered his head and gave the longhorn bull version of a purr. The old fellow purely loved the attention.

With a final pat, she walked on, knowing he'd likely want more scratches. She waited for his nudge once again. Sure enough, the bull lightly butted her, and she turned back to give him more attention just as a voice echoed across the meadow.

"Roz, look out!" The shout whirled her around. Morgan was riding toward her. Behind him were the thick woods on the west end of the meadow. He leaned low over his horse, galloping so fast she frowned. He shouldn't work the horse so hard unless it was an emergency.

Big Red bunted her again. She stumbled a few steps, then saw Morgan draw his rifle from the boot on his saddle.

What did he think needed shooting? Stepping back, she ran into Big Red on one side and Patch on the other. She ducked behind their horns and slung an arm around the neck of each critter as she watched Morgan charge across her meadow. Suddenly the charging slowed, then dropped to a trot, and finally to a walk as Morgan drew close.

His eyes studied her, frantic, confused. She thought she saw fear there too, and she'd never seen Morgan show much fear.

He reined in his horse, slumped forward in the saddle until the saddle horn had to be poking him in the belly. Then he dismounted while holding on to the saddle as though his knees might give out. He fumbled a bit but managed to get the rifle back in its scabbard.

"What's the matter?" she asked. "Why did you get your rifle out?"

Morgan steadied himself, then looked between Patch and Big Red. "I-I saw that bull butt you. Longhorns are dangerous, and I thought . . ."

She knew then what the rifle was about. "You were going to *shoot* one of them?" Her irritation, which was quiet but always there, flared now to red hot. She let loose of her friends and marched right up to Morgan, glaring at him. "You will do no such thing! I've known these animals a lot longer than I've known *you*, and they're my *friends*."

She clenched her fists. Only sheer willpower kept her from punching him in the stomach.

Morgan stared at her as though still confused. "But . . . you told me you kill one of 'em for the beef every year. You eat your friends?"

She turned away. Looking right into Big Red's eyes helped with getting control of herself.

And then she heard him chuckle, then laugh, then howl with laughter. She whirled to see him bent double. She had to admit, she was fighting a smile herself, and she wasn't sure why.

Through his laughter, he managed to say, "Do you keep a few as strangers?" He looked up and started in laughing again.

Then movement caught her attention, from the direction Morgan had just come. It was Jesse. She noticed a sack of some kind tied to his saddle. What were her menfolk up to now?

Instead of punching her husband in the gut, she whacked him on the shoulder. "Don't you dare kill any animal raised on this ranch without consulting me."

He nodded and straightened, still chuckling like a half-wit.

"What in the world is Jesse carrying?" she asked.

Morgan mopped his eyes and glanced behind him. "Turkeys."

"Turkeys? Morgan, we can't eat more than one at a time." It was a good-sized sack.

"I found where they nested earlier and laid a trap that would snare them but keep them alive. Didn't you see the second coop I built yesterday?"

Roz frowned, shaking her head. No, she had not seen it.

"Well, that's probably because I built it back in the trees a bit." He pointed to where Jesse had stopped and dismounted, the sack in one hand. He set it on the ground but kept hold of the top to keep it closed.

She could plainly see the chicken pen, but now Morgan had built a second one just behind it.

He took her by the hand and led her toward Jesse, who

was a good distance away still. As they walked, Morgan said, "I could swear I saw that huge bull bunt you in the back."

"His name is Big Red."

Shaking his head, Morgan muttered, "She names her cows." Then he went on, "I've worked with longhorns a time or two, and one thing I learned is that they're mighty dangerous. More wild animal than farm animal and, I've been told, as dangerous as a wolf. And just as apt to turn on you and attack."

Roz looked back over her shoulder. "Truly?"

"Yep, I was told never to walk amongst them because they could go from placid to vicious in a heartbeat."

Roz felt her brow furrow as she considered her herd. "I've never seen one speck of wild in them. I walk amongst them all the time." She gave her husband a small smile. "So you were trying to save me?"

Morgan went from holding her hand to wrapping an arm around her shoulders and pulling her close. "I was scared to death for you, honey. I'm sorry I upset you about shooting your pets."

"And I don't eat the older ones; I don't need that much meat. I usually kill and butcher a yearling bull. I've had some trouble with the bulls fighting each other and learned which ones are the most troublesome. By doing that, I've found it helps to keep the herd calmer."

Morgan nodded, then called to Jesse, "Go ahead and put 'em in the pen."

Jesse sprang into action. He opened a little door, shoved the bag through it, let go and swung the door shut. A turkey shot out of the open end, followed by another and another. Ten in all.

"Are those for—?"

"We can't eat the chickens, Roz, leastwise not very often. We need them for eggs. Now I don't have to go hunting quite so often. We have two coops now, one for chickens and one for turkeys. I doubt they'd get along very well if we penned 'em all together." Morgan blew out a breath. "Now, let's see if one of your gentle giants is tame enough to let me milk her."

Roz gathered up her courage with both hands to ask, "Why didn't you tell me you were doing this?"

Morgan, watching the turkeys flutter and test the fencing, suddenly turned to face her, a frown on his face. "What, so you could tell me it's a bad idea?"

"No, because it's a wonderful idea and it's smart. You know, ever since we got here and set up a household together, you stopped talking to me. You stopped telling me what you're thinking. Why, Morgan?"

Morgan reached up to scratch his head and knocked his hat off. Jesse, close to hand, caught it because Morgan didn't seem to notice. "You mean you want me to?"

Roz felt herself struck dumb. And that was just a big old part of her problem, wasn't it? Being blunt was all she could manage. "Yes, I want you to."

Morgan tipped his head from side to side. "I reckon I'm not used to talking much, and I'm not used to being a . . . a rancher. Wait, am I a rancher or a farmer?"

Roz shrugged. "Rancher, I reckon."

Morgan continued, "Well, I don't know much of what I'm doing, so I'm not exactly making plans. I'm just thinking up things and trying them out on the spot. I work alone most of the time. The business of transporting prisoners isn't my usual work. I've never had someone to talk to, not much anyway. But neither have you, Roz."

"That's true. I suppose I'm not used to talking either. But I see you talking to Jesse all the time."

Morgan looked at her son, who handed back the hat. Morgan grinned and tugged it back on his head. "There are things to teach him. We find ourselves talking about all sorts of things, don't we, Jesse."

"Yep."

"Well, let's try and talk to each other more, all right? I find myself wishing we could." Roz felt less irritated than she had in a long while.

He nodded. "I'll try and come up with more things to say to you, and when I'm thinking over plans rattling in my head, I'll speak them out loud, and we can discuss them." He smiled as he slid his right arm around her shoulders, his left arm around Jesse's shoulders, and turned them both so they could all look at the turkeys, poking about in their new pen.

As they stood there, Roz found herself feeling a bit guilty for wanting things to be different. Maybe this was the beginning of getting used to married life.

18

Morgan thought getting yourself married was the best idea any man ever had.

He could tell Roz was happy, too. It was turning out that they were the best matched pair who ever lived. And he loved this place. The Sawyer Ranch. The SR. He needed a brand, and he had to register it. He was playing around with a shape and size in his head, but he hadn't settled it yet. When the time came, he'd need to make sure it wasn't already taken. There were plenty of things to think about and now talk over with his wife.

And he needed to stop panicking every time a one-thousand-pound bull came up to Roz or Jesse to be scratched. That was going to take some work to stop that.

He and Jesse, working together, moved the turkey and chicken pens every few days over to fresh grass. As they edged the turkey pen along, the birds took turns flying at the edges.

"Never knew turkeys were so fierce," Jesse said.

"Me neither. I suppose when you shoot them in flight, you can't get a sense for how they'll act up close."

They got the coop moved by picking it up about an inch

off the ground, too low for a turkey to get under, and moving sideways, scooting unwilling turkeys along. As they finished, suddenly that same chill climbed up Morgan's spine. Without reacting outwardly, he peered into the woods nearest them. He couldn't shake the feeling that someone was out there.

Morgan noticed everything. When out hunting, every smell, sight, and sound was sharper. The cold, smooth iron of his rifle felt as if it were an extension of his own hand.

"Let's go on back to the cabin, Jesse, and help out your ma for a while. I've got some scouting to do, but it's a one-man job, and I need to wait until dark to do it."

They were now well into September with the days getting shorter, so it wouldn't be long before the ranch was cloaked in darkness. Summer was indeed waning, the leaves turning color and starting to fall.

Jesse gave him a look of dissatisfaction. Morgan had thought the kid might pout and fuss about wanting to stay outside longer or go scouting with him. But the boy was too smart for that. He caught Morgan's serious tone, however carefully Morgan had said the words, and understood there was more going on without being told.

Roz had raised him to be a wise young man, skilled in the ways of wilderness life. Morgan was teaching him how to hunt and read a trail, but thanks to Roz, Jesse was already skilled in those areas, too. He liked having a son like Jesse.

"And you and your ma are going to have to stay inside until I return," Morgan added, hoping the day would never arrive when he wouldn't come back . . . and these two would be left alone again. Thankfully, Bowie would be visiting them, along with a few of his brothers, maybe Tex and Owen as well. Tough men. Morgan was looking forward to having them around for a bit.

He, Roz, and Jesse had been at the ranch two weeks already. Hadn't Bowie mentioned he'd ride up to see them in a week or two? The man could be coming any day now. Maybe Morgan had sensed Bowie or some of the others out there. Deep down, though, he didn't think it was them he'd sensed.

Jesse gave Morgan a firm nod, his eyes bright and curious. Hadn't Roz told him that her son was born in September? He recalled her saying she wasn't sure of the exact date but that he'd been born in the fall when the days were the same length as the nights. They'd have to pick a date and make that the boy's birthday.

Being a young man who didn't know his real birthday, well, Morgan could recognize that such a thing mattered.

He put a hand on Jesse's shoulder, and the two of them strode toward the house. Morgan wished instead he could turn and face the woods. Face whatever trouble was out there.

The boy walked with him out into the open meadow. They veered around the little stream that curved through the grassland before turning back and flowing into the forest.

Morgan decided right then and there that he wasn't coming back to the cabin later until he'd figured out who'd been roaming their woods.

When they stepped inside the cabin, it took Roz about one second to sense trouble. Busy at the fireplace with her back to them, she whirled around and gave Morgan a strange look.

"Is there coffee ready?" he asked.

She usually kept a pot warm at the back of the fire. She furrowed her brow as she reached for it.

"Let's all sit down," said Morgan. "We need to talk."

Roz felt everything in her go cold. Though she wanted to pepper Morgan with questions, instead she resisted the urge and clamped her mouth shut, telling herself to listen first to what he had to say before asking him anything.

All she knew was that trouble was brewing somewhere. She'd had to face a number of trials since Morgan had come back. Honestly, her life had been as routine as the rising sun before she got her heart's desire and the love of her youth returned. There were blizzards. A cow occasionally got injured. Sometimes their food became meager. She'd been forced to shoot a wolf and a couple of rattlesnakes and had struggled to keep clothes on their backs and shoes on their feet. Meanwhile, the snow piled up, the wind blew bitter cold. Except for all that, no real trouble really.

But ever since Morgan had returned, there was trouble aplenty.

She brought the coffeepot and two cups to the table and poured some for him and then herself.

"Someone has been watching me from the woods," Morgan began, taking a sip from the steaming cup.

She didn't ask who it might be. It could be anyone, and yet one person came to mind right away.

"If it was someone friendly," he went on, "they'd've made themselves known, come in to talk to us. Nope, it's no one with good intent. I'm waiting until dark, then I'm going out there. And I won't be coming back until I've found out who it is and settled this."

Roz still didn't talk. All she could think of to say was *Stay with me*. And he wouldn't want to hear that. Finally, she thought of something she dared to say out loud. "What do you need us to do?"

Something sparked in Morgan's eyes. Pride maybe. Something good. He approved of her reaction. All the more reason not to start begging for him not to leave her. Not to take risks. Not to go out into the wilderness and face the danger alone.

"Stay inside. Keep the door and windows latched. We haven't talked about it, Roz, but there's a loose shutter in the room we share."

Her pa's room. It was the largest of the rooms. She'd moved in there with Morgan shortly after they'd settled here. There was an empty room between them, then Jesse's room. She preferred the larger room and the bit of space it offered as well as privacy. Nodding, she asked, "What about the shutter?"

"The latch on it is broken. I planned to fix it sometime before winter but haven't gotten to it yet. The shutter closes tight, though, and won't blow open in a storm. Sometimes I'll slip in through that window, maybe for a meal or to sleep for a bit. If I do come in that way, it's before the sun rises or after it sets." He grinned. "I'm glad now I delayed fixing it. And don't you get ambitious and fix it, or I won't have a way inside during those times."

"Can I ask how you know a stranger's been watching you from the woods? Did you hear someone or—"

"The crickets went quiet. A bird fluttered off a branch it'd just landed on. And I smelled him. A man who wants to be sneaky oughta take a bath now and again."

That almost got a smile out of her, but she couldn't quite manage it. "How long will you be gone?" Yet she already knew the answer to that.

"However long it takes, Roz."

That wasn't the true answer. The true answer was until one of them was dead. Or maybe it wouldn't come to that. Maybe Morgan would find the mystery man, see that he was an odd, half-mad hermit who liked watching people but with no harm in mind.

She doubted all of that, but she wasn't about to say it. "All right, we'll stay here and shut everything up tight. The turkeys will be okay for a while without their coop being moved since you just did that. Do you . . . ?" Roz hesitated.

Morgan looked her in the eye. "Do I *what*?"

"Do you hope to hunt for this man without him realizing he's being hunted? If you do, you should go out at night and be around the ranch during the daytime, acting like everything is normal."

It was Morgan's turn to hesitate. "I'm hoping it won't take that long. I mentioned about coming through the window in case of trouble, but maybe you're right. It's a good thought. Thank you for telling me that." Then he nodded and said, "Let's eat now, and afterward I've got a few supplies to pack for the hunt."

Before Roz could stand and get their supper started, Morgan quick leaned toward her and kissed her soundly. "You're a smart woman, Rosalind Sawyer. Don't ever hesitate to speak what's on your mind. We'll do better out here with both of us thinking."

It was a compliment. Roz hadn't had many of them in her life. It warmed her heart until it nearly burned, and because she was afraid there might be tears in her eyes or maybe just a blazing pleasure from her husband's kind words, she stood and moved to the stove.

Morgan got the plates out, Jesse jumping in to help set the table, while Roz worked on preparing the meal.

19

Roz crawled into a cold bed and was struck by a feeling of loneliness. How had she lived all those years, cut off from the rest of the world out here with only Jesse for company? How had the two of them survived?

She rolled onto her side so that the empty bed wouldn't be something she felt with every breath and stared at the back wall. Solid rock. The floors also were of stone. Pa had built this house up against the canyon wall, facing the meadow. She'd always thought of it as a fortress. She'd never noticed the busted shutter latch that Morgan pointed out.

After breathing a prayer for her husband and son, she flopped onto her back, longing for sleep to overtake her. *Think of something else*, she told herself.

When they first arrived home from Fort Russell, it had been a relief. She'd quickly grown tired of being around all the people, horses and wagons, the train with all its noise and smoke. When she saw the train in town for the first time, its enormous size had shocked her, left her gaping at it.

She'd heard Morgan and Owen talking about how the train tracks went all the way from Denver to Cheyenne, but the train wasn't running. They'd had to ride horseback from Denver to Fort Russell. If they had been traveling by train, they'd have arrived at the fort in a single day.

If they'd gone by train, there'd've been no gunfights. They wouldn't have been driven up into the mountains. Morgan would've never come home. And there she was, back to dwelling on her husband and getting all stirred up.

She was glad to have seen the fort and Cheyenne. So many different kinds of things to buy in every shop they went into. And the food was delicious and of such variety. Up here in the meadow, she and Jesse had lived on meat and vegetables mostly. They had a productive garden, and Pa had figured out how to get corn to grow, and they ground it for corn pone and cornmeal porridge, all dressed up with honey.

Now Morgan wanted eggs and milk. She'd never considered such a thing. And they had bought bags of flour and white sugar, canned peaches, hams, and side pork. Morgan even suggested they get some pigs and raise the animals themselves for the pork. That way they wouldn't have to make the trip to town as often. Their cupboards and root cellar were now filled with an array of food she'd never imagined.

But after all the time away, Roz had been so relieved to see her precious meadow again. A part of her wanted to hole up here like a rabbit forever. And while at first it had been a novelty to have Morgan with her, his presence had naturally meant changes to normal life as she'd known it, which she now realized was quite *abnormal*.

Ma Bridger had been so kind to Roz, she wished she'd brought the older lady home with her. Roz needed to learn so many things. But were they necessary things? Roz admitted now, lying in her lonely bed, that she hadn't thought so. All the things they'd bought and hauled home. The skills Ma had tried to teach her. She hadn't taken it seriously, and right now she was torn between frustration with herself for not paying better attention and frustration at the whole world for not realizing how Roz lived was just fine. In fact, everyone should change to live like she'd always lived.

Except she didn't want a return to the loneliness, nor the fear of losing Morgan. No amount of struggling with so much change made her want to give up love, to give up her husband. Instead, she wanted to head out into those woods and help him. Surely she could track down this intruder.

Yet that was, above all else, the thing she'd been forbidden to do.

"Ma?"

The voice jerked her out of her reckless wish to get out there and help Morgan. Jesse stood on the other side of her closed door.

"Come in, Jesse. What is it?"

"I can't sleep for worrying."

"I'm not sleeping for wondering and worrying about Morgan either. How about I get up, and we have a bite to eat?" Roz wished she had a cookie to offer her son. Something to give him a little pleasure when worrying weighed so heavily on the boy.

Then she remembered. "We brought a few sticks of horehound candy home with us. How does that sound?"

Jesse smiled in response.

Roz reached for the lantern beside her bed, wondering about lighting it. Wondering about being watched by someone in the woods. Doubting every move she made. Then, because she wanted to cheer up her son, she lit it and turned up the wick. They hadn't had kerosene for years. It was something Pa used to bring home they'd long since run out of. When it got dark, they went to bed. That was it. Well, no more.

Picking up the lantern, wearing her pretty blue nightgown, she said, "Let's get the candy and go sit by the fireplace for a while and pray over every worry we have."

"Let's do that," Jesse said. "Pa said we'll go to town again soon. We can buy more candy when we go."

Roz reached over and squeezed Jesse's shoulder. He was getting taller, almost up to her chin. Her son wasn't a little boy anymore. She dreaded the thought of something happening to Morgan, for herself but also for her son. They'd both gotten mighty used to having the company of a fine man.

There was something about the nighttime. As Morgan moved silently through the woods, searching, listening, he wondered what it was in him that loved hunting at night? And alone.

He understood a bit how the nighttime animals must feel. It was their time to hunt. Most people avoided the dark, headed for home to beat the sunset. Not Morgan. For some reason, he didn't mind the darkness.

He paused, waiting and watching, sniffing, almost tasting the night. Someone else was out here. They were hunting, too.

He stayed low to the ground, out of sight of the one he was looking for. Below the drooping limbs of the scrub pines and the gnarled, stunted baby oaks that couldn't find enough sunlight to grow big but fought for life without it.

He was careful not to snap a twig or set a rock rolling. Mindful of the sound of his deerskin pants brushing up against a tree, mindful of his breathing, his heartbeat. He moved forward, waited, then moved again.

He'd hunt all night, all week if need be. In his head, he was hunting for the Ghost, yet he couldn't be sure. Therefore, he didn't allow himself to assume anything. The way the night frogs fell silent. The way the breeze sounded when it curved around something, or someone, that wasn't a usual part of forest life.

Morgan had noticed that the frogs had *not* gone silent when he entered their kingdom. But now someone was here that they didn't accept as part of their home.

His ears tuned to the direction of the humming wind. This mysterious intruder thought he'd come to stalk Morgan and his family—to steal, to frighten, to do harm. Waiting in the night in utter silence just as Morgan did. Whoever was out there considered himself a hunter. A predator. But tonight he wasn't the predator. He was the prey.

Morgan hoped the man was arrogant enough he didn't believe anyone could find him. It would make all this easier.

He hoped, but that hope was heavily laced with doubt. It would be anything but easy.

Every night for a week and still nothing. Morgan saw the wisdom in Roz's advice that he show himself around the place during the day, and he had to find time to sleep. So he went home around dawn, slept a few hours, then showed himself. There'd been no choice when he couldn't track his intruder down. He'd found so little evidence of anyone, he began to wonder if he was imagining the whole thing. Yet a little voice inside him said different, that he wasn't just imagining it.

The first three days he stayed out in the forest day and night. Finally, in desperate need of rest, he went home before dawn, crawled in through the broken shutter to find Roz already up and gone from the room. She'd heard him come in and met him about the time his boots hit the floor.

She smiled, and he wondered how he could miss anyone as much as he'd missed her.

"Sleep now," she told him. "There'll be food ready when you wake up."

So he slept and ate and went about doing chores, like moving the turkey and chicken pens, gathering eggs, seeing to the horses and cattle and such. Come full dark, he was on the hunt once more.

He decided to venture deeper into the woods. He had a notion as to where the intruder—the Ghost most likely—might leave his horse, but that was a distance away. He couldn't bring himself to leave Roz and Jesse alone for so long. One of these days he might have to chance it, but for now, he stalked a man who stalked him in the night and slept in the daytime. He had to get some sleep, or he wouldn't be sharp enough for the hunt.

He slept about four hours, which wasn't quite enough stretched over days. But it was all he'd been able to get because by midday, his sleep was broken by quiet whispers in the cabin and the smell of good food.

He'd get up, eat with them, then go out and show himself in case the Ghost was watching, but Roz and Jesse did most of the work.

Tired and frustrated, Morgan's nerves became frayed after a week. He'd started snapping at Roz and growling at Jesse for the few hours he was awake and around the place. They'd begun doing all the chores, watering the horses and keeping an eye on the grazing cattle, gathering eggs in the chicken pen and whatnot.

When Morgan was fully awake and able to help, he got to work on a winter coop that would protect their flock in adverse weather. Neither Roz nor Jesse had much skill for building, but they worked hard at his side and took up as much of the labor as they could.

With Roz and Jesse gentling a cow that'd just given birth, Morgan insisted he milk her because he was the only one of them that'd ever milked a cow, and the new mama was nervous and prone to kicking. For a few days, Morgan was providing milk to his family. Then Roz and Jesse caught on and started milking her themselves; the cow seemed less nervous when it was one of them. Soon Jesse claimed it as his own job. Sure enough, the cow, one of Roz's pets, preferred the boy do the milking.

Morgan should have been proud of them, but it was hard to fight the feeling of being shoved aside by these two who'd always managed alone. But though Roz and Jesse were managing alone all right, she preferred not to live that way anymore, at least Morgan hoped she did.

Morgan said to his wife, "I don't want you to go out of the house when I'm not here or if I'm asleep. It's too dangerous."

"But most the work is outside, Morgan. And you need to sleep. Jesse and I aren't ones to sit around inside all day. Anyway, the greatest danger is during the night, isn't it?"

Morgan fought to not yell at Roz. What was wrong with

him? He blamed his temper on exhaustion and maybe feeling like a failure.

"What if we—?"

"Enough, Roz." He waved a hand at her, and she stepped back, eyes wide with alarm. "Good chance I've thought of anything you might suggest." His heart about stopped from the fear in her expression. "Sorry," he said. "My temper is short from the long nights. I guess I don't need you criticizing how I'm doing my job trying to keep us all *safe*."

There at the end, some folks might judge him to be yelling. Roz's jaw went taut. She looked to be one of those folks. Jesse did too.

And Morgan felt a wave of shame for not having a better handle on his tongue. If living with his pa had taught him anything, it was that a man like that was hard to live with.

Before he could say anything more, Roz nodded her head hesitantly as if afraid to speak. Finally, she said, "Don't forget, we decided to call September twenty-first Jesse's birthday." She glanced at her son. "That's tonight, but I suppose we can put it off. When we talked about a date, we hadn't figured you'd be busy."

Morgan tried to shake off his bad mood and the exhaustion. "No, tonight's fine."

Roz nodded. "I'm making him a special supper. I picked out one of the smaller turkeys and plan to roast it. We'll make the day memorable."

Which meant she'd been outside in the turkey coop, right on the edge of the woods. He didn't mention it for fear of what might fly out of his mouth. He just nodded, tugged on his hat, and called out, "Jesse, come with me. The horses need to be ridden so they don't forget how to behave."

20

Roz had a birthday party planned for her son. His first one ever.

She was mighty sure he was eleven, though she hoped she never had to prove it.

She knew nothing about birthday parties. She herself had never had one that she could recall. Maybe way back when Ma was alive, but that was all lost somewhere in her memory.

"I'm glad to celebrate you being born, Jesse," Roz said.

She'd put Jesse between her and Morgan at the small square table Pa had built. The table was pushed against the wall next to the door to the unused bedroom, the one that'd been hers until she married Morgan. On past that empty room was the door to Jesse's room.

"I remember well the day you were born," she went on. "Fall was coming to the meadow. The trees were changing color. Pa had just gotten back with a deer, and I made a venison roast for supper. I know now I was having the pains of childbirth, but I had no notion of what to expect. Ma died before she could teach me much of anything.

"When you were born, I felt like I finally knew what love

was. I understood how my parents loved me in a way I never had before. My life is so much better for having you in it."

Jesse's face lit up. Morgan looked relaxed and interested, even with the dark circles under his eyes and the furrows of worry cutting into his forehead. The poor man had been mostly quiet, and after they'd agreed to talk to each other more! And grim from the stress of knowing someone was in the woods near their home with no good intent.

Roz felt grim herself, but tonight she wanted to enjoy her son's company, and it looked as though Morgan was going to try as well.

"What was it like to have a baby join the family, Ma? Was my pa happy to have a son?"

Herman. Roz didn't even try to control a shudder. "Your pa wasn't here that day, and I thank the Lord for that blessing."

Morgan made a strange noise that she didn't understand. She looked at him, but he said nothing.

"You've said before he was a worthless man and you didn't get overly sad when he died." Jesse said it matter-of-factly, as if it was a story he'd heard many times before.

"Yep, the night you were born, my pa was still alive and present. When I mentioned how the pains came and went, faster and harder the whole day long, he said the baby was surely on the way. He remembered it from when I was born. He didn't seem overly interested, but he was looking forward to seeing you. He went to bed as usual after supper, and you were born a few hours later. Strange business birthing a child, but you've seen the cows be delivered of their calves, so you know what it's like."

She noticed Morgan rubbing his forehead like he was trying to smooth out the creases of worry. He had his head lowered so he was staring almost straight down.

"Sure. And then you found out you'd had a son."

"Yep. I showed you to your grandpa in the morning. He said we could all just hope and pray you didn't turn out like Herman. We'd both liked Herman at first, but he didn't amount to much."

"And Pa came home to die and got to meet me?"

Nodding, Roz patted Jesse's hand. "It was the summer when he came. You were getting toward your second birthday. Pa had been dead for some time by then. When Herman got here, he was mighty sick with an ugly open wound above his knee. To cut it off, I'd've had to—"

"Roz!"

She cut off her story, startled at Morgan's tone. "What?"

"Stop."

"I'm just telling Jesse about the night he was born." She glanced at her son, hoping he'd tell her to go on. She noticed Jesse looked a bit green, his eyes sort of frozen on her face. "Don't you want to hear about that night, Jesse?"

"We've wandered some from that night, Roz."

"Um, I guess I heard enough, Ma." Jesse sounded tired, that was the best she could describe it. "Th-thanks, but you can talk about other things now. Like milking the cow or something."

"Talking about the cow is something we do every day. I'm trying to make your birthday special."

"Y-you did."

Jesse ran a trembling hand across his forehead, which had tiny beads of sweat on it before he wiped them away. His slight shaking reminded her of Morgan, who seemed to suffer in a similar way. She hoped the two of them weren't coming down with something.

Morgan was left tired, frustrated, and disappointed by Jesse's birthday celebration and the horrifying story Roz had just told and heaven knew what other details she'd planned to include. He leaned back in his chair and crossed his arms. "We should talk about happier things."

"Happier than the night my son was born?" She smiled fondly at Jesse and didn't seem to notice the boy might be fighting to keep his supper in his belly.

Morgan tried desperately to think of another subject to talk about. "You could have made him a birthday cake, Roz."

Roz turned and gave Morgan a look, her smile changing to a frown.

"It's a good birthday." Jesse sounded nervous as he glanced from his ma to Morgan.

It spiked Morgan's temper because she'd clearly upset Jesse.

"I-I'm sorry, Jesse," Roz said. "I'm sorry your birthday meal wasn't nicer." Then she spun on Morgan and said, "The days are getting shorter now, and you're either gone or sleeping. We have to be completely silent when you're here and asleep and stay inside when you're away. And making a birthday cake is . . ." She quit talking then, as if needing to scowl at him was sapping all her energy.

What was she so mad about? Morgan's jaw tightened. "I'm not *gone*. I'm right out there in the woods yonder. And I'm sleeping because I was out hunting in the night. Should I just ignore that there's someone lurking in the forest around our home?"

Morgan felt like he could almost hover near the ceiling and watch himself act this way, all riled up, and wonder about the strange, cranky man below. He dragged in a deep breath, fighting his fractious temper.

"Well," said Roz, "if there *is* someone out there in the woods, all your nights hunting haven't turned up much, have they?"

Her words felt like he'd taken a pointy stick right in the gut. Rising slowly, he leaned forward, glaring at his wife, who seemed to be irritated with him beyond any words he'd just said. "You don't think I know what I'm talking about? You think I'm *imagining* that we're being watched by someone who seems to act more like a ghost than a living, breathing man?" He suddenly remembered what had started all this. "All I meant was that you should have maybe made this more of a birthday party."

"If you'd wanted a cake, you should've said so."

"Birthdays need a cake." He'd never had his birthday celebrated, but he'd seen a few birthday cakes in his life. Or heard of them. He couldn't remember exactly seeing one.

The cabin door swung open. Morgan whirled to face Bowie Bridger in the flesh. Behind him stood Owen, Delaney, Tex, and Stella. They were all staring at him, looking as though they'd heard every word he was ranting. And of course they had since he'd yelled those words.

They all stood there frozen for a long moment.

Delaney gathered her wits first and shoved past Bowie, who'd shaved and cut his hair and put on clothes not made from animal skins. He looked all in all more civilized than

Morgan imagined him ever looking. In fact, Morgan was surprised he even recognized the man.

"Roz, Morgan, we're here." Her cheeks a bit flushed with embarrassment, Delaney soldiered through the awkwardness and pulled Roz into a hug. "Are we too late for supper? We've brought our own food, so there's no need to concern yourselves if we are."

Roz came unfrozen, and the fear—yes, Morgan saw fear—faded from her face. "I roasted a turkey for supper." She gestured at the remains of their supper. "Come in, all of you, and eat. Y-you can put your horses up later."

They all surged inside, talking now in hearty voices.

Morgan was given handshakes and pats on the back. Then into the chaos, he said, "I'll see to your horses. You go ahead and eat something."

He stormed outside, glad of an excuse to quit talking to his wife. He heard the door close behind him, a little late. Owen and Tex were coming after him. They were accustomed to seeing to their own horses, or maybe they weren't that hungry.

Bowie, though, stayed behind with the others in the cabin. Morgan felt a little sorry for the man.

"So," Owen said, grabbing the reins to his and Delaney's horses, "how's married life treating you, Morgan?" He and Tex both broke out into howls of laughter.

They were lucky men, too, because Morgan let them laugh.

21

Roz got busy serving everyone the rest of the turkey dinner.

"Bowie, I'm glad you came along." She sliced the meat and handed him a bowl of potatoes to pass around, then told the legendary mountain man the goings-on at the ranch, including the mystery man who, according to Morgan, was stalking the woods nearby.

Bowie hadn't been legendary to her; she'd never heard of him before they arrived at Tex and Stella's camp. But she'd been told he was a man of legends and had assumed it was true.

As she shared the details to the extent Morgan had told them to her, his eyes grew narrow and thoughtful.

"Do you think it could be Wildcat Duncan?" Delaney asked, reminding them all of Bowie's suggestion after they'd asked him about the man who'd lurked around their camp.

Roz glanced at Stella, who was listening intently. If the idea concerned her, she didn't show it.

"And you're sure this is the same man who stalked your camp while you were searching for Tex and Stella?"

Roz shrugged. "No, but when I think of what that man acted like then, this one here sure reminds me of him."

"If it is Wildcat," said Bowie as he started to eat, "he could've heard about Morgan killing Stella's brother, Leland, when he opened fire on you. Maybe he's out for revenge for the sake of the family."

"My family is fierce about loyalty. That might make Uncle Lenny act that way, but he wasn't around when Leland got shot. And my family fell right in to following after Clive, so they didn't tell anyone about it." Stella hesitated. "Except the last two of Uncle Gordy's sons ran off after Leland was killed. I suppose it's possible they found my outlaw uncle somewhere."

They all ate in silence for a time, no doubt thinking of all the what-ifs.

Roz had concocted a rich gravy, and they had mashed pumpkins from the garden. It had been a good meal, although she wished she'd known about the tradition of the birthday cake.

She should have told Morgan she'd never heard of birthday cake and didn't know how to make one. Instead, she'd been embarrassed to admit she was a failure as a wife and mother, and then she'd likely insulted him. She couldn't recall what all she'd said in the heat of the moment.

She only knew he hadn't liked it, and now she'd ruined her marriage. He'd probably ride off with his friends when they left. For the first time ever, she wondered if Herman had abandoned her because of *her*. She'd always blamed him, but maybe it was her fault. Maybe she just wasn't a woman a man could love.

Considering her guests, she wondered if they would be

here at all if it weren't for her marriage to Morgan. The three who'd remained at the house with her were eating as if they didn't have a care in the world, not asking about the shouting Roz was sure they'd heard coming from the house. She was grateful for it.

Jesse served himself seconds of everything. He as good as started over with eating the meal. The growing boy was always hungry, it seemed.

And then Roz had an idea. "Delaney, do you know how to make a birthday cake?"

"Ma, don't fret about it," Jesse said between bites of turkey. "I liked this meal fine. I don't need nuthin' more."

"I know how to make a cake," Delaney answered. "That's all a birthday cake is, nothing real special except it's made and served on someone's birthday."

Morgan had made it sound like it was a lot more than that.

"Could you teach me how to make one? I'm no hand with anything made with flour."

A smile bloomed on Delaney's face. "I'd be glad to teach you, Roz. If you want, we can cook together every day I'm here. We'll need something to do. The men will be sure to want us tucked in here safe in the house." She glanced at Stella and rolled her eyes.

Stella nodded. "As if we're all delicate flowers."

Delaney laughed. "So while we're hiding out and they face down your ghostly intruder, we can bake."

Roz shoved aside her fears that she'd driven her husband out of her life and smiled. And if he did say he was leaving, she'd make him drive the cattle to town first, every single one of them. At least then she could sell them and pocket the cash money they'd bring.

Ignoring her broken heart, she sat down and scooped up another serving of potatoes and gravy for herself.

"Yeah, these are the same tracks that were found around our camp." Owen crouched down beside one of them.

Morgan knew he was putting off returning to the house. It was soon to be dark when he would continue on with his search for the Ghost. He hoped the men would go with him.

Tex studied the tracks. "He wasn't following you anymore when you found me, is that right?"

"We stole his horse," said Morgan. "I turned it over to the sheriff at Fort Collins. The brand was so clearly reworked, we knew he'd never claim it. It'd be the same as a confession that he'd for sure stolen the animal."

"He probably had to break off the harassment of you until he got himself another horse. How do you reckon he knew to find you up here?"

Morgan had such a creeping feeling of dread, he almost brought up ghosts and their mysterious ways. That was nonsense, though, so he kept his mouth shut.

"We might as well head back to the cabin now, Morg." Owen clapped him on the back. "You look all in. Let's get ourselves some sleep. We can get serious about tracking this polecat down tomorrow morning. If half of what they say about Bowie is true, he may be able to walk straight to where he's hiding."

While it gouged at Morgan's pride something terrible to have to accept that someone else might be better than him in the woods, still, it'd be pure relief to have all this over with. A good night's rest would also help him with keeping his temper from flaring up again after his wife ruined their son's birthday.

"I've only been married a short time, Morg." Owen turned to walk toward the house. Morgan and Tex fell in beside him.

"Don't start, Owen."

Owen nodded. "I got no idea how to keep a woman happy."

Morgan decided to let him start. Maybe Owen had some sympathy for him rather than advice.

"She was telling Jesse about the night he was born, and she started in on what a worthless man his pa was and how she thought she'd have to saw his leg off after he'd badly injured it."

"She had to saw his leg off?" Tex winced.

"I stopped her before she told it all because she was a bit too . . . well, it sounded awful, and it was clearly upsetting Jesse. On his birthday."

"How old is Jesse now? She'd've been little more than a kid herself when she had to decide whether to hack a man's leg off or watch him die." Owen shuddered. "Don't see how that had anything to do with the night Jesse was born."

"She told of how her pa left her all alone to deliver the baby herself."

Looking shocked, Tex and Owen stared at him.

Morgan had been shocked himself. Jesse too. "I thought Jesse was going to run straight out the front door and never come back."

Tex grimaced. Owen looked sideways at Morgan, dismay clear on his face. "Your wife has been mostly alone for years. She'd probably gotten used to just speaking her mind with no notion of how others might take it."

"I reckon I'm that way myself," Morgan said. "Mostly she doesn't talk at all. We're working on that. She needs to learn a new way to speak of things, and how am I, a lunkhead for a fact, supposed to tell her that?"

"And the way you decided to tell her was by yelling at her about birthday cake?" Tex asked.

Morgan shrugged. "She didn't make the boy a birthday cake. It seemed thoughtless, and when I mentioned that—"

"Did you mention it at a shout?"

"I wasn't shouting, was I?" Thinking back on it, he'd say Roz had done much of the shouting, not him.

"Morg . . ." Tex gave him a light punch in the arm. "You were yelling for a fact."

His shoulders slumped. "Being married is a tricky business."

"I haven't found it to be so." Owen kept moving toward the house and Morgan's doom. Would she take up yelling again? Would he? In front of everyone?

Morgan glared at Owen. "You're probably more careful with her because you're scared of her pa and her brothers."

"Did I tell you about the time her other brothers showed up, Jedediah and Crockett? They'd gotten wind of Delaney and Boone coming to the fort and decided to go visit her. The whole family being together was . . . you're right, I'm mighty careful around them. A tough bunch. But I don't mind it so much. Maybe a man needs to be that way with a woman. Maybe having us here will help you, Morgan."

"What would help me is a full night's rest. I think I'll stay in tonight. I'm worn out and that's the truth. But maybe with your help later, we can catch up to the Ghost and get my married life back to being normal. With or without a birthday cake."

They reached the house just as Bowie swung the door open.

"You don't look like the same man, Bowie," said Morgan. "All that fur gone off your face. It's good to see you again."

"Roz told me all about your mystery man, haunting your woods like some kinda ghost. I'm real interested. I'm going to hunt around in those woods tonight." Bowie swerved around Morgan and headed out.

Another person around here who wasn't much of a talker.

Morgan almost protested, almost went along. But then he peeked inside the house and saw Roz talking to Delaney while Jesse, still sitting there at the table, hadn't yet eased up on his ma's turkey dinner.

Morgan drew a deep breath and let it out slowly. Thankfully, things inside the cabin looked to have calmed down some.

He was determined to find his bed and get himself some sleep. Maybe Bowie would catch the Ghost tonight, and then it would all be over. The Scriptures said clear as day that pride was a deadly sin, and Morgan thought his pride to be all tangled up with his temper. Well, pride and exhaustion. Maybe his pride could take a little beating now and then to keep him humble. And while Bowie was beating him at his greatest skill, Morgan would be sleeping away.

He missed his pretty wife, the woman he'd been yelling at just a few minutes ago. She probably wanted nothing to do with him right now. Add in a houseful of visitors and he probably wouldn't be able to talk with her tonight.

"If you'd wanted a cake, you should've said so." She'd yelled that at him.

"Birthdays need a cake," he'd shouted back.

He wondered how hard it'd be to make a birthday cake. He knew how to make hot cakes. A birthday cake had to be similar. Maybe Owen or Tex knew how and would teach him.

22

Roz didn't get a chance to tell Morgan that if he was leaving, he had to drive the cows to town first. Once he crawled into bed, the poor man as good as passed out and slept solid through the night without stirring.

The only talking they did the next day was in the middle of a crowd, and so nothing got settled. The next night he went ghost hunting again, so Roz had Stella stay in her room.

Stella gathered up several blankets to sleep on the floor.

"You can share the bed." Roz rose up on one elbow and looked down at her guest. "Or I can move to the floor."

Stella smiled at her from her pallet on the hard floor. "I've slept on the ground so much, a bed feels strange to me. I had one at the fort, of course. Ma made me take it."

"Hester makes you call her Ma, too?" Roz wasn't surprised to hear it.

Stella shrugged from under her blanket. "I was afraid to disobey her. She's a formidable woman."

"True." Roz flopped onto her back. "Tell me, how is Tex? I saw the cast was off his arm."

"That's what took us so long to come. That and his swollen

knee, his occasional wretched headaches, and his ribs and back."

Roz hated to hear the list of injuries the poor man had acquired and knew Stella was speaking only of the most serious ones.

"The doctor pushed hard to get him to stay put at the fort for a couple of months. In the end, Tex was so restless, the doctor sawed the cast off his arm and bid him goodbye."

"I wasn't sure if you'd come. I thought you might just settle into fort life and stay there."

Stella had a smile in her voice when she answered, "I couldn't do much settling. I listened to a lot of talk about the possible identity of that mysterious intruder that was harassing your camp. Bowie thinks it's my uncle Lenny Duncan. But I don't believe it. Lenny always travels with his family, just like my branch of the family does. Why would he be alone out here skulking around your cabin, and slipping around your camp before this?"

"Why would anyone be doing that?"

"Good point. Anyway, I know where Uncle Lenny—"

"He's the one they call Wildcat, is that right?"

"Yes, but I have trouble thinking of him by that name. Anyway, I know where he lives. Of course, if he'd go home, then he wouldn't be here bothering you anymore. I told Tex and Owen I could possibly help track him down, and staying in town was getting on my nerves."

"I can imagine! All those crowds. The fort alone was overwhelming."

"It was. And so they let me come with them. I'm not sure what's going to become of me next, but in the meantime, I'll keep riding along with the Marshals."

There was a stretch of silence, and then Stella asked, "So is married life a terrible business? It wasn't easy for my ma, but Pa did have a soft spot for her."

Roz was startled by the question. "It's mostly nice. But I can't seem to get used to having someone else on my ranch, making decisions, doing things I'd normally do. Even though the thought of him leaving me here alone again is terrifying."

"You think he'll leave you? That would be low-down of him."

Roz sighed. "I don't know. He was so angry at me for not making a cake for Jesse's birthday party. Could be he'll just ride off with Owen and Tex when they leave. My last husband took off on me. Maybe all husbands are like that."

"My pa and uncle rode off and left me alone with my ma and little sister and my aunt. And it sounds like Grizzly Bridger does that, too. Yep, all husbands must do that."

"My pa didn't, but I think he stayed around because my ma had died. Maybe pas only leave wives, not their children." Roz pondered that for a few seconds. "I'm going to miss him terribly, the big half-wit."

"Would you like me to stay here and live with you if he leaves?"

Roz rolled onto her elbow again and looked down. "That might be nice. I suppose, though, you'll end up yelling at me too after a while. I really don't think I know how to get along with people."

Stella gave a sigh. "Well, I could build my own cabin not far away. Then we could have some distance from each other those times we're not getting along."

Another stretch with neither of them speaking. Stella

sounded sad in the darkened room when she broke the silence. "You must not want me to stay, then, huh?"

"It's not that. You can stay. I'm just imagining how Morgan would react if I told him he needs to build his own cabin. Anyway, whether he rides off or not, you're welcome to stay. It gets lonely up here, and it's worse when the snow is twenty feet deep. Yep, we should build that second cabin."

"Thanks. I'll plan on it. Between the two of us, we should be able to build a little house."

"Jesse sure is a big help these days."

"I'll help out however I can," said Stella. "And I know how to make a cake if you still want help with that. It's been a while since I made one, but Ma taught me the right way. I think I remember all that's needed."

"It's settled then. I'll sure miss Morgan, though. I've gotten right fond of him." It was a more casual way of saying she loved him with all her heart, and him riding off would be the next thing to killing her. She wondered how a woman went about getting a man to love her back. Then she thought of him yelling about cake. "That is, I'll miss him when he's not hollering at me."

Morgan didn't really want to go back in the house.

After his first good night's sleep in over a week, he'd gotten outside early, wanting to delay talking to Roz. He had to figure out if he should say he was sorry or demand she do so. Or should they just continue not speaking to each other for the rest of their lives?

He and the other men had done a few chores to make sure

the new horses were fed and settled in, and then they'd done a little scouting in the woods.

Bowie said, "We need to stop now before we trample on tracks and mess up the trail this sidewinder left behind."

"You're sure it's the same man I talked about following us when we were searching for Tex?"

"I never saw his tracks, but it sure seems likely."

"We call him the Ghost," Morgan said.

Bowie tipped his head to the side. "That makes sense, although you'd think a ghost would have better things to do than wandering around in those woods."

"You'd think whoever this is would have better things to do." Morgan's frustration returned, adding to his confusion over his wife and why the woman refused to bake a cake for her son's birthday once he had pointed it out. But Morgan didn't say that because Jesse was along with them. He didn't think it was proper to criticize the boy's mother in front of him.

Probably not proper to criticize her in front of anyone.

Instead, he turned his attention to Big Red, grazing not far away. He'd gotten used to being around the old longhorn. He was huge, but as harmless as a house cat.

As Morgan strolled up to his four-legged friend, Big Red looked up curiously.

"Morgan, what are you doing?" Tex had grown up on a cattle ranch in Texas and knew longhorns.

Morgan kept going. When he was close enough, he scratched Big Red between the ears. The critter tilted his nose up and closed his eyes, his usual blissful reaction to someone scratching him.

Tex ambled up slowly, steadily reached out a hand, then scratched the bull.

Big Red opened his eyes, and it was as if he knew Tex was a cattleman. He took a step forward and leaned his head against Tex's denim pants and seemed ready to catch a nap.

Jesse came up beside Morgan and slung an arm around Big Red's neck. Patch and a few others in the herd wandered toward them.

"You know this behavior isn't normal, don't you?" Tex asked. But he didn't stop scratching the friendly pet.

"I almost shot him the first time I caught sight of him coming up behind Roz and bunting her, which was his way of begging for attention."

Owen started scratching Patch, the red-and-white cow that reached them first.

"Before I could do anything, I saw Roz was playing with the old monster. And when she figured out what I'd intended, she tore a strip off me." Morgan thought of Jesse, of all he didn't know, and added, "I've been mighty confused ever since, I reckon."

Owen walked over to join them, patting Patch's neck. Then Patch's red baby they called Little Red came up and nudged Owen to get his attention. A late-spring baby, his horns had grown nearly a foot in the month since they'd come home. Roz said that was normal. Morgan thought it was a lot to ask of the little guy to carry those horns around, not to mention learn not to get them tangled up with anything.

Owen began scratching the baby, too.

"There are more coming," Bowie said, who didn't seem inclined to pet anything. "You said the bull there bunted Roz when he wanted to be petted. When you stop, do you have to run for your life?"

"I usually have Roz to distract him while I get away. Jesse, what do we do? I'd like to move the chicken and turkey pens before we go in for breakfast."

Jesse laughed. "You go on. I'll distract them for you."

"That sounds downright cowardly of me," Morgan admitted.

"I'll be fine," Jesse assured him.

Morgan nodded, and the four men headed for the pens. They started with the turkeys, each of them lifting a side and edging the woven crib along, keeping it low to the ground so the turkeys couldn't escape.

By the time they had the chicken pen moved, Jesse was there and picked up four eggs.

Morgan had a bright idea. "Run those in to your ma and tell her we're hungry. We'll be there shortly."

Jesse snatched up more eggs and held them in his shirt, then walked carefully to the house.

Morgan turned to Bowie, almost unrecognizable with his hair cut short and his beard gone, and Tex, who was still a little rattled from petting a longhorn, and finally Owen, the only other married one in the group.

"I think I'm making a hash of being married," Morgan began. He looked from one man to the other. They were cool characters. They didn't give much away as to what they were thinking. Unfortunately, they couldn't quite disguise the fact that they thought he was right.

"All I told Roz was that she should've made a cake for Jesse's birthday dinner, and she got real mad at me."

The three men exchanged looks. Owen, an old married

man of two months to a very agreeable woman, chuckled and said, "I guess you'd better learn to live without cake, Morgan."

"I had myself a cake every year for my birthday," Tex said. "My ma was fond of making 'em."

Bowie scratched his chin and asked Morgan, "What does she usually do for a birthday?"

"She's never done nothin'. I suggested a birthday party for Jesse, and Roz liked the idea. And she made a real good meal. She's a fine cook. I asked her . . ." Morgan's voice trailed off. He tried to remember. What had he asked her exactly?

Owen helped him out. "You said she told the story of the night Jesse was born."

Morgan dragged the Stetson off his head and whacked his leg with it. "Jesse looked badly shaken by the story, and I was only trying to change the subject."

Bowie shook his head. "You should do that talking thing you mentioned. If you spoke in a harsh way about the cake, she doesn't know you were upset because of the story, not the cake."

"You could be right about that," said Morgan thoughtfully.

Then Bowie added, "If she's lived up here for years with no runs to town and no flour to speak of, maybe she doesn't even know how to make a cake. Did you tell your wife you expected a cake and just assumed she'd know how to make it? How would she, Morgan? If her ma died young, and her pa didn't bother with birthday celebrations, she might have no notion about such things as cakes."

Morgan didn't like admitting he was wrong. But if he could admit it to himself, maybe the telling of it would come natural-like. He sure hoped so. "All right," he said with a big sigh. "Should I apologize in front of everyone or ask her outside to do it privately? Should I wait until later or do it right now? Should I—?"

Owen stopped him talking with a clap on the shoulder that was a little harder than was necessary. Either way, it was a mercy because it made him shut his mouth.

"Let's go eat and then wait until dark before we start hunting," Owen suggested.

Morgan fell in beside Tex, and they started for the house. He was getting close when he smelled the hot food and picked up the pace. Then he thought of his angry wife and dropped back to let everyone else go in first.

Roz hadn't slept well, but when she finally woke up the next morning, she was alone, and she hadn't heard Stella leave.

Dressing quickly, she left her room to find the menfolk gone, including Jesse. It was an early-rising crowd, it seemed.

Delaney and Stella were drinking coffee at the table.

Stella poured Roz a cup. They only had four cups in the house, left from all those years back when it had been just Pa, Ma, and her. But like all folks who'd spent time around a campfire from time to time, they carried tin cups in their saddlebags, as well as plates, forks, and knives. All of those had been unpacked and arranged on the table.

"Did the men say they'd be in for supper, or are they heading out to hunt?" Roz asked.

She wanted to run out of the house and find her husband and promise him she'd learn to bake a cake and just generally learn to use flour. She thought that was what was bothering him, but she honestly wasn't sure. Men could be confusing.

"They'll come in to eat, then slip out after dark," Stella said. She went and dragged the chair from the head of the table, moving it to sit beside Roz. "Tomorrow we'll start baking." She scooted closer to Roz. "Truth is, I know only a little about baking. We didn't go to town when I was living with my ma and little sister. Pa would bring some flour home on occasion, and we'd have pancakes and biscuits for a while. A loaf of bread even, if Ma kept the sourdough alive. Hard to do without flour, but it helps if you rarely use it."

Delaney looked from Stella to Roz and back. "We'll do lots of baking and learn together."

Roz nodded. "Then maybe Morgan won't ride off and leave me?" She turned to Stella. "You can stay even if he decides to stay."

Delaney reached over and rested her hand on the back of Roz's. "Did Morgan say he's leaving you?"

Roz looked at Delaney. She felt her brow furrow. "Don't all men leave, at least for stretches of time? My pa didn't, but Herman sure did."

"Roz and I talked last night about how my pa and uncle did, too." Stella took a drink of coffee. "He was gone more than he was home. How about yours, Delaney?"

Delaney looked a bit stunned. "Now that you mention it, yes, Pa left us frequently. But he always came back."

"Herman came back a couple of times before he died. And he was home when he died, so at least I don't need to wonder what happened to him."

Delaney gave her head a little shake.

"And my pa came back with my brothers." Stella seemed

to be looking into the past. "We were always relieved when they rode off again. Most winters it was like our peaceful home being invaded by a pack of bears looking for a place to hibernate. Growly, furry, bad smelling, hungry all the time."

In a small voice, Delaney asked, "Do you think Owen will leave me, too?"

The three of them looked at each other. Roz thought the feeling of sorrow was shared among them. "Maybe not. At least for now, he'll be working at the fort. I didn't mind Herman leaving, leastways not much. It's different with Morgan, though. I never cared much for Herman, but I like Morgan real well."

"I *love* Owen." Delaney's eyes got watery, and her voice broke.

The door swung wide open, and Jesse came in with eggs. It was just as well. Roz was afraid the women would make each other cry before long, and she didn't want any part of that.

"Pa said they're coming right after me, and they're hungry."

Roz shoved herself to her feet. She had a venison roast heating in the oven with potatoes stewing on the stove. Delaney had made biscuits, and Roz thought she could do that herself now.

As the women pitched in to help with the meal, Jesse poured himself a glass of milk. They had milk now because Morgan had taught them about milking a cow.

They were eating better now. If only she knew what in tarnation to do with flour.

Stella got busy draining and mashing potatoes, then slicing up a rasher of bacon they'd brought. Delaney used flour and the roast drippings to make a much nicer gravy than Roz had ever made.

The door behind her swung open again, and four men strode into the house.

Roz looked at them and thought they all stared at her funny, then looked away too fast. She wondered what the polecats had been up to.

23

Over supper, Morgan said, "We're gonna work on building winter coops for the chickens and turkeys until it's full dark. Jesse, you can help. Then we're heading into the woods. Bowie thinks our varmint has been staying away during the day, so maybe he won't know we're out there. Once we leave, we won't be back until we got the Ghost rounded up." Yet Morgan doubted it'd be that easy.

"I'm not going on the hunt." Tex tipped his hat. "I'm still healing up, and I'm the least of you mountain men in the ways of tracking."

"Don't be so hard on yourself, Tex. You were mighty good in the wilderness." Stella jumped in real quick to defend the man. Her doing so made Morgan wonder about the two of them.

"If you want to come back through the bedroom window, we'll make sure we aren't sleeping under it. Stella slept on the floor last night. You'd've landed on her head."

"You had to sleep on the floor?" Tex asked.

"I insisted on it. I had blankets aplenty, and being up off the ground is making me go soft."

"I do think one of the men should stay here," Tex said. "I'm volunteering. The women are capable enough, and I'd reckon Jesse's good at keeping an eye out, but there's no sense in all of us men leaving them for the night."

Roz nodded. "Thank you, Tex. Well, Delaney's going to help me make a cake tomorrow. Maybe we can all celebrate Jesse's eleventh birthday again." She couldn't help wringing her hands as she looked hopefully at Morgan.

He wondered what was going on inside her head, but this wasn't the time or place to ask her. Nor was it the time and place to apologize to her, not with everyone staring at them. He supposed it would keep. At least she wasn't glaring at him anymore.

"Let's go build those coops," Owen said after they'd finished eating.

Soon the men were heading outside, with Jesse tagging along.

Morgan wondered about that cake, second-guessing his reluctance to talk to Roz. He should have taken the time to apologize to his wife before setting out on a hunt that might take all his attention for days.

Despite Tex's arm not yet being one hundred percent healed, he proved himself to be the best builder among them. He had firm ideas about where each coop should go and how it should be built. Morgan had never thought of nesting boxes, but Tex said they were necessary for a proper coop.

They had the little buildings nearly finished by the time the sun went down.

"I'm going to wait until the ground is all the way covered with snow," said Morgan, "before I put the birds in their new coops. Right now, all they eat is grass and bugs."

Tex said, "I noticed you've got corn growing."

"Yep, pretty dried out now, what's left of it. Roz grinds it up for cornmeal."

"If it's not all ground, you can crack it and feed the birds that. Or I suppose they'd eat cornmeal, too. If you can get by without it, save it back for the chickens. I reckon you can just let the turkeys go and catch a new batch next spring."

Tex was full of information, as was Owen, who said they'd had chickens back in Iowa. Morgan learned more than he wanted to.

Jesse had wandered off and was playing with his pet longhorns. Judging by his and Roz's success with the normally prickly animals, he was a little surprised they hadn't tamed any bears or mountain lions. A wolf or two. Maybe a rattlesnake. He wouldn't put it past them to try. This family needed him around, and that was a fact.

"Let's go in, Jesse!" Morgan hollered. Like cowards, he, Owen, Tex, and Bowie headed for the house before they had to deal with overly friendly monster cattle.

After dark, just as the men rose to head into the forest for however long it took, or as Roz suspected, until they got hungry or cold, Roz told Morgan that Stella was going to stay and live with them, and she'd like him to add a room onto the house.

"You're staying?" Tex froze with his Stetson not quite on his head. Then he lowered his hand and gave Stella a confused look. "Why?"

Roz had expected a reaction from Morgan, not Tex, which she thought strange.

"I told you I don't know where to live in the world, and Roz asked if I'd like to stay here. I figured it was a good idea."

"I'd enjoy the company," Roz said. "And Delaney and Owen need to return to Cheyenne for his job." She turned to Owen. "But if you get tired of that work, you and Delaney can come back here. Bowie and Tex, you're welcome to stay as well. We can always build more rooms or cabins. There's plenty of food. Plenty of most everything." Roz felt her excitement grow to think of so many friends being close by.

Morgan slid his eyes to Tex. "You talked of getting out of the Marshals Service when Owen and I did. It'd be nice to have a few more people up here with us."

Tex shook his head as if he'd just climbed out of the river and was flinging off water. "I've never given living in the wilderness much thought." He focused on Stella again. "Are you really thinking of living here?"

Stella shrugged. "You know I don't want to live with the menfolk in my family. They're always moving around, never settling anyplace. Staying here will give me a chance to think things over. Summer's done with, and winter comes early. It makes sense to settle somewhere, and it doesn't have to be forever. But yes, I like the idea. Away from crowds but not completely alone. And I'm so far into the mountains, I don't think my family would ever find me up here."

"You're hiding from them?" Roz asked.

"It seems that way, doesn't it? I hadn't thought of it as hiding so much as staying out of their way . . . somewhere they could never find me."

"Yep, that's hiding." Roz got up from the table as the men rose to leave.

"I suppose it is." Stella sounded glum.

"We can decide later about 'forever.' For now, stay for the winter." Roz smiled and gave Stella's shoulder a gentle squeeze.

Jesse asked, "Can I go into the wilderness with you, Pa? I've been working on moving around real quiet, reading tracks and such."

Morgan nodded at the boy as he pulled on his heavy buckskin coat. "And you're gaining skills every day. I'd take you if I didn't think we might be up all night, maybe gone for days. Let's do it when I'm not gonna be away for so long. Right now, I'd like you to stay here with Tex and help keep an eye on things. That's an important job, too."

Jesse promised to do as he was told, his spirits remaining cheerful. Morgan had turned him down without crushing him. He'd even made Jesse feel like staying back with Tex and the women was a noble job. Roz appreciated Morgan for that.

Roz loved him deeply. It was a shame she didn't know how to make him stay with her. She'd've just sat right down and cried if it wouldn't embarrass everybody, most especially herself.

Morgan looked at her and gave her a firm nod. It felt like it was a goodbye just for her. Then he led the way out.

Owen stopped to give Delaney a kiss or two.

"Be careful." She touched his cheek gently.

He nodded, pulled on his coat, and left.

Bowie went out next without paying any mind to anyone.

"I'm going out for a bit, but I'll be back before long," Tex said to no one in particular, then gave Stella a confused look. That made no sense at all to Roz, but then she didn't know much about people.

The last to leave, Tex closed the door behind him and was gone. In the few moments the door had been open, Roz realized how much the temperature had dropped. She pictured her ranch three feet deep in snow. If not tonight, then soon.

"Do any of you know what chickens and turkeys eat if they can't find grass?"

Delaney seemed to search inside her head. Stella shrugged.

"Pa says we have enough corn to feed them if we break it up." Jesse knew because Morgan had told him. Roz wished Morgan would talk to her more like he did Jesse. "But it has to be cracked corn, Ma, not cornmeal like we make for corn pone."

"Well, I guess the man has got everything figured out." She spoke a bit sharply, but it must not have been so bad because nobody paid her much attention.

"Did she seem odd to you?" Morgan asked Owen.

Owen turned to him and arched a brow. "No, but it's odd that she invited Stella to live with you."

"Stella can't live out here. That's ridiculous." Tex was trudging along beside them, his hands thrust in his pockets.

Morgan noticed snow filtering down from a pure white sky. They were nearing the end of September, plenty late for snow to be falling. "Tex, are you really going to quit being a Marshal and live here with me, too?"

"I've never considered such a thing. If you have to add a room on for Stella, you'd have to add another one for me. Or maybe I'd just build my own place. I've already written to the man who appointed me as Marshal. He understands how much I'd gotten hurt. My arm isn't going to be fully mended and strong again for a while yet. He released me from the Marshals Service. I figured I might go on home to Texas. These cold winters don't agree with me."

Tex seemed a little grumpy. It annoyed Morgan because he was the one with the problems. It seemed like Tex was being a little selfish to conjure up problems before Morgan's were solved.

As the four of them reached the edge of the woods, Morgan and Owen said their goodbyes to Tex, who would be making his way back to the house, still too injured to be traipsing about in the woods, especially at night.

They then turned to Bowie, who said, "I'm not going to stick with you; it's better if we split up. With the snow now, we'll be leaving tracks everywhere. It's not heavy enough yet for that to be a problem, but at the rate it's falling, it will be before the end of the night. Spread out and lay up like a net. Let's hope this ghost of yours walks into it."

Morgan was glad someone was paying attention to what mattered. "I'm going to keep moving until the snow starts collecting under the trees. I'll be heading deeper into the woods, see if I can find the Ghost's horse or catch him coming on foot. There's a deep gully to the west I doubt a horse can cross. I wonder if he crossed that on foot. I'm going that far to see what I can find. Besides, if we stop moving now, we're likely to freeze solid before we catch anyone."

Bowie seemed to consider that, with Morgan and Owen waiting to see if he had more to say. Finally, Bowie said, "It's gonna be a long night since we're hamstrung by the weather. The animals are huddled in their dens. They'd usually be the first warning of someone in the woods. No birds will stop their singing because they won't start. And be careful if you start shooting."

Morgan considered that an insult. Sure, they all had guns. Morgan hadn't bothered with a rifle, which was for distance and greater power. But he wasn't going to start shooting at someone at a distance. Visibility was gonna be bad. Add to that he didn't *want* to shoot anyone, friend or foe. Oh, he'd done his share of shooting. Hard to avoid as a U.S. Marshal. But it left him sick, and he didn't go to shooting anyone who wasn't trying their best to kill him or someone else. It troubled him that it had been his gun that had killed Stella's brother Leland during the ambush that took the life of one Marshal and injured another, as well as Delaney's brother Boone. That had been a dark day.

Still, he didn't plan on doing any shooting tonight. Whoever the Ghost turned out to be, he hadn't shown an inclination to open fire on them. And anyway, it kept echoing in his head that he might in fact be his own pa.

His pa who'd maybe gone mad.

And Morgan didn't want shooting his pa on his conscience. Not for the first time, he was seized with a desire to see Pa again or at least find out if he was alive or dead. He reckoned he might never know which it was, but the ache of living the rest of his life without knowing, well, he hadn't expected it. He didn't know what to do about that ache.

Owen looked up at the white flakes drifting down. "Maybe if this turns into a heavy snowfall, the Ghost will break off haunting you until winter's over. I don't see how he can hope to skulk around out here without leaving tracks. We're not the only ones who are hamstrung."

"Well, if he does wander off somewhere for the winter, I won't have to go looking for him again till spring arrives." Morgan peered into the woods. He should've ridden his horse. "But I'd as soon get this settled now," he added, then gave a nod to Owen before tramping off into the forest.

He was hoping to track down the Ghost tonight. He'd go deeper into the woods than he'd ever allowed himself before. And Morgan wasn't coming back without him.

Before they bedded down for the night, Delaney wanted to write out the recipes for cakes and cookies and breads, then get started by mixing some ingredients together.

"I can't read," Roz pointed out, "so there's no sense in writing anything down. You know, your ma had me bake some bread once, but when I got home and tried doing it, it came out all wrong."

"There's a lot of steps to it. It's easy to forget one or two, and that's when things tend to go awry. But with some practice, you'll be baking proper cakes and such in no time."

Roz sure hoped so. But wondering what the men would be doing overnight was driving her mad. "You think if I learn about baking, Morgan will stay around?"

"Is Pa going somewhere, Ma?" Jesse asked. The boy was lingering close by and had overheard their talking of Morgan.

"I reckon he will," Roz answered honestly. "Some men like to wander off from time to time."

"Are you sure? I want him to stay here." Jesse seemed upset. She understood how he felt. She was upset herself.

"He got real mad when I didn't make you a birthday cake.

We're hoping if I learn to bake one, he might not be tempted to leave."

"He wasn't mad about the cake, Ma."

Roz turned to her son and noticed the other women do the same. "He wasn't?"

"Nope." Jesse was busy swiping the bowl of cake batter with his finger and licking it clean. Delaney said that was traditional.

"Well, that's what he was hollering about."

"Yep, but the things you said about my pa and the horrible way he died were what got Pa worked up. I think he didn't like you talking that way, so . . . well, maybe you could've left out some of the worse details about possibly having to saw my pa's leg off."

Delaney whipped her head around to stare at Roz. "You didn't mention *that* when you told us Morgan was hollering at you."

Roz frowned and tried to remember back. "He never said a thing about anything but the cake."

"But he told you to *stop talking*, remember? I think he felt bad that Grandpa went off to bed and left you to birth me alone, too. That seemed to darken his spirits a bit."

Delaney winced. "You were all alone when Jesse was born?"

"I was with Ma when Sissy was born," Stella offered. "We talked a lot about such things. Your pa should have stayed with you. I know it's terribly personal, but a woman shouldn't be left all alone during the birthing if it can be helped. Maybe Morgan thought that and felt bad for you."

Roz looked from one to the other, all three faces serious. "You're saying I'm wasting my time learning to use flour?"

Delaney said weakly, “It can’t hurt any to learn to bake. While the cake is baking and the bread is rising, maybe we could stir up some biscuits.”

Roz had never been so confused in her life. Should she not talk about anything that others might find upsetting? But how would she know what would bother someone until after she said it? She was clearly no judge of such things. And if that was true, it seemed even more likely Morgan would wander off soon, possibly forever. The thought hurt because she liked him a whole lot more than she ever did Herman. She even loved him.

24

Morgan trudged along in the thick woods amidst the settling dusk. The snow was coming down more heavily with every passing minute. He felt pretty sure now that he knew which direction the Ghost came in from. Through trial and error, he'd eliminated most directions. If he didn't get it right tonight, there was always tomorrow.

He wanted to put some distance between himself and his cabin and the men helping him. Having Tex stay back at the house with the womenfolk and Jesse eased his mind.

If he kept on walking in this direction, he'd come to a deep gully. He knew from experience that the Ghost's horse wouldn't cross it, even though his horse had crossed plenty of them. It was just as well Morgan was on foot.

He'd gone as far as the gully in the early days before the Ghost showed up and remembered it from when he and Roz explored this land as kids. He'd gone into these woods as far as he dared a few times, but he was always haunted by the image of the Ghost watching Morgan mosey right past him, then going to the cabin and doing heaven-knew-what to Roz and Jesse. But he'd searched everywhere else, including looking for a horse tied up in the woods, and he hadn't found anything.

Tonight Morgan was going as far as he needed to, and if the Ghost slipped past him, he'd be dealing with plenty of trouble from Bowie or Owen, even Tex back at the house if it came to that.

But what if the Ghost turned out to be his pa? Shaking his head to dispel that notion, Morgan walked faster. About the time it was full dark, he had to slow down. His night vision was sharp, and snow brightened the night, but there wasn't a star in the sky, the clouds heavy with the moon nowhere to be seen. He'd walk right into a tree if he wasn't careful.

The snow continued to fall, yet there wasn't enough to cover the ground yet, not completely. Hundreds of years of fallen leaves could take a heavy snow before they'd show any tracks without careful inspection, especially in the dark. So Morgan wasn't overly worried about that.

But keeping quiet did worry him. He was good at it, but moving in true silence took time, and he wasn't taking that time because he wanted to cover the distance.

He realized then that he'd come upon a trail, and it looked like a trail that got some use. Had he done it? Had he finally gone far enough that the Ghost wasn't being so careful? He did his best to stay alert, to listen for any sounds and look for anything that didn't fit.

Maybe the Ghost had seen how far out Morgan was willing to go, and beyond that point he'd given up a lot of his stealth. It was dark enough Morgan couldn't read tracks, but the trail itself was wider than the usual forest trail worn by deer. Maybe it was worn because a man had walked it every night for the last few weeks and hadn't realized that with time, Morgan would come.

That time was tonight.

Tonight was the night. The Ghost smiled to think of it. The snow coming down lightly told him it was time.

He'd enjoyed taunting Marshal Sawyer. A worthy adversary. The Ghost hated to see the end of it. Yes, he knew that Sawyer had been searching for him. It hadn't taken long to figure it out.

He respected the man's skill. In truth, he'd been searching for the Marshal while the Marshal had searched for him, and they'd never met up. Both too quiet. Both of them skilled at hiding their trail, their very existence, fading into the thick timberland like, well, a couple of ghosts.

But the fun was over now, and the Ghost could only regret it. The snow and the coming winter would not be denied.

And though Sawyer was skilled, his wife and child were not. And it'd always been about the woman. He'd known she lived up here, but when he traveled with his boys, they'd left her alone. She had nothing worth stealing, after all. But now that he was alone, his sons off on their own, with himself roaming far and wide while he decided what to do next, he'd happened upon them in the wild.

He'd wanted a new family. She even came with a son. He'd start a new family with them. When that blasted Marshal had bested him, he'd known where to find her. He'd come here hoping she'd return home, but then she'd brought the Marshal with her.

Now he wanted this meadow, along with the cabin, the

cattle, the horses. He wanted the woman and the child, too. It all called to him. Sure, he had his own place, but it was wretched compared to all this. That cabin in the meadow . . . a man could call it a castle.

Tonight he'd slip past Sawyer and head straight for the meadow. He'd take the woman for now, and once Sawyer was dead, he'd move into the cabin with his new family.

The time for fun was over. Tonight he'd stop playing games and get serious.

Tex started heading back to the cabin, but not too fast. He had to figure out what to do with the rest of his life before he reached it.

One thing he knew for certain was that he wasn't leaving Stella up here alone. It would be like Morgan having two wives, not in the most serious or meaningful sense, of course, but with two women around, Morgan could find himself on the wrong end of things and fast. Or was Roz planning to start her own town? That was ridiculous in a place like this. No, what they needed to do was drive their herd of longhorns to Fort Collins, sell them for the beef—even the one-ton pet bull—and then Morgan could get a job within a hundred miles of *something*.

Though his friend might be tough enough to stay alive up here, Tex knew this place wasn't favorable to living—even if no one else would admit it. He glanced overhead at the snow coming down. The temperature was dropping, and the snow blew down the back of his neck like icy fingers. Here came winter.

Tex had lived through plenty of Colorado winters. None

up this high in the mountains, but with several feet of snow nonetheless. He wanted to go back to Texas, but he couldn't do so if Stella stayed here. He wasn't sure why he couldn't; he just knew it for a fact. He needed to convince everyone to leave this place, and they needed to do it now, before there was nothing resembling a trail to get out.

He thought of those awful trails they'd followed up and down canyon walls to make it to this meadow and shuddered to imagine them coated with snow and ice. Where he came from in Texas, the land was laid down flat instead of standing on its side like it did in Colorado. Oh, there were some rolling hills and river valleys, rugged land cut through with a huge canyon called Palo Duro. In his opinion, Texas was the finest state in the union, and he had probably oughta get all his Marshal friends to move down there.

Owen, though, was probably stuck up here. The Bridger family he'd married into were settled in Wyoming. But Morgan and Roz, Jesse, and Stella? All of them needed to pack up for the trip to Texas, and they needed to do it before this snow got much deeper.

As Tex stepped out into the open meadow, the snow falling heavier with every passing minute, he paused to marvel at the beauty of it. Sure, he saw the appeal of the place, but good gravy, the cold and inconvenience were outrageous.

Tex walked through the scattered herd of longhorns, some grazing, some lying down for a night's rest. A few looked at him while chewing their cud, but they didn't run and kick and attack like proper longhorns.

He thought of Jesse hugging that monster he called Big Red and hoped the kid didn't fully understand what happened to a longhorn once he was sold to a butcher shop.

It was pure stupid to walk too close to these cows. Longhorns were dangerous. Tex would have to learn to fear them again after this. He suspected the cows would be glad to remind him they were dangerous by trying to kill him. If Morgan and the rest came with him to Texas, Roz and Jesse would have to learn caution, too.

Tex finally approached the cabin, went inside, and swung the door shut against the falling snow. After the others greeted him, he said, "I suspect Bowie will be staying in those woods overnight—the man's probably used to it. And Morgan seems bent on spending the night out there. But Owen's likely to give it up after a while and come back before sunup."

Delaney nodded and said, "We were all just getting ready to go to bed."

Happy to be in a warm cabin, Tex shrugged out of his coat and hung it on a peg near the door. He should probably feel ashamed for staying back with the women and the kid, but he couldn't quite manage that. It was freezing cold out there in the woods, and Tex didn't care one bit for snowy winters. Right this minute, he missed Texas so bad his teeth ached, along with his still-healing arm.

And he was so tired, he was falling asleep standing up. Grabbing his bedroll, he said, "I'm gonna sleep out here next to the fireplace."

"Stella, you can sleep in my room again," Roz said. She sure seemed to love having houseguests. "Delaney, you stay in your room in case Owen shows up." She hesitated. "Will Owen remember he might land on Stella if he comes in through the window in my room?"

"He won't come in that way," said Tex. "Morgan did that because he didn't want the Ghost to know he was out hunting him. Owen said he won't come in quiet like Morgan did. He'll knock on the front door, which is solidly locked. He doesn't want to sneak up on a houseful of edgy men and women with guns."

Tex nodded at Jesse, who had a gun like everyone else, though it wasn't out at the moment. Including the boy in the group as one of the grown-ups had the sleepy kid straightening up and smiling.

He regretted leaving so late in the season, as if he didn't know how early the snow came. But he'd been pushing his luck stalking Sawyer, and now the ground was covered with snow. Though his tracks could be wiped out, it'd take time and every ounce of his skill. And he couldn't take the time to do that, not tonight.

He'd leave his tracks then, and he'd hightail it out of the country and never come back.

Smiling at the recklessness of it all and feeling confident that he'd managed the whole thing perfectly, he moved quietly to the cabin's broken shutter. He'd seen Sawyer slip inside this way a few times.

He peeked in and saw her lying there, sleeping like a baby. The sight made him smile again. He dropped to the floor in the woman's room . . . soon to be his woman.

He landed on someone and had to bite back a yelp of surprise. The boy? But no, it was another woman. Whoever it was grunted when he landed on her, causing her to squeak in a girlish way.

If it'd been Morgan, this would've been his chance to kill

the man. But that had to come later because the woman started squeaking again, and he had to keep her quiet.

Using the butt of his pistol, he knocked out the other woman before she could make another sound. He turned toward the bed. By some stroke of luck, his woman hadn't awakened. Silently, he used the rope he'd brought along to bind the unconscious woman on the floor. A wicked desire to take her along had to be controlled. He couldn't carry them both.

Once she was dealt with, he rushed to the bed and gagged his woman. She was soon fully awake. He had no desire to bash her in the head, though he would if he had to. He quick tied up her hands and feet just as he would a calf at branding time. He'd considered she'd be in her nightclothes, so he wrapped a blanket around her, then bound her tight with more rope.

He'd come thinking the boy might stir, so he'd brought double the bindings. Once again he came ready for trouble, and it paid off. His woman strained against the ropes as he slung her over his shoulder and clambered out the open window.

Now, moving fast and on foot, he hurried to where his horse waited, a long way off. Sawyer wouldn't begin tracking him until he got home and realized his woman was gone. With barely stifled laughter, he wondered how long it'd take Sawyer to give up his nightly hunt, then go home to find his woman gone and their guest bound and battered. No doubt he'd start hunting again without delay.

Well, he could go on following tracks forever because the Ghost would vanish long before anyone could catch up to him in the wilderness.

One thing niggled at him, though. Where had that other woman come from? He'd assumed it was just Sawyer, his woman, and the boy. With his visits mostly at night in recent days, it had been a foolish mistake to assume anything.

It didn't matter now anyway. In fact, he regretted that he was going to have to quit the country to avoid Sawyer, who was sure to come after him on a rampage.

He usually spent the winter holed up in his cabin, not far from where his family and friends had settled. And now with his woman.

With the snow falling fast, it was winter for a fact, no matter what the calendar said. So he'd take her home with him and worry about claiming this meadow for himself come springtime.

Roz was tied up so tightly, she could hardly move a finger. And the gag made breathing near impossible. She was cold, too. Her feet were bare. She was still in her nightgown, wrapped in a single skimpy blanket.

But none of that mattered. What did matter was that she was being stolen like a sack of gold. And out of a houseful of people no less.

This man had to be Morgan's ghost. He was quiet enough. Why hadn't Stella noticed him? Why hadn't Tex heard anything? Why hadn't she?

Roz was annoyed with herself. She had to admit, the man was skilled when it came to stealthy movement. She'd been bound and gagged so quickly, by the time she became aware of what was happening, it was already over and she couldn't move a muscle.

She saw no way to call for help and no way to fight him, certainly no way to run. But there had to be something she could do. It was shameful that a woman as knowing in the woods as she was, as alert to danger, as wise in the ways of wild animals, had no idea of what to do to get free.

She settled in to consider when to attack and, more importantly, how to go about it.

A violent wrench of her body knocked him into a stagger, and she threw herself off his shoulder. He dropped her, then just scooped her back up and kept moving forward. He hadn't made a sound. No rage, no blows or threats spoken. The man remained silent. A shiver rushed through her that had nothing to do with the cold and snow.

Roz knew Morgan was out there somewhere, as were Owen and Bowie. Woods-savvy men who'd be on the alert, listening for unusual sounds.

He didn't drop her again. His grip was like iron clamps, holding her in place. It felt like anger to her, and she had a surge of fear. She saw no sense in making him even angrier with more escape attempts.

Her hands were trapped at her waist by the blanket and tied besides. The cold pressed against her almost as hard as the fear. Though wrapped in the blanket, she could feel herself getting colder to the point of freezing. Even if she somehow got away from him, she'd then have to fight her way free of the ropes and run for home in the snow on bare feet.

Her eyes weren't blindfolded, nor her head covered, yet all she could see was his back. If he'd've dropped her on a steep slope, she might've fallen a far distance. Far enough it'd make considerable noise, and far enough he might just run rather than chase her down the slope to gather her up again.

Lifting her head slowly so as not to draw his attention, Roz tried to figure out her surroundings. He'd taken her into the rugged timberland, having left behind her beautiful meadow. He was dodging trees, not running but striding along fast.

She noticed the tracks he was leaving in the snow. If someone came after her, it'd have to be fast because it was obvious he was leaving the area. He couldn't stay around here now that he had a prisoner. How far did he have to walk to reach his horse?

Morgan had mentioned to her that the Ghost must be hitching his horse a good distance from the meadow because Morgan had never found it. She watched for some chance to get away and prayed she'd know it when she saw it.

If only she could scream. Doing her best to move slowly and not attract his attention, she worked on sliding the gag out of her mouth by rubbing her face against her shoulder. It gave her something to do as she waited for the right moment, looking for her chance to roll down a slope like an escaping log.

The gag inched down. Yes, she would become a screaming, escaping log. And that might make all the difference.

Tex woke up in the middle of the night and for no good reason. He couldn't figure out what had disrupted his sleep. Had it been a noise? After listening for a long time, he fell back asleep, sure it'd been nothing but a gust of wind or a wolf howling.

He awoke again at dawn, this time to the sound of a fist pounding on the front door. Springing to his feet, he rushed to the door. "Who's there?"

"It's Owen, Tex. Let me in. I'm sick of this cold."

That quirked a smile out of Tex, and he slid the heavy wooden bar aside and opened the door. Owen, shivering, hurried inside and headed straight to the fireplace to warm himself.

Delaney had heard the men talking and came out of her room, followed by Jesse from his room.

Tex got busy building up the fire while Delaney helped Owen out of his heavy coat. "I wonder why you didn't wake up Stella and Roz," she said.

"Better go check on those two, Delaney." Then Tex felt a sudden chill that had nothing to do with the winter weather.

Delaney was back in seconds. "Owen, Tex, get in here!"

Owen was fastest to respond, but Tex and Jesse were right on his heels.

Stella was tied up and lying unconscious on the floor. The shutter on the window stood wide open, and Roz was gone.

Tex knew without a moment's considering. She'd been taken by the Ghost.

Owen rushed out of the room, pulling on his coat as he raced for the door. Tex was only a few paces behind him. Once outside, they rushed around to Roz's window. The sky had begun to lighten with the coming sunrise.

"There!" Owen pointed at the Ghost's tracks in the snow.

"He didn't even try to hide them," Tex said. "That tells me he's quitting the country; he wouldn't leave a trail like that otherwise. C'mon, let's ride."

They ran to the corral and started saddling the horses.

"Should we come, too?" Delaney asked. She'd run over to the corral, putting on her coat at the same time.

"You and Jesse stay here, take care of Stella." Owen swung up onto his horse.

"We'll find her!" Tex shouted, hoping that woman-stealing vermin heard him.

How long had she been gone? Tex remembered then the sound he'd heard in the night. Only the faintest of noises and then he'd gone back to sleep. He was furious at himself for not getting up and looking into it.

To Owen, riding beside him as they followed the tracks in the snow, he said, "We'll get Roz back, and while we're at it, we'll round up the Ghost, too."

They thundered into the woods.

25

At last, Morgan found the Ghost's horse. It had taken him all night, but he'd done it.

The snow had stopped, but not until it'd piled up a good three inches at least. It was cold but not bitter. Morgan, born and raised in the mountains, knew how to bear the cold, knew how to keep his fingers and toes from freezing.

Morgan crossed the gully he'd been long searching for and found a place that was sheltered and comfortable enough for a man to survive. He settled in just as the night was losing its fight with the coming day.

Though tired, he stayed watchful, denying himself sleep. He'd once snuck into a swamp in eastern Virginia and stayed there, silently watching as the entire Army of Northern Virginia marched past him just ten feet away. A few of their horses looked at him, but not one Confederate soldier knew he was there. As soon as they were out of sight, he hightailed it back to his camp with the Army of the Potomac, armed with military intelligence that would later help the Union side to win the next battle.

Despite the Ghost's ability to move around with spooky silence, he was just a man, one who could be bested. Morgan had stolen his first horse when they were out searching for Tex and Stella. No doubt the Ghost had seen from a distance that his horse was gone and so stayed back. Given the man's sly ways, Morgan had decided not to chance letting him slip past them and ride away.

This time, Morgan wanted to face the Ghost head on. If Morgan tromped around the man's horse, he'd leave tracks in the snow that would send a warning to the Ghost.

The sun rose. The wind whipped up for a bit as it often did as daylight overcame the darkness, but then the wind died and the sun grew brighter, easing the worst of the chill.

Morgan focused on the horse. It had an altered brand that didn't look fully healed. He wondered who'd been robbed this time. That had to rule out his pa.

Why did he still think the Ghost might be Pa? It couldn't be. Pa was no horse thief. Whatever else his pa was, he was an honest man. True, Pa had threatened to shoot him on sight. Even so, he'd never turn horse thief, and Morgan wouldn't believe different without solid evidence.

If this horse turned out to be stolen, then his pa wasn't involved in all this.

Why did it set him off so badly to think it might be Pa? Maybe because what was likely to happen next could break out into shooting trouble, and it made him shudder to imagine he might have to draw a bead on his own pa.

It surprised Morgan how much he wanted to see the cranky old badger again.

She was a skinny woman. The Ghost couldn't help but feel a little smug about that because he still had a long way to walk to get to his horse.

He chuckled to himself as he thought of how feisty she was. The way she'd tried to throw herself off his shoulder told him nothing with her would be easy.

And that suited him just fine.

Yet his nighttime wandering had gotten old. He missed the others. He'd needed to do something else for a time, and he had. But now he wanted to get back to his friends and family. That now included this woman. His woman. He chuckled again, thinking of her.

She had some fight in her, but he wouldn't want a woman who didn't. He'd never thought to get another woman since his wife died, and he hadn't felt the lack of it. But following her and the Marshals had set him to longing for one. The minute he'd gotten himself back in the saddle, his yearning over this woman had him heading straight for her meadow.

Sawyer had a Marshal's badge. Well, there was no Marshal work to be done up here. The Ghost decided right then that he'd help himself to the house in the meadow, the woman, and the child.

Problem was, Sawyer was too watchful. Which was something the Ghost respected. Sawyer had yet to see him, he was sure of that. Too many times, though, the Marshal had come close to eyeing him. The Ghost had to keep on edge to stay out of sight. It'd been hard on his pride to admit that Sawyer had everything he wanted.

It couldn't be allowed to stand.

He had one last treacherous stretch to cover. Down a gully, then back up, and there he'd find his horse. He'd made it.

He was tempted to stand the woman up on her bare feet and let her loose, let her walk down the narrow gulch on her own. It was pretty steep. And carrying her might throw off his balance.

Only the bare feet stopped him.

That restored his pride in a way because he was taking care of her. That was what a man did for his woman.

She'd quit her wiggling. He wondered if she'd fallen asleep or maybe passed out. Either one was good since he had his hands full walking down this trail with snow underfoot.

As he reached the low point in the trail, he noticed that dawn had passed and turned to full daylight. He trudged up the other side of the gully, and as he reached the top, he stepped on a snow-covered stone. It caused him to slip and stumble, then suddenly reel back.

Roz had waited and watched and then waited some more. She'd never tested his grip for fear it'd remind him to hang on tighter.

And then came the chance she'd been waiting for.

The Ghost stumbled backward, his arms loosened, and she hurled herself off his shoulder and screamed, "Help! Morgan, help!"

She wrenched her arms free of the blanket and clawed at the ground as she rolled downward and away from him. She stopped herself by grabbing a narrow shelf of rock just as overhead something slammed into her captor.

Roz found herself dangling from the ledge, chilled to the bone, still half wrapped in the blanket. Looking down into the gully, she saw it was a long drop to the ground below.

While the opportunity had seemed right at the time, she hadn't picked a good spot in which to wrest herself free of the Ghost.

She screamed Morgan's name again, and then a gunshot rang out, followed by another . . . and another.

Not letting himself get distracted, Morgan kept his eyes on the place where the Ghost's horse stood tied to a small tree about fifty feet away. Nothing much to see except that the Ghost had hitched the critter in a way that allowed the buckskin gelding to graze and lie down if it wanted to. This was a man who looked to the care of his horse—except for stealing it, of course.

As Morgan was pondering the Ghost's skill in the wilderness and his fair dealings with a stolen horse, a scream rang out. A woman's scream . . .

Roz!

Charging out of his hiding place, he ran straight at the man who was clawing at a woman's figure wrapped in a blanket as she rolled down into the gulch. Morgan had crossed that slope. He knew the fall from there would be a deadly one. And as she vanished over the edge, it struck him hard that he loved her.

Of course he loved her. He'd loved her from the first, even back when they were youngsters. But this had hit him like a hammer. He loved her, and she was falling to her death! Morgan rushed after her.

The man whirled around and drew his gun with the reflexes of a rattlesnake. Morgan quick drew his own gun. The man fired, then fired again. Morgan dove to the ground, avoiding getting hit by the bullets, then fired back at the man. Though Roz was out of sight, he heard her screaming. She was alive!

It was all the encouragement he needed. He took aim and fired his gun once more.

The Ghost shrieked as one of Morgan's bullets hit home. Then the man began staggering toward his horse.

Morgan never considered for a second going after him. Instead, he hurried to the edge of the gully and went right over it. For a split second, he thought he was following Roz in a plunge to his death. His heart ached with regret that Jesse would be left without a pa. His life with his sweet wife would end too soon.

Then he hit solid rock and stopped. Just feet from the top of the gully. He was down just far enough to block the gunfire from above. Bullets whizzed past him, shattering rock that sliced at his hands and face. But none hit him.

Roz dangled from a ledge. Her bound hands were hooked around a stone. That alone had saved her.

Morgan caught her hands, then her arms, and pulled her up as hoofbeats sounded from above them. He lifted his wife and set her on more solid ground, relief and joy washing over him.

"This ain't over, Sawyer!" The Ghost's shout echoed in the gully. They heard him ride off. Just as the hoofbeats faded away, another man came tearing up the other side of the gully.

Bowie Bridger!

He looked after the running horse, then quick holstered his gun and turned to kneel on the edge of the gully. "Let me help you."

Between Morgan and Bowie, Roz was raised to the safety of higher ground.

Morgan whipped out his knife and cut the ropes binding her hands while Bowie worked on the rope that kept the blanket tied around her.

The two of them set her free, and with a stifled sob, she flung her arms around Morgan's neck.

Morgan looked up at Bowie. "Thank you."

Sounding grim, Bowie said, "He meant it, Morgan. This isn't over."

The Ghost rode fast, every so often howling like a crazed wolf. He was heading to where he was planning to go with the woman.

"Where did that other woman in Sawyer's cabin come from? And who was that man who'd popped out on the gully trail?"

He realized he was talking out loud. A man who prided himself on staying silent. But he saw the newcomer and Sawyer were on foot; nobody was getting a horse across that gully, which meant they couldn't come after him. He could talk a little if he wanted to.

"Where did the other two people come from?" The Ghost didn't like making mistakes, and he'd made a serious one this morning. He'd been sure beyond any doubt that Sawyer, the woman, and the boy were alone.

Yet there had been two more people with them. When did they arrive?

He didn't like it. It made him feel like a fool, and that

rubbed him raw right down to the bone. And he wasn't going to let it stand.

But for now, he had to fall back. He glanced down at his hip. Bleeding still. Feeling the ugly wound, he decided it was a deep graze only. The bullet hadn't broken a bone or gone inside to rattle around in his innards.

But it hurt bad enough to make his raw feeling doubly raw. Was it the work of Sawyer or the newcomer? The Ghost was always ahead of everyone else—faster, smarter, wilier. But today he'd been thwarted, made a fool of, and shot to boot.

Nope. He wasn't going to let this stand.

But he needed to heal up, and winter was coming on. He considered what to do next. Either he rode home now or he'd have to stay out here all winter.

There was plenty of space between him and Sawyer now. He should stop, tend his wound, stanch the bleeding. But he was spooked by what had happened back there. Something inside told him to keep riding.

The choice as he saw it was to get away or go back and kill every man and woman in that cabin, except for the woman he'd claimed as his own. He'd have plenty of time then to tame her, and later when he returned home, they'd all see he'd brought with him a real prize of a woman.

He decided he needed to put more distance between himself and Sawyer, although he was still weighing whether to go home or not. He couldn't just head straight home like a whining child running to his mama.

For now, though, he'd keep on riding . . . at least until the chill that rushed down his spine eased off some. A man needed steady nerves to be a ghost.

26

Tex had been pushing his horse to a dangerous speed in the uneven terrain since the moment he'd heard the gunshots ring out.

He reached the top of another of those endless valleys to be climbed down just as Morgan popped up in front of him, carrying Roz.

Dark clouds scudded low overhead, and a strong gust of wind told Tex the snow he'd hoped was done falling was in fact returning with a vengeance.

Roz lay in Morgan's arms shivering. She was barefoot and in her nightgown, wrapped in a blanket. But very much alive and well.

Swinging down from his horse with a sigh of relief, Tex said, "You have her. Thank God."

Bowie came up next.

Morgan asked, "Can I have your horse, Tex? I need to get Roz out of the cold."

"Yep, I'll walk back to the cabin. I've been in such a tearing hurry, scared to death when we found her missing. Then when I heard the shooting . . . well, I can stand to cool down a little. Stella was knocked cold and tied up. Delaney and Jesse are caring for her, but someone needs to get back so they aren't alone."

Owen rode up beside Tex and swung down. "Bowie, you've been out all night. You can have my horse. I'll walk back with Tex."

Bowie shook his head. "I don't mind walking. You go ahead and join Morgan."

Morgan mounted up and took off, still holding Roz tight. She never uttered a word.

Once they were out of earshot, Tex said, his voice as cold as the winter snow, "Where's the Ghost? Let's go round him up."

"He's long gone by now," Bowie said. "And I doubt you can get your horse down that steep gully and back up in the snow. We had no choice but to let him go since we were on foot. His last words—no, his only words—before riding off were to Morgan, promising him he'd be back." Bowie raised grim eyes to Tex. "Then he howled like a madman. I've never heard the like. The Ghost, whoever he is, isn't going to stop coming. We're gonna have to stop him."

Tex's jaw tightened.

"I'm riding after Morg," Owen said. "See if I can be of some help."

"You're the best of us at doctoring, and Stella might need you. And check Roz's toes. It wasn't a fit night to be outside barefoot."

Owen gave a nod as he urged his horse toward the cabin.

Tex and Bowie started for the cabin on foot.

"How long until we can get a horse across that gully?" Tex asked.

"If it keeps snowing, it'll be spring before it's passable. If it warms up, maybe before that. With the next snowfall, the Ghost's tracks will be covered completely. But I could find him regardless."

Bowie made it sound like a promise.

"What happened out here?"

Bowie told all he knew, which wasn't much. "I spotted his trail from when he grabbed Roz. Easy to read as a newspaper headline. His feet were bound up in rags just like you said, so I knew it wasn't Morgan. I went after him fast as I could move. I was most of the way up the far side of that gully when I heard Roz scream."

Bowie shook his head and swallowed hard. "Then guns started firing. Somehow she'd gotten away from him, but it was right at the edge of the gulch when she did. She was hanging from a ledge a little way down. Her wrists were tied up, and she'd looped them over an outcropping of rock or she'd've fallen to her death. Her screams let us know where she was. Morgan must've already been there because he came out with his gun drawn as soon as the screaming started. He's pretty sure he wounded the Ghost.

"I came along in time to help Morgan pull Roz up over the edge. We were untying her when the Ghost galloped off. If Morgan did hit him, it must've only been a graze because the varmint looked as lively as ever. And there I stood with no horse, and no way to go after him."

Bowie sounded angry at himself. Tex understood because he was furious at his own failure. He'd been right there in the house when Roz had been taken and Stella attacked.

"Now tell me what happened at the cabin?" Bowie wanted

answers as much as Tex did. "How'd the Ghost get past you?"

"I was woken up in the night for some reason. I know now that he must've made a noise when he knocked Stella out and tied her up. I woke up but saw no reason for it. I listened, heard nothing, then fell back to sleep like some innocent, trusting child."

The snow came faster, the wind picking up speed. They moved along briskly and hadn't gone far when Owen came back leading two horses. He should've stayed to help with the doctoring, but he hadn't, and Tex didn't waste his breath complaining. Owen handed the reins to Tex and Bowie, turned and rode off again. This time they were right on his heels.

Tex was scared sick over the memory of Stella's unmoving form on that bedroom floor. He wanted to do a little screaming himself that he'd been so unaware. Morgan said the Ghost was good at moving around undetected, and Tex knew it to be the absolute truth.

When they reached the open meadow, Owen took off at a gallop toward the cabin.

"He should've let us walk," Tex muttered.

"Let's see what we can do to help." Bowie picked up the pace, and they reached the corral in a matter of minutes.

But to Tex's way of thinking, it still took way too long.

Morgan carried Roz straight to the fireplace, knelt to set her gently on the floor, then moved quickly to the woodbox to build up the fire.

Roz was shivering, and her teeth chattered audibly. Delaney came out of the bedroom and gave a cry of relief. "You found her! Roz, are you all right?"

Roz nodded, her arms wrapped around her body. "I h-heard Stella was hurt. How b-bad?"

Jesse hurried to his ma's side, his face tight with concern. "What can I do to help?"

"Rub her toes," said Morgan. "They're so cold it's dangerous."

Jesse peeled back the blanket, lifted one foot, and rubbed it vigorously between his palms.

"Stella?" Morgan repeated Roz's question.

"She still hasn't come around. I've pressed cool cloths to her forehead and . . . well, it seems that's the limit of my doctoring skills."

Morgan looked into Delaney's eyes and saw the worry there. He suspected he had the same look in his own eyes. "Owen, Tex, and Bowie should be here soon. Owen's good at doctoring—maybe he can do something to help her."

Once the fire was stoked, Morgan said, "I'll carry Stella in here. That way we can see to them both at the same time."

He hated leaving Roz even for a second. He needed to see to warming her up. But he wasn't gone much longer than a second. Stella lay unmoving, no moan of pain even.

He stretched her out on the floor beside Roz, who was sitting up. Shifting around to Jesse, Morgan said, "Now, let's take a look at Roz's feet."

Her toes reminded him of little cubes of ice. He'd known men who lost toes and even feet and legs because of the cold. It was a mean business cutting off someone's toes, a business he had no stomach for.

Praying fervently for healing for both women, an idea

popped into his head. Moving fast, he unbuttoned his coat. Only now did he realize he was still wearing it. He tossed it aside, then unbuttoned his shirt and the front of his long-handles. Then he drew Roz's feet toward him and pressed them against his belly.

Roz gave a shuddering gasp.

His head snapped up. "Can you feel that?"

"Y-yes. It hurts." She tugged one of her feet away.

He pulled it right back. "That's a good sign, Roz. If you're feeling pain, it likely means your feet aren't dangerously frozen. Let me warm them up." Morgan glanced up at Delaney. "Could you start a pot of coffee? A hot drink will help her warm up inside."

Delaney flew into action as if desperate to be given something to do.

Morgan pressed his big hands over both of Roz's feet. "Jesse, go fetch your ma's red shirtwaist and her black riding skirt." He looked at his shivering wife and smiled. "I suspect she's tired of all and sundry seeing her in her nightgown."

"I'm not changing clothes out here in front of everyone." Roz's cheeks pinked up in a blush.

Morgan noticed white patches on her cheeks. He hadn't seen them before. Cold could be dangerous in lots of different ways. That vicious man had a lot to answer for. Morgan remembered the Ghost's shouted threat that he'd be back and his shrieking like some kind of banshee. Or madman.

"Bring a blanket too," he said to Jesse. "We can rig a screen with it so she can get dressed right here, and she'll have her modesty."

Jesse hopped up and went to work.

Morgan glanced at Roz and whispered, "He needed something to do. He's scared for you. He wants to help."

Roz had a stubborn look on her face like she'd been prepared to refuse the idea of changing. But the mention of Jesse's fear and his need to take care of her softened the expression.

"Stella's in her nightgown, too. As soon as you get changed, we can use that blanket to cover her."

Jesse was back fast. "I brought the blanket from my room for Stella."

Delaney set the kettle of water next to the fireplace. The cabin was small, so she'd heard Morgan's plan to get Roz dressed. "How are her feet? Can you let them go for a little while? You and Jesse hold up the blanket, and I'll help her change into something warmer." Delaney gave Roz a smile. "I'll bet she could do it herself, but I might as well help out if I can."

Morgan felt Roz's toes for a moment. He wasn't satisfied. "How do they feel?"

She wiggled her toes against his belly. "They ache." A violent shiver stopped her from talking for a bit, and then she went on. "And t-they itch until I w-want to claw at them."

"They're going to be fine, then." He sure hoped he was right. "Let's get you dressed. Then I'll warm them some more."

It didn't take long to get the blanket set up as a screen, and for Roz to pull up her skirt under her nightgown, then shift from the nightgown to the shirtwaist. Delaney helped, and it was done before Morgan could start nagging. Soon he was back with her feet against his belly.

"Jesse, your ma's face looks cold. Come and lay both your

hands on her cheeks. We'll get her warmed up and then we'll try to bring Stella around."

Morgan rested worried eyes on Stella, then looked at Roz, who met his gaze. She was as worried as he was. Then she looked back at Jesse and smiled at the boy with the sweetest smile a ma could ever give to her son.

Jesse pulled his hands away. "The white patches are mostly faded."

"Thanks, but maybe keep on warming my face a little while longer."

Jesse returned his hands to her cheeks. The connection between them was strong. All their years together. They'd welcomed Morgan into their family, but he wasn't yet a part of what they shared together. He wanted to be, though.

Delaney crouched beside Stella with a wet cloth to rest against her brow. The woman didn't move.

"Remember when Boone got shot in the head?" Her brother Boone had been traveling with them from Denver to Fort Russell when they were ambushed by the Duncans, Stella's family.

"Sure, I remember. We were afraid he was dead. Your brother is a tough man."

Delaney nodded. "He didn't wake up for several days. She's not bleeding like he was, but she's got a terrible lump on her head. I'm afraid Stella took a blow as wicked as the damage done by the bullet that grazed Boone. She might be a while coming around."

Morgan turned back to Roz. "Let me see her face, Jesse."

Jesse lifted his hands. "I think you're better, Ma."

Roz pressed her own hands against her cheeks and nodded slowly.

"Can you fetch her a cup of coffee, Son? A hot drink oughta be about the best thing for her right now." As the boy hurried to get the coffee poured, Morgan said to Roz, "I think your toes are going to be all right." He looked up from her pink toes and smiled at her.

Jesse, back with the coffee, carefully handed the steaming cup to his ma. "I'll go pour you a cup too, Pa."

"Thanks." Morgan set Roz's feet on the floor closer to the fire.

"Now, what else can we do for Stella?" Morgan studied the silent woman, still as death. "Tell me again what went on here." Morgan looked at Roz. "Tell me everything you can remember about the Ghost."

Before Roz could start, the door swung open. A draft of cold air gusted in, along with billowing snow. Owen, Tex, and Bowie stepped into the cabin. They shut the door quickly, yet the temperature in the cabin still dropped twenty degrees in the short time it was open.

Owen looked at Delaney, then down at Stella. He shed his coat and went to Stella. He exchanged long looks with Delaney that made Morgan itch for that same kind of closeness in his own marriage. He remembered then the shocking realization that he was in love with his wife. And he was determined to tell her so just as soon as he had a moment alone with her.

Tex and Bowie were soon out of their coats and drinking the hot coffee. The cabin was mighty full of people now, and it struck Morgan that all of them could be stuck living here for the winter. With the gullies and passages leading out of the valley slick with snow, it would be dangerous on horseback, and no one was leaving here on foot.

"Let's go back over everything," Bowie suggested.

Morgan told about his night and finding the horse.

Tex talked about waking up to find Stella unconscious and Roz gone and the moment he'd awakened in the night.

After letting Tex rage about being duped, Morgan said, "The Ghost was almost completely silent when you consider he was just a room away from you all. Going through the window, knocking Stella out, tying her and Roz up, then jumping out again. One tiny sound, not repeated."

"I might've made that sound, Tex," Roz admitted. "I saw him for about two heartbeats while he gagged me, tied up my hands and feet, and wrapped me in the blanket. I tried to scream but only managed to inhale loudly is all."

Tex's eyes strayed to Stella. Shifting restlessly, he set down his coffee cup and went to her side, across from Owen.

Morgan decided he'd had enough of the floor, and the room had warmed up enough that Roz could get up, too. It was getting crowded in front of the fire. He rose and helped her up.

Jesse stood beside her, offering her his arm. "If you're warmed up now, Ma, come and sit at the table. I'll get you more coffee."

Roz ran a hand over Jesse's white-blond hair. The two of them were a matched set for sure. Morgan wondered what Herman had looked like, but then he banished the foolish thought. There was no need to be jealous; Herman was gone.

"I'll sit for a few minutes, and then I'll start on breakfast."

"We'll see to it, Roz." Morgan took her arm as they moved to the table. "I'll get your shoes and stockings. Now that your toes are safe, the shoes will give you added warmth."

She smiled and nodded. Morgan hovered for a minute

before running to the bedroom for the shoes. He was back directly.

Owen, on the floor beside Stella, talked about his time in the woods yesterday. He didn't see or hear anyone, but he'd gone to the south side of the woods while Morgan headed west, and Bowie went his own way.

"I found his tracks after he'd left a new trail going away from the cabin," Bowie said. "Not many tracks to speak of, but he probably got here before the snow came down heavier. I didn't see any signs of our tracks from yesterday either."

Tex nodded. "He wasn't being careful of leaving a trail. With the snow, that'd be next to impossible anyway, but he didn't even try. I took that to mean he was heading out of the country. I know now it was because he had Roz and was taking her with him somewhere."

Tex gave Roz a somber look. "We were sorely afraid that if he had you, he was planning to quit the country, and then we'd never see him again." Morgan moved to help put the stockings on her feet. She waved him away with a grateful smile and took over the job.

"Did you get a look at the Ghost, Roz?" Owen asked.

"From what I remember, he had a full bushy beard like most men wear up here in the wintertime. It was dark, but with the fresh snow, the room was a bit brighter than usual." She fell silent, thinking, then looked down and lifted the kerchief at her neck. "This is his. It's thin leather, I think." She removed the kerchief and handed it to Morgan.

"It's buckskin," he said. "Some mountain men use leather to make kerchiefs instead of cloth. Makes sense, I suppose. He's a skilled woodsman, so why wouldn't he dress like one?"

"He pulled the blanket over my head, slung me over his shoulder, and climbed out the window. He was fast and strong. I wasn't struck by him being a huge man. I don't think he's as tall as you, Morgan." Roz shook her head. "I'm not much help, am I?"

Bowie cut in, "Can I fry up some eggs? I need to eat something and then I'm heading back out there. The Ghost was running like mad and clearly wanted to get far away from here. But I'm not trusting that. Even though I'm tired, I'd like to go back out for a bit, see what I can find."

Delaney got up and started heating the skillet while Bowie began slicing bread.

Morgan studied Roz for a few minutes to make sure she was all right.

She rested her hands on his face just as Jesse had done for her. "Thank you for saving me, Morgan." She kissed him sweetly. Not proper in front of everyone, but he couldn't say he minded it much. "Thank you all." She looked around the room. Everyone gave her a nod and a smile, then went back to work.

Everyone but Stella.

"If you think it's safe, I'd like to sleep for a while," Roz said.

"You can have my room, Ma," Jesse offered. "It'd be safer. You shouldn't sleep in your room until that window gets fixed."

She gave her son a firm one-armed hug. "I'll certainly sleep better in your room. Thank you."

"I'll have that window fixed before dark," promised Morgan. "The Ghost must've seen me go into the cabin that way.

Then the vermin used it against us." He shook his head in disgust.

Bowie brought the bread to the table, a stack of plates, and forks. Delaney added a ball of butter Jesse had made with the butter churn Ma Bridger sent home with them.

Delaney came back with a plate piled high with scrambled eggs.

Roz ate a bit, but exhaustion swept over her, and she headed for Jesse's room.

After she did, Bowie grabbed his coat and left the cabin.

Owen left Stella, still unconscious, on the floor, but Tex stayed beside her. Without commenting, Delaney filled a plate with eggs and handed the plate to Tex where he sat.

Morgan had the window fixed and latched tight before another hour had passed. Owen bundled up to find Bowie and take a shift standing guard.

Morgan found a corner of Jesse's room and lay on the floor, sleep-deprived after a long night in the woods.

"Come on up here, Morgan." Roz drew his attention before he could fall asleep. While there wasn't hardly room in the bed for him, Morgan shoved aside the blanket he'd rolled up in and crawled into bed with her regardless.

He whispered, "Roz, I'm so glad you're here. Safe and not half frozen." He wrapped her in a hug.

"Every time I shut my eyes," she said, "I remember. I don't scare easily, but waking up like that . . ."

He hugged her tighter.

"If you hold on tight and stay close, maybe I can push aside the terrors and get some sleep."

"I'm not going anywhere, Roz." He almost told her he loved her, but he felt her muscles start to relax, her breathing deepen. She was on the verge of sleep, and now wasn't the time for talking.

Turned out the smaller bed was plenty big because he held her so close. Before long, he felt her doze off. Only then, with her resting in his arms, did he dare let himself follow her by drifting to sleep.

27

Roz woke up alone and wondered how long she'd slept.

The time of day was impossible to judge because Jesse's room had no windows, and the back wall was made of solid stone. She felt as safe as if she were still wrapped in her husband's arms.

Yet she wasn't safe exactly. Morgan was gone. She hadn't felt him leave, but she'd known about him planning to take a turn guarding the place. She missed him. She should've stayed awake last night to talk with him more, to thank him privately for saving her. Tell him how much she loved him. Instead, she'd slept, and now another day would have to pass before she had any hope of spending a few moments alone with him.

Roz got up and, after getting dressed, left the room to find Tex asleep on the floor beside Stella. Delaney was crouched nearby, pressing a cool cloth to Stella's forehead.

"She hasn't come around at all?" Roz saw that the shutters were all closed, and the fire burned brightly. She couldn't tell the time of day here in the main room either.

"She stirred once," Delaney replied. "That's a good sign,

but her eyes never opened. I hoped to get her to drink a little water, but she hasn't woken up enough for me to give her any."

"What time of day is it?"

"It's midmorning."

Roz gasped. "I've never slept this late in my life."

"It was a bad night for you. Resting is a good idea," Delaney reassured her. "Bowie came in and slept for a time. The men have been taking turns keeping watch. Now they're all outside, except for Tex."

Tex shifted and sat up suddenly, turning to frown down at Stella. Shaking his head, as if the sleep could be knocked aside, he said, "It's gotta be my turn to stand guard now."

"There's coffee ready if you want something hot to drink first. There's bread too and jerky if you're hungry. I told Owen that if they gave me some warning, I could make up a plate of food for everyone."

Tex looked solemnly at Stella. "She should be waking up by now."

Since he spoke the plain truth, neither woman commented. What would be the point?

Shoving himself to his feet, he grabbed a fistful of jerky and sliced himself a chunk of bread, then disappeared outside.

Roz went straight to the coffeepot and poured two steaming cups. Delaney joined her at the table. Roz met Delaney's worried eyes. Bowing their heads, they each said a prayer for Stella.

Morgan studied the slope in front of him as the snow came down in earnest.

"The Ghost hasn't come back up that slope—neither walking nor riding," said Bowie. He didn't seem like the kind of man to say the obvious, so he must've felt it was necessary.

Morgan raised his eyes to the far side of the gully. Every imaginable trace of a trail was deeply buried now, and it wouldn't show itself again until the spring thaw. Even then there wouldn't be much of a trail left to see.

With a heavy sigh, Morgan said, "You know we're not apt to catch him until spring, don't you?"

"If I stay up here with you," Owen said, "I'm trusting my father-in-law will hold my job for me." He looked at Bowie. "Grizzly is your pa. What do you think of that?"

Bowie shrugged. "Things slow up when winter hits. I don't know much about forts, but maybe that's true of this one as well."

"You're wasting your time asking, Owen." Morgan reined his horse around to head home. "There's not gonna be much to do here over the winter months. There's hunting to be done, of course, but even without that, we have the turkeys and chickens."

Owen frowned. "I suppose we can always work our way through your herd if the winter stretches longer than normal."

He sounded annoyed that he was trapped here and looking to goad Morgan into being annoyed, too. "Just don't eat any cows Roz considers as her friends."

After a long, hard, cold day, they all burst out laughing, and it was a relief.

"Well, I figure the Ghost is probably gone for the winter," Morgan said. "If that turns out to be true, then I can relax a bit, turn my thoughts to the winter and adding a room onto the cabin." He looked at the men riding with him. "Maybe two rooms."

"Even with the snow, we can still get a couple of rooms added if we work fast." Bowie sounded like a man who'd built a cabin in a snowstorm before. "We can put a second fireplace in between the rooms to keep them warm. That should keep us plenty busy."

Morgan had been looking for a chance to ask Bowie a question he dreaded asking. Now seemed a good time to ask it. "You've wandered in these mountains for years, Bowie. I take it you know 'em well."

"As well as any man alive, I reckon." Bowie swung down off his horse as they reached the corral.

"Have you . . . ?" Morgan hesitated, drawing Owen's attention, and figured that meant he was acting like a half-wit.

"Have I what?"

He decided to plunge forward regardless of the consequences. "Have you ever seen or heard of my pa, Amzi Sawyer?" Morgan noticed Owen's already rapt attention sharpen further.

Bowie scratched his chin as if that'd help him think better. "I've heard tell of him but never met him. You know what a vast wilderness this is, but there ain't that many people in these mountains. So when you sit around the campfire with others, you tend to hear stories about most everyone there is."

"I'd like to know what you've heard. I'd like to know if he's . . . if he's alive."

Bowie kept scratching his chin. It seemed to Morgan that Bowie remembered well enough, but he wasn't sure just what he ought to say. And Morgan figured that for a bad sign.

He forged ahead regardless. "My pa left me a letter telling me not to come home after the war. Telling me he'd kill me on sight. My brother died fighting for the South, and I fought for the North. Pa landed his grief directly on my head, blaming me for my brother's death, even though the battle he died in was hundreds of miles from where I was fighting." After a moment's pause, Morgan added, "Roz said he stopped by their place on his way out of the country, and he seemed half mad. That's all I've heard of him in nearly ten years."

Bowie nodded and said, "He was known to be a wandering man. I heard of him around Hahns Peak; there was a gold rush there around 1865. But there's no gold there anymore. I don't know as anyone found much anyway."

"A gold rush? Pa never talked much about seeking out gold."

"I've not heard from anyone that he died either. I did hear once that he was living in an Arapaho village in Oklahoma, but that was two years ago now. It was said he'd taken an Arapaho wife and had children with her."

That news was like Morgan getting slammed against solid rock with stunning force. Could it be true? Did he have brothers or sisters he hadn't known about?

"Do you want to see him?" Owen asked quietly.

Morgan turned to his friend. "It seems foolish, but I-I think I would."

"Oklahoma ain't that far away," said Owen, "not if you took the train south out of Denver."

"'Course, your pa might've moved on from there by now." Bowie sounded doubtful.

The three men stood in silence for a long moment. Then they got back to leading their horses into the corral.

Morgan had a lot to think about. Did he want to see his pa again? Was the man settled somewhere with a new family? Thinking of his pa brought with it a boiling mix of love and doubt and fear.

Shaking all that aside for now, Morgan noticed that the grass near the corral wasn't much covered with snow. The wind had swept into the meadow in a way that piled up the snow at the south end, leaving the northern part mostly clear of snow. He shook his head. A man could never tell what strange sights winter would bring.

It didn't take long to finish building the two winter coops. The other men and Jesse helped Morgan move the turkeys and chickens to their new homes. The turkey flock was getting smaller, as they harvested one for a meal now and then.

Back at the cabin, Stella still lay stretched out on the floor. From where Morgan stood near the fireplace, it didn't look as though the woman had moved a muscle in the hours he'd been outside. She was covered by a warm blanket, and a second blanket had been folded and placed under her head.

Where would she sleep? Yep, they needed two more rooms added on the cabin for certain. Or maybe Morgan should just build a hotel.

Roz crouched in front of the fire, stirring something that gave off a savory smell. Delaney had biscuits baking, and there was a loaf of bread rising on the counter by the dry sink. With Delaney here, they were definitely making better use of their flour.

"Well," Morgan said, "the snow is deep enough now, we reckon the Ghost is long gone, at least for the winter. Even so, we'll be keeping an eye out for him." He led the way to the table while Roz brought over the coffeepot and tin cups.

"We can't depend on the hope of good luck, Morgan," Roz said. "He's too sneaky and—"

"Uncle Lenny, no! No!" A wavering voice had them all whirling around.

Stella, her eyes closed, head tossing from side to side, struggled to sit up on the floor. Again she cried out, "Uncle Lenny, stop!" She gasped, clasping her head with one hand, then rolled flat on her back.

His eyes wide, Owen looked at the others. "Uncle?" Then he rushed over to Stella just as Delaney dropped to her knees beside the fretful woman.

She was out cold again.

28

Tex sat on the floor, leaned up against the side of the fireplace. Stella was unconscious again. He'd known plenty of injured people who'd been a while coming around. He shouldn't be this worried.

"We should carry her into a bedroom." Tex had suggested that before. They'd debated it amongst themselves. Yes, she'd be more comfortable in the bedroom, but here in the main room they could all keep an eye on her. That seemed important when a woman was unconscious, no matter how hard the floor.

Stella had come around yesterday, spoken those few words, and then gone right back to sleep. She'd been left here on the floor overnight, and they'd taken shifts sitting with her.

No one had gone out to search for the Ghost, or Stella's uncle, who had to be what she'd meant by calling out his name. Unless she'd been dreaming of something else to do with her uncle.

"Morgan, go into Jesse's bedroom and pull the mattress off the bed and drag it out here." Roz wanted to make

Stella more comfortable. Or maybe she was willing to do or say anything to shut Tex up. He admitted he'd done a fair amount of out-loud fretting. Which really wasn't like him.

It was midmorning, and breakfast was over. Tex had managed to get a few drops of water down Stella's throat. She'd moved a bit, trying to avoid drinking it, but Tex had overpowered her without much trouble.

"She's going to be all right," Delaney said as Morgan got up to fetch the mattress. "Remember when Boone first regained consciousness? He woke up slow, slept more than he was awake for a time, and seemed dazed for a while afterward. He said he was seeing two of everything, and his head hurt every time he so much as looked up or down or sideways."

Owen came in from outside. Tex noticed his friend had grown restless. They should probably get him out of here before they were all snowed in for the winter. But if they did, Morgan and Roz and the boy would be on their own.

"If you're up for it, Delaney," said Owen, "I think we can still leave before we're snowed in for good; otherwise, we're likely to be stuck here till spring. The sun is strong today. Snow is melting. If we go right now, we can get up and down the gully back toward—"

"You want to leave?" Bowie was outside more than he was in the cabin, but right now he happened to be here.

Owen turned to face Bowie. "Of course I do."

"But didn't I hear you say you hoped my pa would hold your job for you? I figured you'd want to stay here for the winter and protect your friends. I can help get you out if you really want to leave. If you recall, I came along to show Morgan how he could drive cattle out of here."

"I'd kinda forgotten that," Owen said. "But we were talking about getting out yesterday morning."

Bowie shook his head. "No, you were talking about chasing after Wildcat or whoever it is. You know you can't get across that gully, not with a horse."

"Is there another way out of these mountains?"

"There is. The trail out will close after a time, though, about when the snow piles up to be ten or twenty feet deep."

Tex shuddered. He was definitely going home to Texas next chance he got.

"But it's open now," continued Bowie. "It'll probably be passable for another month yet. It passes through lower ground, and there are some tight corners. We'd have to walk along a stream for a time, too."

Owen turned to Delaney. "What do you think? Do you want to head back to the fort?"

Delaney looked from Owen to Stella. "I do, but if we've got another month, can we wait until Stella wakes up? I'd be hauling a load of worry home with me if she's not up and around before we go."

Owen seemed to ponder her words, then said, "I only said we could go now because the trail I thought we'd need to take is just barely open. But if there's another way out . . ."

Delaney nodded. "Good. It's settled then."

"All right. Morg, after you get the mattress for Stella, let's start in with building more rooms onto your cabin."

Morgan shrugged. It struck Tex that more thought oughta be put into building the rooms than what Morgan was putting into it. Yet he needed something to do, and he was in fact a fine builder, even if his arm wasn't quite what it should be.

Tex stood and looked at Jesse. "You can come along, too.

You might as well learn what you can. You did a fine job helping with the coops, but adding a room onto a house is very different from that."

Jesse jumped up and raced for his coat. Tex started pulling on his coat. It looked like everyone was restless, not just Owen—who looked at Delaney, then Roz. "Why don't one of you come outside with us? Stella doesn't need both of you at her side. One of the men can stay with her, too. Watching over someone who's ailing doesn't have to be women's work."

Delaney and Roz looked at each other. Delaney said, "Go ahead. It's your cabin. They oughta at least tell you what they're gonna do to it. They might listen to any idea you've got."

Roz grinned. "First thing is an entry at the front door. We get a blast of cold air every time it opens, and it's aimed right at Stella. I've never paid much mind to it. It's just the way things are. But we can change that."

Morgan, all bundled up, brought Roz's coat to her and helped her on with it. "We'll see to it. An entry shouldn't take long."

Tex took one more look at Stella and wondered what it would be like to leave her behind to ride off with Owen and Delaney. They'd been together mostly every day since they'd gone over a cliff together. She'd had to leave him at night, back at the fort and here at the cabin, but even when the doctor made him stay in his office to be cared for, she'd been there most of the time when he'd wake up.

He didn't like the idea of leaving her. And Morgan needed someone here to help fight off mad ghosts, so Tex wasn't going anywhere. Winter or no, the idea didn't bother him.

For now, he had trees to chop down.

Roz had spent some time in the cold and worn off some of her restlessness. The men decided to build a hallway across the front of the house rather than tear open the walls to connect the new rooms to the main cabin.

Then she'd gone inside and taken over for Delaney, who had baked bread and started a ham baking that she'd found among the things Ma Bridger had sent home.

Roz had never eaten ham before in her life, and it smelled so good she almost started in on it while it was still roasting. Instead, after Delaney went outside, she knelt beside Stella just as her eyes flickered open.

Roz gasped. "You're awake. You've been unconscious for so long, we've been worried."

Stella started to push herself up, and Roz remembered that the effort had knocked her out before.

"No, be careful. Don't overdo it. I'll help you sit up, but first I'm gonna get you a cup of water. We have to be careful of your head."

"Why?"

"Because you took a hard hit," Roz said. Then she saw a cup of water close to hand, left there by Delaney. The woman was a dab-hand at managing things in the house.

Roz slid an arm around Stella's shoulders and eased her forward, afraid she'd move too fast and cause harm. When Stella was raised enough, Roz gave her a sip of water and waited until Stella swallowed it.

"Are you all right? Can you take another sip?"

Stella nodded.

"Slowly. I'm afraid with your empty stomach, you might cast it up if we go too fast."

Stella blinked. "More please."

They were slow about it, but eventually Stella drank the whole cup.

"Thank you. Now, can you tell me why I'm"—Stella glanced around—"stretched out on the floor?"

"First, let's get you off the floor . . . I mean, if you think you're up to it." Roz pulled a chair over so that Stella could immediately sit down if she needed to.

It was slow going because Roz was careful and Stella a bit wobbly, but they got her up.

She looked so normal, Roz smiled. "You've been so quiet for so long. It's wonderful to see you awake and alert. You got hit in the head by . . . well, maybe by your uncle when he snuck in here to kidnap me. You said his name, but you've been unconscious for three days. You woke up once for just a minute and . . ." Roz told her all about it.

Stella nodded along. "Uncle Lenny. I do think it was him. He must not have recognized me in the dark. He wouldn't have clubbed me over the head if he had. Leastways I'd like to hope he wouldn't have."

Roz got her a slice of bread and more water. Stella ate slowly but steadily.

"I feel better with something in my belly. I've really been unconscious for two days?"

"Yes," Roz said, "and I'm so relieved you've come around. Everyone will be so glad to see you awake. The men are outside getting started with adding more rooms onto the cabin. You're all welcome to stay here with us for the winter. But if you decide you want to leave, Bowie says he knows a way to get you out."

"I still like the idea of staying here with you," Stella said. "I don't know much about living in a town—I'm not sure it would suit. But will Uncle Lenny attack us again?"

"With the snow now, we're hopeful your uncle can't get across the gully. That's where he kept his horse the night he kidnapped me and attacked you. He galloped off after Morgan saved me, and now we don't have to worry about him again . . . at least until the spring. Or so we'd like to believe." Somehow just saying that made a chill rush up Roz's spine.

The door swung open, and the men and Jesse trooped inside.

Seeing Stella sitting up, one by one they smiled. She was soon surrounded. Delaney hugged her. Owen checked her head wound and said, "You've still got an egg-sized lump."

"It's lunchtime," Delaney stated. "How does ham sound?" She went to work on it, and Roz did her best to watch every move her friend made, hoping to learn more cooking skills.

The men got the table set, and Morgan grabbed the coffeepot off the stove and poured everyone a cup. By the time they were settled, Delaney and Roz were putting food on the table as everyone else, including Stella, passed the ham around.

"Now, what can you tell us about your uncle, Stella?" Owen poured more coffee all around, offering Jesse a cup as well.

"Uncle Lenny Duncan. I think you said he's called Wildcat Duncan on the wanted posters. Well, that's the nickname my pa gave him." She went on talking about her uncle, the family scapegrace, for a while.

"Where is he?" Tex asked. "He's a wanted man. I've seen

the poster. And now he's kidnapped a Marshal's wife and assaulted a woman. He needs to be stopped."

Stella met Tex's eyes for a moment before she set her coffee cup down. "I've never had much use for my family. My ma was a fine woman, and my aunt and younger sister were fine people as well. But my pa and my brothers, Uncle Gordy and his sons, well, I never want to see them again. And for sure I never want to be forced to live their wilderness life ever again. Still, I was raised to hold dear loyalty to family, and even after what he did to me, it hits hard to be asked to help you find and arrest my uncle."

Stella looked at Roz and touched the tender lump on her temple. "But you're right. He's more than a fool who lives a mountain man's life. He's dangerous. Striking out at me the way he did, he didn't care if I lived or died. Taking Roz away from here on a cold night with bare feet and no care for whether she froze in the course of his reckless plan? A man like that needs to be stopped. And I know right where he is. I suspect he's run for home. He always spends the winter there."

"And you know where home is?" Tex asked.

"I do. I told you how we lived on the outlaw trail in a place called Robbers' Roost?"

The Marshals all nodded.

"I remember," Tex said.

"He lives there. It's remote and well hidden, but I can show you where it is. He lives right near where I grew up. What's more, I know which trails are closely watched and which are quieter back trails where we can slip in unseen."

"Will you take us there, Stella?" Tex had a grim, apologetic look on his face.

Roz could tell he didn't like asking a woman to betray her kin. But he was doing just that, and Stella was nodding at him.

Rubbing her bruised head, she said, "He's never been unkind to me before, and he protected us from the outlaws who lived at Robbers' Roost. I know . . . or at least I *hope* he wouldn't have harmed me if he'd known who I was, but that doesn't excuse him. I heard once that Jesse James loved his mother and was good to her. But he killed fifteen or twenty people and was involved in countless robberies. Just because you're decent to your family doesn't make it all right to be a criminal. My uncle needs to be stopped."

"Are you sure about guiding us to his—?"

Stella held up a hand, interrupting Owen. "I'll help you, but we can't get to him till spring. At least we can't get in if he got home. If he was blocked by snowdrifts, he might still be wandering the wilderness, but chances are he got back in. I suspect he thought he could grab Roz, ride fast and get across those treacherous mountain passes and be locked away from anyone coming after her—locked away until spring. It'd take all he had to get through those passes with this much snow. And more has likely fallen since he rode off. We'd never make it."

The U.S. Marshals stared at her for a moment, then exchanged glances.

Before they could start interrogating her, she said, "I'm going to stay here with Roz and her family. The rest of you can leave if you want. We'll be here come spring, waiting for you to come back. Then I'll guide you to Robbers' Roost."

"I'll stay here for the winter, too." Tex sounded like a man who'd made up his mind. "I'm not leaving Morgan here alone to handle that varmint if he comes back."

Roz felt her spirits lift. None of these men were stronger than Morgan, but another man to stand guard and to fight if need be suited her just fine.

"I'll stay too," said Bowie, nodding his head. "I'd be content here if Morgan will let me build my own room or even my own cabin."

"I do think Delaney and I should go, just so we don't end up lining the whole side of the mountain with cabins." Owen looked at his wife. "Does that suit you?"

She smiled at him as if it pleased her greatly to be asked. "It does."

"All right then. Delaney and I will be back up here as early as we can make it in the spring."

"No," Morgan said. "We'll get out as early as we can, but it's hard to know just when that will be. We'll ride to Fort Collins and send a wire. With the train you can get there fast."

Nodding, Owen said, "When would you say the trail to Robbers' Roost opens up, Stella?"

"Late May, and that's a mite optimistic. But I think we can fight our way in by then. It can't be a large group, though. There are narrow places we'd have to hide away in if we meet up anyone along the way, and only a few of us can fit in them. If you bring an army, you could maybe round up half the criminals in Colorado, but you'd never get close enough to try."

"Then we'll make sure it's safe here," said Morgan, "and leave the women—all but Stella—and go root out that kidnapping coyote."

Roz gasped. She thought it was a quiet gasp, but it must not have been quiet enough because everyone turned to stare at her. Morgan was looking very closely. She knew she loved him and that she'd miss him, but that seemed to just be the way it was . . . unless she refused to put up with it.

"I'm going too," she stated.

Morgan's eyes narrowed.

Roz glared right back at him. "Jesse and I are good on a trail, but maybe you can spend the winter teaching us more."

"I'm not taking a woman and her child to a gunfight."

Roz refused to accept that. "I believe I told you when you showed up here that I wasn't letting you out of my sight for the rest of your life. I reckon I can't make you stay here, but I can follow along wherever you go."

Morgan gave his head a hard shake. "I'll come back as soon as we arrest a few dozen armed men, Roz." Then in a quieter voice, one that sounded almost hurt, he asked, "Don't you trust me?"

She could only speak the truth. "Men have always left me, Morgan. You left. My pa stuck around until he died, but that's another kind of leaving. Herman left. Delaney's pa left. Stella's pa left. Don't all men leave? Then come back if they've got a notion to have a roof over their heads for a while? Well, I'm not the kind of woman who likes that idea."

Morgan stood, shoving his chair back with a harsh scraping. "I need to talk to my wife."

Owen helped Delaney move Stella into a bedroom. Tex and Bowie stepped outside, Jesse right behind them, and soon the sound of axes chopping and felling trees rang out across the meadow. Before another moment had passed, Delaney and Owen slipped outside as well.

Morgan pulled Roz out of her chair and drew her into his arms. He had things to say, but first he wanted her to know it all came from being hurt and befuddled. In fact, he'd spent most of his time mighty confused since the day he got married.

He held her close. She leaned against him, and yet it was as if she were steeling herself against what he might say. And because he was a man of few words, it didn't come easy to express the sweet words a woman was wanting to hear from her husband. He wasn't sure what sweet words even were.

Deciding he needed to look her in the eye when he talked, he caught her shoulders and moved her away just far enough.

"Roz, hearing you say that, well, what I, uh . . ." Morgan was stumped. Especially as he thought of how his pa had left him, too. *Did* men always leave? "Have I ever lied to you, Roz?"

She didn't answer right away. "I can't remember you lying, but we haven't known each other that long."

He gave her a gentle smile. "You're thinking about now. As adults we haven't known each other long, but we did know each other for a long time when we were youngsters."

"You mean before you left me?" Roz's voice broke, and he saw her eyes fill with tears.

True, he had left her before. *Please, God, give me the words . . .*

"I talked about chasing after that low-down Wildcat Duncan, but I planned to come right back."

"Herman always came back, too. Eventually."

She didn't even seem all that upset. Demoralized but fully accepting he'd leave her.

Then Morgan thought of one thing that was as true as

the sunrise. "You know, when I found Wildcat's horse tied up and was waiting there for him, I had a real strong desire to take him prisoner and lock him up for good. But then he came up that trail through the gully right toward me, and before I knew he was carrying something, I heard you scream and saw you throw yourself off his shoulder and roll over the edge of the steep gully . . ."

His voice failed him for a moment, and he rested his forehead against hers as he remembered the terror he felt, the fury, the desperation to save her. "I ran right toward a loaded gun to save you—all I could think about was to get to you before it was too late."

He held the most important person in the world tightly in his arms. And that was when Morgan knew.

"I love you, Rosalind Sawyer."

Hearing her little gasp gave him hope that he'd maybe come up with the right words, the sweet words a wife might want to hear from her man.

He pulled back to lock eyes with her again. "I won't leave you, Roz. You're right. It's a fool idea to take a woman and child along to climb into a dangerous hideout of the worst vermin in Colorado, but I'll do it if that's what you want. Even though I plan to come right back after we're done, I don't want to be away from you that long. I love you, and anywhere I go from this day forward, you have my solemn vow that you'll be at my side the whole way." And Morgan meant it all the way down to his soul.

Her eyes widened as he talked. The tears were replaced by a gleam in her eyes. "I love you too, Morgan. I always have, although when we were kids, it was a different kind of love. But now it's the purest and most forever kind of love

I could imagine. Thank you for not leaving me." She threw herself into his arms.

Her words of love echoed like the drumbeat he'd marched to during the war. They stood holding each other as he heard another tree crash to the ground outside the cabin. The axes then went to work shaping the logs for building more shelters for the winter ahead.

When finally Morgan released her, he stepped back and smiled right into those gleaming eyes and the mile-wide smile that was just for him. "All right. Let's go help build a couple of rooms onto this cabin. Together."

She nodded as she swiped her wrist across her eyes. "Together."

29

The rooms being added to the cabin were coming along well. Overall, the cabin was in good shape, ready to handle the harsh winter weather.

Stella's recovery came slow, the bump on her head still tender. She slept a lot of the time and was unsteady at times on her feet. Sometimes she struggled with speaking. But she was improving little by little, and Morgan and the others hoped that, in time, she'd heal up completely. They all coddled her as much as she'd allow.

Owen and Delaney were going home with promises to meet up with everyone in Fort Collins in the spring.

Morgan realized how long he'd been working with Owen Riley and wondered if he'd ever see his friend again. The West had a way of swallowing people up.

There'd been no sign of Wildcat Duncan, and Morgan had been looking real carefully. He figured Duncan had gone home for the winter, but he didn't believe it enough to quit being watchful.

"I'll be half a day guiding these two out of here," Bowie said as he finished the last of his breakfast. "I'll ride into town with them and bring a few supplies back," he added, sounding confident about getting there and back to the cabin without much trouble.

"Do you need a packhorse?" Morgan asked. He wasn't doing much riding, what with all the snow. He also had serious doubts whether Bowie was going to be able to find a way to town. But he reminded himself that he was talking to Bowie Bridger, who knew his way around these mountains better than any man within a hundred miles.

Morgan decided to keep his doubts to himself.

"Yep, a packhorse would be appreciated. Maybe a couple of them. Tex, why don't you ride along with me part of the way? I should be able to show you the route far enough so you can figure the rest out yourself. That'll help you as far as driving the cattle come spring. Probably not a bad idea to know the way out in case something keeps me from getting back up here." Bowie's eyes turned narrow, cold even. "Remember, I want in on the hunt for Wildcat Duncan. I owe him for the way he hurt Stella and Roz while I was on watch."

The man's expression was grim to the point of pain. Morgan almost said something. He didn't want anyone to carry around such a burden of guilt or anger, especially when it'd been him who was most responsible.

Delaney hugged Roz like she was taking leave of her best friend, and then she did the same with Stella. Even Jesse got a hug. Morgan braced himself to duck and run if he had to. Delaney just looked at him and grinned, then gave him a salute she had to have learned from her pa.

Owen shook his hand and clapped him on the shoulder.

Tex said, "I'll be back before nightfall."

They all mounted up and rode off, their horses wading in the deep snow.

Morgan stood with Roz, Jesse, and Stella and watched them go.

Then Roz said, "I've learned to bake a cake, Morgan. And Stella says she'd made one before, though they never called it a birthday cake. The two of us are going to make one to have with our supper."

With a wide grin, Roz led the way inside, Jesse and Stella on her heels.

"I'm gonna go check the cattle," said Morgan, "and the chickens and turkeys need cracked corn. I'll look for eggs while I'm at it." He watched his family and Stella move into the cabin and wondered at the life he'd stumbled into. However he'd come to be here, he found it suited him just fine.

He turned to face the snowdrifts, the cold, and the coming winter. They were safe now, or as safe as anyone could get in this world.

Tex was back before nightfall, wanting to show Morgan the way out just because it was so unexpected he thought someone else should see the strange, winding trail.

It took Bowie four days to make his trip. He'd left with two packhorses but came back with four. It looked to Roz as though the man had found a surprising number of things to buy when in town.

The winter was going to be a comfortable one, if you didn't count ten feet of snow as far as the eye could see, howling winds, and the bitter cold—and Roz didn't count those. She'd lived with deep snow, wind, and cold through the winter all her life, and she would again this year. Her cattle were used to it. Her son was used to it. Bowie had to be used to it. But Morgan, Tex, and Stella might be in for a shock.

"Cracked corn aplenty," Morgan said, looking at the bulging burlap sacks loaded onto one of the packhorses.

Tex was back to working with Morgan and Jesse on the cabin. Tex had seemed the easygoing type to Roz, but now without that much to do, he acted a bit desperate to find something to keep his hands busy. His arm seemed to be working all right, and if it hurt him to use it, he never complained.

Roz had plenty of ideas. They needed beds in the two new rooms, and firewood laid up since they now had two fireplaces. That all needed to be done. And Morgan was talking over whether to put down a wood-plank floor throughout the whole cabin.

Since Pa had built it on rock, Roz had never considered laying wood on top of stone. Still, if the man needed to invent things to do, who was she to discourage him?

As the winter months unfolded, Morgan began to ease off on his concern about Wildcat Duncan possibly returning to their meadow.

By Christmastime, Roz wondered if she might have a baby on the way.

By the first thaw of spring, she was sure.

In the dark of night, in bed cuddled up to Morgan, she said, "Listen to the water dripping off the roof." Though the snow was deep and would be many weeks thawing, it sounded like spring was arriving.

"Looks like we made it through the winter okay." Morgan pulled her closer, her head resting on his strong shoulder.

"Was it hard for you, Morgan?" Roz asked. "Can you stand living up here? We don't have to stay . . ."

"I lived in Pa's cabin for going on ten years before I left for the war. I knew what was coming. But Pa's cabin was always cold. In this cabin, built into the side of the mountain and with snow so deep on the roof, we're tucked in safe and warm. All in all, it's been a good winter."

He seemed to be drifting off to sleep. He drew in a slow, deep breath that was the next thing to a snore. He often fell asleep fast and deep after they'd shared intimacies. She didn't want that. Not yet.

"Morgan, I have something to tell you: I'm expecting a child."

The breath turned from a snore to a snort. "W-what did you say?"

She didn't repeat it. She was two inches from his ear. He'd heard her well enough. He wasn't claiming deafness, only disbelief. Well, what had he expected considering the way they carried on in the night?

"You for certain can't come on the hunt for Wildcat Duncan, not if you're in a . . . a family way."

The dull stumbling of her heart shocked her. "I guess I knew you'd leave me given the chance. I'd hoped you wouldn't, but—"

Morgan silenced her with a kiss. He'd promised her after all, and she knew he was a man of his word. But maybe just this once, he'd break his promise in some misguided attempt to protect her. And he'd come back, eventually.

She sensed the battle waging inside him.

And then his arms tightened around her, his breathing

becoming unsteady. With her head resting on his chest, she heard his heartbeat speed up.

"Roz . . . you wouldn't be safe out on the trail."

She let the silence between them stretch a bit before she replied, "And you're sure I'll be safe if you leave me here alone?"

He kissed her forehead, her nose, her lips. "We'll settle this in the morning. I know nothing about a woman expecting a child. Maybe Stella has some memories of her ma and how a woman is to act."

"I've had a child, Morgan. You don't have to ask Stella, just ask me."

Morgan reached over and turned up the lantern. His eyes met hers in the dimly lit room. "I promised I'd never leave you, Roz. What I'd like to do is stay here with you. But that Wildcat Duncan seems like a madman to me. He's likely to come back here. I have to find a way to stop him before he hurts you and Jesse and now the baby." He heaved a sigh and shook his head. "I can't take you in a delicate condition to a gunfight or leave you behind with a child coming. That would be breaking my word. There's a churning in my gut to protect you, but it seems no matter what I do, it'll put you in danger."

"I want to be with you, Morgan. I'd prefer to face the danger with you at my side than sit here alone, fearing you might be killed or . . . or maybe you just decide to stay away for a long stretch of time."

Morgan nodded. "Maybe we should pack everything up and move somewhere else for a while. We could drive the cattle to town first thing in the spring, use the money to set up in a place far away from here. Tex has mentioned going back to Texas. Maybe we could find a home there. Or when Owen and Delaney come for a visit, you and Delaney and Jesse could ride for Cheyenne while I round up Duncan."

"We can't do that. Stella has to go with you, and it's not proper for her to ride along with a crowd of men."

That seemed to stump him. Roz thought Morgan looked confused as to what was proper and what was not. Little as she knew of the ways of the world, she was clear on that.

"Maybe Stella can give us a good enough idea about the trail to Robbers' Roost that we could have her go with you and Delaney. That way, you and Jesse can settle in at Fort Russell with the Bridgers. You'd be safe there, or—"

Roz kissed her husband soundly. "Don't think up any more choices right now. You already have too many to ponder. You've got some decisions to make, husband."

"*We* have some decisions to make, Roz."

"Knowing you love me makes any decision easier," Roz said as she snuggled closer to Morgan. "It was what my heart most wanted."

They settled in for the night. She dozed off while listening to the snow drip off the roof, content to be in the arms of the man who loved her.

For more from Mary Connealy, read on for an excerpt from

Forged in Love

Available now wherever books are sold.

Keep up to date with all of Mary's releases at MaryConnealy.com and on Facebook.

ONE

AUGUST 1870
PINE VALLEY, WYOMING
NEAR THE WIND RIVER MOUNTAINS

A bullet slammed into the side of the stagecoach carrying Mariah Stover, her pa, and her older brother.

"Robbers!" The driver's voice roared in the hot Wyoming summer as the crack of a whip lashed, driving the horses faster. "Everyone, fight or die!"

Mariah heard the man riding shotgun on top of the stage land on his belly and open fire from the roof.

Bullets peppered the coach.

Mariah sat between Pa and Theo, facing the horses. Pa, a Civil War veteran, snapped his Spencer repeating rifle into his hand and fired out the window in a steady, rolling blast.

Theo threw himself to the opposite seat, occupied by two men who looked terrified. He aimed, fired, and fired again with his Colt pistol. Pa's rifle echoed the pistol in a steady volley of gunfire.

Mariah dug for the pistol in her satchel and checked the load. She looked out the window to her right. No one there.

Her pa and brother were tough men used to Western ways, who knew that civilization was often left behind at the town's edge. You just had to hope the uncivilized wouldn't follow you right into town.

You protected yourself, or you died. The stagecoach driver had it right.

Pa fired out his window while Theo used the window beside the two others. Both men looked more city than country, and if either of them had a weapon, he didn't produce it. Instead, they just slid aside for Theo.

Mariah gripped a six-shooter. When Pa paused from firing his Spencer, the one he'd gotten in the war when he'd been a sharpshooter, Mariah shouted, "Lean forward while you reload."

Pa did so without looking or speaking, focusing completely on his rifle and trusting her to be tough, competent, and ready.

Mariah watched out the window and saw four men riding ever closer, blasting away. One of them went down, likely from the gunfire of the man on the roof.

She aimed and fired, aimed and fired, and kept going, trying to get the most out of her flying lead.

They were miles from town. No way to get help before these gunmen finished their fight, died trying, or were driven off.

"Get back!" Pa hollered.

Mariah needed to reload anyway, so she gave way to Pa's superior marksmanship.

A cry from overhead ended the gunfire from the shotgun

rider. Mariah saw him plummet from the top of the stage. As the three remaining outlaws rode past him, two of them fired into his body.

Pa growled in disgust at the vicious killers. He opened fire again. Mariah had her gun ready to go when she saw someone coming up beside the window on her side. She whipped her head around in time to see the rider empty his pistol into the city boys until they were riddled with bullets.

Her hair came loose from its knot on the back of her head and blinded her for just a moment as she cried out in horror. Then she glared at the skinny blond man. An ugly scar cut across his left cheek and through both his upper and lower lips. She pressed her body against the door and leveled her gun just as she heard a snap from under the belly of the stagecoach—an axle giving way.

She opened fire on the gunman as the stage skidded sideways. Crimson bloomed on his left arm. He brought his gun up with a wicked smile that revealed one of his front teeth was missing right in line with the scar. Their eyes met. He aimed.

The stagecoach tilted wickedly toward Mariah's side and slammed into a boulder alongside the road. The gunman fell back to avoid the boulder. The stage hit so hard the door flung open, and Mariah fell out. She felt the weight of the stage smother her.

More guns fired. Pa's Spencer fell silent, then Theo's Colt stopped blasting.

A bullet hit her in the side. White fire blazed in her belly as the stagecoach settled hard on her.

The world went dark.

Mariah's eyes flickered open from where she was caged by . . . by something. Voices sounded from outside. She tried to cry out for help, but the weight on her chest was so heavy she couldn't draw a breath to manage it.

"They're all dead—just like always."

"What about the woman?" Whoever said that sounded on edge. "First woman we've ever killed. I don't like it. And the Stovers. What were they doing on this stage?"

"Like it or not, she's dead. Crushed under the stage, and I got a bullet in her just to be sure."

Mariah stopped trying to call for help.

"I'll get the strongbox."

A bullet blast made her flinch, which hurt everywhere.

A third voice asked, "Is there a good haul?"

"No, only a couple hundred. When we stripped the bodies, we got a couple hundred more."

"I thought this stage had a payroll on it for Fort Bridger?"

"We got bad information, or they pulled a switch, sent the money by another route."

"Maybe they know there's a leak. Maybe he needs to die. I don't like talking outside our group."

"He don't know why I was asking. He don't know nothin'."

"He'll put it together when he hears about this robbery."

"The horses broke the traces and got away, too. We're too close to town. We've gotta clear out. When those horses go storming into town, a rescue party will come a-running."

"You sure everyone's dead?"

"You helped kill them, same as me."

"The Stovers were good folks. This is a bad business."

The stage was pressed to Mariah's face so that she saw the dark wood and nothing else. She couldn't move her arms or legs, could barely draw a breath. Her head was pinned and aching. The pain was dizzying, and it came from every part of her.

Her belly was the worst, but her chest felt like it'd been smashed out of shape. Her vision blurred as she fought for each shallow breath. Her whole body was crushed.

Finally, she heard horses galloping back the way the stagecoach had come.

As much as those men terrified her, being left alone was almost worse. Tears slid from the corners of her eyes as she thought of Pa and Theo.

Thought how it felt like she was already in a coffin.

Clint Roberts was loitering outside his diner, hoping to catch Mariah's attention, when he saw the stagecoach team charging into town. The stage he'd been watching for wasn't behind it. The thundering hooves and wildly out of control speed told of panicked horses. He could think nothing but the worst. "Sheriff, get out here!"

Clint sprinted for his horse, penned up in the corral behind the blacksmith shop. He'd already lost one family. It would kill him to lose another one. The Stovers certainly didn't count him as family, but he'd begun to count them.

He didn't ride in from his homestead every day—it was an easy walk. But today he'd hoped Mariah and her family would be back, and he'd wanted an excuse to stop in, get his horse, and say hello.

The sheriff burst out of the jailhouse, saw the stage horses, and raced for his own mount tied to the hitching post. Willie

Minton, the town deputy, was only a pace behind. Other men were coming, too. They all knew the stage was in trouble. And the trouble might be ugly.

Clint was galloping before he reached the edge of town. The stage had been late, so he hoped that meant they'd been close to town.

Mariah. Mariah . . . Please, God, let her be all right.

He'd been waiting until he felt established before he approached her, or, better to admit, before he approached her flinty-eyed father. Maybe even better to admit, he'd been waiting until his heart healed enough to risk sharing it with someone again. As he galloped up the trail, he was sick to think he'd left it too late.

Had he failed Mariah just as he'd failed his family?

Two

Mariah wasn't sure if she'd passed out or was just so dazed and under so much pressure from the stage that time meant little to her. She startled when she heard a voice.

"That's John and Theo." A voice she knew well.

"It's got to be the Deadeye Gang." Another familiar voice. Sheriff Joe Mast. A man she trusted. She tried to cry out, but she barely managed a wheeze. No one heard.

"Everyone's dead. Most robbers wear masks when they hold up a stage, take everything of value, and ride off without killing anyone," the sheriff went on, sounding furious and grief-stricken. "John and Theo were tough men. If they couldn't hold off those men with Sculler on the roof fighting, no one can. The stage line should have outriders."

"They did for a while, but no one's struck around here for a year." Mariah recognized Willie Minton's voice. "We thought they'd moved on. Who ever heard of outlaws taking a year between robberies?"

"Where's Mariah?" That first voice again. Clint Roberts, who owned the only diner in town. But he wouldn't normally ride with the sheriff. "I know Mariah rode out with her father. They were going to a funeral down in Laramie."

There were sounds of movement. Men striding all around.

"You don't think they'd take her, do you?" the sheriff asked.

Mariah wheezed. It was the only noise she could make, and it sounded about like a gust of wind.

"They've never done such a thing before," Deputy Minton said. "But have they ever killed a woman before?"

"Not too many women out here." The sheriff strode off to Mariah's left. "I've never heard of a woman being on a stage that got robbed by this bunch."

"Have they ever found such a beautiful woman as Mariah?" Clint thought she was beautiful. Not many did, as she worked alongside her pa and brother in the blacksmith shop and tended toward trousers, bulky leather aprons, and soot.

"Look down here." Clint's voice sharpened. "That's a corner of her skirt."

Footsteps pounded toward her. She wheezed again. This time, with them close and paying attention, it was enough.

"She's still alive," Clint said. "Sheriff, hitch the horses to the stage so we can lift it. I'll only need a few inches. Just enough to drag her out."

He crouched low and looked under the stage while there were more sounds of activity. "Mariah, we'll get this off you and get you to the doctor. Hang on."

Hang on? She didn't have much else to do.

She wanted to ask about Pa and Theo, but she knew enough and couldn't get a word out anyway.

Clint drew her out, his hands under her arms. Once Mariah was clear of the stage, he shouted to the men riding with him, "I've got her."

The stage dropped back to the ground with a crack.

He knelt beside her, checking for broken bones.

"You're bleeding." He was scared to death of what harm had been done.

"I hurt all over."

"I'm taking you to town." He slid his arms under her and lifted, knowing it hurt. Hating it.

The sheriff was at his side.

"I'll get her to the doctor," Clint said.

"Go on. We'll be along when we're able." The sheriff gave Mariah a worried look and didn't mention bringing in the bodies.

The bodies. Mariah's family. Clint wanted to blame himself for that, too. He knew this trail was dangerous. The stagecoach robberies had seemed to stop, but he could have ridden along. He could have gone out to meet the stage. One more gun. The sound of an incoming rider. It might've been enough to save everyone.

With the sheriff's help, Clint swung up onto his horse and kicked the little black mustang into a gallop. He didn't have the will to go slowly, even if it spared Mariah pain. She would hurt whether he went slow or fast.

He looked down to apologize and realized she had fainted. Kicking the horse to go faster, he hoped it was only a faint.

Please, God. Please let her be all right.

Doc Preston took one look and went into action. "Get

her in the back room. Mariah . . ." The doctor spoke quietly, grief already in his voice as Clint laid her down. "John and Theo were with her?"

"Yes, both dead. Mariah was pinned under the stage and left for dead. Heaven knows what injuries she has from the weight of the stage."

The doctor focused on the worst bleeding. He got a wicked knife out and slit the front of her dress to reveal an ugly bullet furrow cutting along her belly just below her navel. He then took a pad of bandages and pressed them to Mariah's stomach. "Hold this down hard while I get a needle and thread."

As the two of them worked together, Clint told all he knew about the stage. They'd been at it awhile when Nell came charging in, with eyes only for Mariah. "Let me help."

Sheriff Mast was a few minutes behind. He looked from Mariah to the doctor to Nell and, finally, to Clint. Gravely, he said, "I need to be alone with the doctor for a few minutes. Doc, can you spare these two?"

"Uh, well, yes."

"I'm not leaving her." Nell set her jaw as firm as granite.

"Neither am I," Clint said.

"Um . . . Nell, I guess you can stay. But, Clint, please go on out. Let us talk in private. It's a matter of the crime. I'm not ready to talk to you about it yet."

Clint glared at the sheriff, and for a minute he wrestled with leaving. He wanted to tell the sheriff he wasn't man enough to make him leave, but something in the sheriff's expression convinced him this wasn't a request made lightly.

Clint jerked his chin down in a nod. "I left things undone at Le Grande. I'll be right across the street."

He stalked out. Leaving her felt like tearing his own skin.

The sheriff stepped into the kitchen of Le Grande as Clint hung up the last of his pots.

Clint had left the back door unlocked, hoping he'd get news about Mariah and wanting to make it easy for anyone to get to him.

What he saw in Sheriff Mast's eyes twisted his gut. "What's wrong?"

The sheriff lifted both his hands as if to stop Clint from speaking. Or to push away the words that had to be spoken.

"I'm sorry, Clint." The sheriff stared at the floor, unable, it seemed, to meet Clint's eyes. "Mariah didn't make it."

Sheriff Mast turned to face the door connecting the kitchen to the dining room. Clint thought he was leaving, and he leapt forward to grab the man's arm.

But the sheriff wasn't going anywhere. He just stood and stared at the floor.

"She wasn't that bad. What happened?"

"Doc thinks maybe a broken rib punctured her lung or her heart. Maybe a head injury. He isn't sure."

"No." Clint pushed past the sheriff and ran for the doctor's office.

"Clint, wait! No, come back here."

But Clint ran on, sprinting through his dining room and out onto the street.

Mariah, Mariah. Please, God. It can't be.

As he ran, he saw the undertaker, Jim Burke, outside the mortuary, building a box. He had a big stack of wood for all the coffins he needed to make.

Including Mariah's. No. No. No.

He was vaguely aware of children playing in the schoolyard and Pete Wainwright, Pine Valley's mayor, standing outside his general store.

He slammed through the door to the doctor's office. Doc Preston came out of the back room and firmly clicked the door shut behind him.

"Clint, go on home. You can't be in here."

"She wasn't hurt that bad. Are . . . are you sure?" How could a doctor not be sure? Stupid question, but Clint had to ask. "Let me see her."

"No, Clint. Nell's with her, and she doesn't want any company. Go on."

"I will not *go on*," Clint shouted. "What happened?"

The sheriff rushed in.

Clint turned and saw through the open door that Jim Burke had quit building, and Pete Wainwright had taken the wooden steps down to the street.

"Come away, Clint," the sheriff said.

"I will not leave here without seeing her. I won't." His voice rose with every word. "I can't." He felt the burn of tears in his eyes. He refused to let them fall. He hadn't cried since his family had died, with him nowhere near to help them.

Nell came out of the back room. She shut the door just as firmly as Doc Preston had.

She stood silently. Clint's chest heaved as he watched her. Nell was Mariah's friend. If Nell said he could see her, then he'd be allowed in with no fuss.

"I'm going to see her. I'll knock you out of the way if I have to, Doc. Nell, you can't stop me."

She didn't respond. She looked at the sheriff, who'd come up beside Clint. Clint braced himself to fight.

"We have to tell him," Nell said quietly. "I didn't know you had feelings for her, Clint."

"Don't try and stop me, Nell," he repeated, ignoring her comment about his feelings.

The doctor looked at the sheriff.

"I'll have your word that what we tell you goes no further than this room," Sheriff Mast said with intensity. "Then you'll leave and mourn Mariah fully and publicly."

Clint swiped his wrist across his eyes. "What are you talking about?"

"Come into the back." Nell opened the door and let Clint in. To see Mariah unconscious but breathing steadily. Not dead.

Grief faded, replaced by elation. And fury. Clint boiled over. "What—"

Soft hands gripped his arm, drawing him back from the mad ramblings of his mind. He looked down into Nell's blue eyes. Kind eyes. Not the eyes of a woman who wanted to hurt someone.

"We're saying she died."

Clint waited for more, but Nell held his gaze as if allowing him to take in her single sentence for an extended time.

And then he knew why. "So the Deadeye Gang won't come and kill her."

"She's marked for death," Nell said. "We talked it over, and we think she should be declared dead. We'll bury an empty coffin, then we'll spirit her out of town and send her far away. I'm afraid that's her only hope."

He was going to lose her. But better to lose a living woman than a dead one.

One was a victory and the other terrible defeat. For

Mariah, there was no choice. For Clint . . . he ended up with a broken heart either way.

"Thank you for telling me." Clint touched Nell's hand. He knew loss wasn't new to her. Nell was a widow who'd left her old life behind for the frontier.

"I didn't do it because you were causing a scene and possibly drawing a crowd who'd find out the truth," Nell said.

"Then why?"

"Because hiding her is going to be hard and dangerous. I offered to hide her in the rooms over my shop until she's well enough to travel. But if there's any suspicion that she's not dead, my place is the next place they'd search after her own house. But they might not think to hunt through the rooms over the diner."

Clint had lived above the diner for a while, but now he had a cabin on his homestead. He could easily use those rooms to hide Mariah.

And stand guard much more discreetly. As he fully intended to do.

Mary Connealy writes romantic comedies about cowboys. She's the author of the BROTHERS IN ARMS, BRIDES OF HOPE MOUNTAIN, HIGH SIERRA SWEETHEARTS, KINCAID BRIDES, TROUBLE IN TEXAS, WILD AT HEART, and CIMARRON LEGACY series, as well as several other acclaimed series. Mary has been nominated for a Christy Award, was a finalist for a RITA Award, and is a two-time winner of the Carol Award. She lives in eastern Nebraska with her very own romantic cowboy hero. They have four grown daughters—Joslyn, married to Matt; Wendy; Shelly, married to Aaron; and Katy, married to Max—and eight precious grandchildren. Learn more about Mary and her books at

MaryConnealy.com
facebook.com/maryconnealy
petticoatsandpistols.com

Sign Up for Mary's Newsletter

Keep up to date with Mary's latest news on book releases and events by signing up for her email list at the link below.

MaryConnealy.com

FOLLOW MARY ON SOCIAL MEDIA

Mary Connealy

@MaryConnealy

@MaryConnealy